North Coast

Peter Mansel

North Coast

Oxwich Publishing

First published in Great Britain by Oxwich Publishing in 2014
This Oxwich paperback edition published 2016

Published by Oxwich Publishing
www.oxwichpublishing.com

Paperback ISBN: 978-0-9931505-2-4
Ebook ISBN: 978-0-9931505-0-0

In memory of Myrtle Smith and her vision for Belfast

Chapter One

John Kelly walked into the shopping mall on Belfast's Great Victoria Street, pausing to look in a window display at someone else's memories captured in old picture frames. Great liners, great industries, great times.

'Except they weren't, were they,' Kelly mused.

Our desire for nostalgia, for some other time, another place, smothers current reality. Faces forever frozen in sentimental sepia.

Kelly focussed on an image of a huge liner being launched and he could hear the cheering crowds, the splintering wood and the clouds of rust dust billowing up from the massive drag chains as they raced down the slipway after the ship. Men in caps and hobnail boots lined up next to their liner along the dock, another leviathan lurching towards launch, product of the riveter, the carpenter, the draughtsman and the naval architect.

He checked his watch, brought himself back into present reality and was suddenly acutely aware of a crying child in a pushchair, plastic wheels scuttling along the tiled mall floor and the mother cursing as she struggled to light her cigarette with a neon green lighter, obtained at 'five for a pound'. He moved on.

Time moved on unseen as Kelly took a seat in the waiting area of the train station at the end of the mall. The man in the ticket office was counting change, scraping the coins off the edge of the counter one by one.

An old woman, all coat and arthritis, shuffled towards the ticket window. She grabbed on to the counter with a gnarled hand and got very close to the glass. "Have ye got the train times to Larne," she asked in a loud voice. She wasn't acknowledged; instead the man in the window broke off from counting coins and reached for a Translink timetable, placing it in the revolving change well without looking up at his customer. He pressed down on the lever and sent the timetable through to the woman.

She took the leaflet but opened it upside down, and stared intently at the columns of inverted numbers processing across the page. As her watery eyes gained focus, she realised her error and looked up again at the man behind the glass who was still counting. He noticed her, but without looking up, simply stated "Go through Central, connect after 9.53," the sound of his voice muffled as it came through the glass.

Only partially hearing the advice, she looked tired as she shuffled back towards Kelly, clutching the timetable and said to him, "Are you going to Larne?" stabbing a finger at the timetable.

"No, Marino," Kelly answered and noticed that the woman's brow knitted together for a second as if the words had landed a physical blow.

The woman sat down heavily next to Kelly and thumbed the cover of the leaflet, troubled and unable to decide what to do. The man in the window, having finished his counting, stared at the tiles on the floor outside his glass box. The red digital numbers on the clock above the ticket barrier moved over to a new hour as Kelly stared at the numbers. The old woman stared at Kelly and then went back to staring at her timetable, not a minute closer to Larne.

John Kelly had always been known simply as 'Kelly' to almost everyone. His father was another John Kelly, as was his father before that and the need to distinguish between them, started as a joke by an uncle, had just sort of stuck.

Now on the train and with a sudden lurch, Kelly's carriage moved ahead, propelling forward the water trapped inside the twin panes of glass next to him. This rose up like a miniature Tsunami, then retreated back along the length of the glass as it reached the other side. The water formed silent waves crashing on a soundless shore as it ebbed and flowed through its constraining channel.

Kelly managed to draw his eyes away from the window and he looked over at a girl on the seats diagonally opposite, watching her mouth as she chewed noisily on a piece of gum. She stopped for a few moments as the boy she was sitting alongside moved closer to her and kissed her, forcing her head back on to the seat. Bored with the gum, she took it out of her mouth and dropped it from her fingertips on to the carriage floor.

"My daddy would kill me if he knew I was missing college," she accused the boy, who soothingly confirmed, "He won't find out will he."

"I went to Donegall Place last Tuesday with Siobhan and I swear we saw my daddy coming along Castle Lane – we had to run into a shop!" she turned to face him square on. "I'm not getting in to trouble again Colin Rogan, it's Mary's 18th next Saturday and we're going to 21 Social."

The boy pulled back from her and with a smile on his face said, "21 Social? You? You'll never get in."

"Mary knows one of the doormen, we're sure to get in and anyway, I've bought that new top 'specially," the girl explained, turning her face away from the boy and out of the window.

Through Bridge End and Sydenham the train went on to reach Holywood. The young couple got off and started to run along the platform through the rain that had begun to fall, darkening the windows of the train to match the sky.

Kelly thought, 'next stop' and as the train reached Marino, he waited for the doors of the now largely empty carriage to open and for the chance to run across the platform to the shelter of the trees lining it. As the train started to slow to a halt at Marino, Kelly was aware of a figure hurrying towards him along the carriage. Turning away to prepare to open the door, Kelly failed to succeed in this and instead he slumped unconscious to the floor as he received a sharp, sickening blow to the back of his head. A momentary awareness of squealing brakes, an echo of a noise as the door opened, then emptiness.

Chapter Two

Kelly felt warmth on the side of his face and was also aware of a dull ache from somewhere inside his head. It felt as though his whole skull was caught in a vice and that someone was slowly tightening the handle.

His hand moved to the warmth and touched something sticky, wet. Opening his eyes he saw two hands in his blurred vision in front of him, but then realised that it was actually just one as the images snapped together. This focus revealed something red on his fingertips – congealed blood that he had picked up after touching the warmth on the side of his face. He lay there for a moment, unaware of where he was but with a vague sense of place, just like the times you wake up in a hotel bedroom or someone else's house and it takes you a few seconds to remember where you are. Kelly tried to lift his heavy head from the floor and was then aware of a loud screech of brakes, a jolt of the train and was then aware of the unmistakable, sharp smell of whiskey.

"What happened," Kelly said with a slur, still unable to move from his prostrate position pressed up against the door as the train pulled into Bangor station. A lady, distracted with holding tight on to the arm of her wayward granddaughter, waited for the train to reach her so that she could press the 'door open' button from the platform as the train stopped and drag her lively ward onto the nearest available seat.

The train slowed to a crawl and stopped. The woman pressed the now lit door button and waited impatiently for something to happen. With a hiss, the doors parted and Kelly's upper body spilled out on to the platform some inches below, leaving his legs trailing behind on the carriage floor. As his bloodied head reached the concrete edge below it bounced off it with a dull thud. The drunken man, reeking of whiskey and slurring something unintelligible, grasped wildly out and made contact with the woman with his bloodied hand.

"Oh my God!" she shrieked, hauling her granddaughter protectively behind her as she struggled to keep her balance. The little girl was screaming on the end of one hand and now Kelly was firmly attached to the other.

"Someone get this DRUNK off me!" cried the woman, "Someone help me!" as her face contorted in disgust and not a small amount of terror.

The conductor of the train, observing the scene from further along the platform, ran along and took hold of Kelly's free arm firmly and dragged his body onto the platform entirely as the woman moved back exclaiming "Bloody drunk!"

Another would be passenger stated "Your girl shouldn't have to see that," and "Why do they let them on the trains, it's a disgrace!"

The woman, now free of her tormentor's clutches looked down at her skirt and realised it was smeared with blood, "LOOK what he's done to my skirt, oh God, he could have been anywhere!" and carried on complaining to the other passengers whilst a businessman and another lady came over to generally join in with the commotion. By this time, Kelly was trying to stand, trying to make sense of his rubber limbs, but only succeeded in falling down on to his knees on the platform and as he did so, an empty half bottle of whiskey fell from his pocket and smashed into pieces on the ground.

A colleague from the station building then joined the conductor.

"You alright Eion?" he said as his huge bunch of oversized keys bounced off his hip as they swung about from his company issue belt. "I've 'phoned the police – he's not in a fit state to go anywhere just now. Was he like this on the train?"

"Well to be honest I noticed him on the floor when we stopped at Cultra, but it's been a quiet run so I left him to sleep it off. God knows when he did that to his head though, I didn't see that on the train, looks nasty."

Eion continued, "Oh well, the police can sort him out now, he probably did that to his head as he fell down, with the drink and all," he surmised, "I'll probably need some details from you for the police – there will be forms to fill in no doubt!"

Kelly had started to crawl across the platform to reach seating along the side and tried to lift himself up so his back would rest against the seat. As he did so, the station employee noticed a growing patch of blood on Kelly's jacket, exacerbated by his second fall to the platform.

"I'm getting you an ambulance as well son," he shouted at Kelly, "you stay there and the police will need to speak to you too," and then he proceeded back down the platform to the station waiting area. Kelly watched him with half closed eyes as overhead a seagull circled and let out a piercing cry as it eyed Kelly with suspicion. The cry echoed in Kelly's shattered head as he drifted off into unconsciousness once more, surrounded by pieces of the whiskey bottle he'd scraped along under him on his platform crawl. The bystanders eyed him with suspicion, unsure whether to approach the blood and whiskey soaked man as the flotsam and jetsam of station detritus swirled about him like the gull overhead in the seaside breeze.

Kelly woke up to find a police officer shaking his shoulder gently and also saw the green overalls of a paramedic close at hand.

"I think he's just intoxicated, he needs a few hours to sleep it off," the officer said, providing his uninformed opinion to the ambulance man alongside him.

"That's as may be, but that head needs stitching in any case," he replied before asking Kelly, "can you walk do you think Sir?"

Kelly's mind became more clear as the minutes passed by and after a few deep breaths he managed to say "I'll be fine, just hit my head . . . I think I blacked out on the train . . . I think someone hit me."

The police officer looked across at the ambulance man and said under his breath, but unfortunately loud enough for Kelly to hear, "Blind drunk more like."

Kelly struggled to his feet, swaying as he did so and said, "I did NOT have a drink, I'm telling you I think I was attacked on the train, I was just on my way home."

"Look Sir, luckily for you the woman you grabbed hold of is just happy that her granddaughter is fine and she's not wanting to take things any further."

"Any further! I didn't attack her, it's me who has been attacked!" Kelly retorted, incensed by the attitude of the officer.

"Sir, I'm going to ask you to calm down – you've plainly had a drink and you don't want to say anything you'll come to regret later," replied the policeman, "let's get you off to the ambulance and get your head sorted and I can take your details from you."

"I have not . . . been . . . drinking," Kelly stated, "why won't you listen to me?"

They reached the ambulance with only a set of steps for distraction en route and Kelly climbed into the back, assisted by the ambulance staff. As Kelly sat there on a chair the policeman said to him, "Look Sir, the conductor on the train found you on the floor of the carriage, you smelled strongly of whiskey and the last of the bottle fell out of your pocket and onto the platform, so shall we start again with this one?"

"Whoever attacked me must have poured the drink down me or something – aren't you interested in that?"

"If you were attacked Sir, you've probably lost your wallet – have you checked?"

"No, I err," said Kelly, fumbling for his wallet and his keys, "no, everything seems to be here," he said, flicking through his credit cards.

"So you're telling me that you've not had a drink even though you would appear to have had one and you've been attacked even though nothing is missing at all from your pockets?"

"Yes, yes . . . I am!" stated Kelly, as the ambulance got ready to make the journey to the City hospital.

Blue, blue sky filled the horizon. The slightest of breezes gently rustled the luxuriant foliage of the surrounding trees of the leafy suburb. Distant sounds could be heard – children playing, birds singing, a radio tuned to classical music. As the sound of the orchestra and the melody built, a woman stood in the hall of a house in Marino. She took a hipflask from her handbag and poured petrol from it onto the hall carpet behind her as she moved towards the front door. She closed the door firmly behind her and crouched down so that her head was level with the letterbox. She lifted the flap, struck a match and calmly dropped the flame onto the carpet with a gloved hand, closing the flap quickly as she did so.

She could hear the whoosh as the petrol caught and as the flames began to spread up the stairs and engulfed the bottom of the curtains. She opened her bag, dropped the matches and hip flask into it and then quickly walked away from the burning house without looking back, leaving it to its flaming fate.

Meanwhile, Kelly stood in the reception area of casualty at the City Hospital, waiting for his taxi home. The police had taken his statement, re-assuring the incredulous Kelly that they would do 'everything that they could' to get to the bottom of the matter and 'find the culprit if he's out there to find Sir'. Somehow, Kelly didn't feel re-assured.

The taxi pulled up. Striding up towards the car door window, Kelly was the very picture of dereliction, Melonin gauze and steri-strips just holding together a shattered faith in his fellow man.

"Where are you going?" asked the driver.

"Marino," said Kelly, happy at least that the hospital staff had found a carrier bag for him to deposit his alcohol and blood stained jacket in to.

The taxi driver didn't speak to Kelly, no chat about the weather, no football results, no enquiry about what he was doing at the weekend, nor indeed any enquiry about his passenger's shattered skull. Kelly was glad of it although he suddenly felt part of an underclass, looked upon with suspicion, aware of the driver's slight fear of his appearance.

Kelly knew the feeling himself, it's just that usually he was the one judging others from afar, the feeling you get when you are aware of someone heading down the street towards you late at night and you try to cross to avoid them and their random lurching movements. The belief you have that the drunk's fate is a self-determined dereliction of decisiveness, the drug user's drowsy stare a selfishly determined desire.

Buildings that were once grand travelled past the window, peeling paint atop cracking stucco. Boarded up, faceless, decaying wrecks of their former selves with Buddleia sprouting from every orifice.

The digital numbers on the dashboard meter determined the fare as Marino's leafy environs welcomed Kelly home.

The taxi driver spotted the fire first.

"Not your house on fire is it?" he joked, smiling at Kelly's face in the rear view mirror.

Kelly's face, pale as the ash that drifted downwards through the breeze showed that it was and his eyes reflected the growing smoke and burning flame pouring into the sky.

Chapter Three

Declan Doyle swirled the ice cubes around his tumbler of whiskey, and stared out from a hotel suite in Lanyon Place over the reflective Laganside waterfront. His eye was caught by the bathroom light as it streamed into the room as Maggie Haugh entered, wearing a towel wrapped around her head and a white hotel robe around her attractive outline.

"Well, did you get them?" Declan asked, swigging back the last of his drink as he sank back into the forgiving sofa.

"Aye, I got them – did you ever doubt me, Dec?" said Maggie, draping herself over the sofa and Declan's lap.

"Doubt you – no, but trust you Maggie – now there's a whole new question."

"I take offence to that, Declan Doyle," stated Maggie, getting sharply to her feet and moving towards the dressing table, "you're hardly known for your angelic personality either, at least I'm reliable which is more than can be said for you."

"When have I not been reliable?" he snarled, slamming down his tumbler, "do I not keep this place on for you – I don't have a view like this from my place you ungrateful . . ."

"Shhh, Declan," purred Maggie, holding her index finger against his lips. "You forget I got used to a view like this when I lived on floor 17 of a council block – granted the lift wasn't as reliable and as for the room service, well . . .!"

"You really are something else Maggie, do you know that?" Declan said, calming down.

"Oh I know that, Declan Doyle, but that's why you like me so much," she said, falling over his lap again so that the towel that had been around her hair fell to the floor revealing long brunette tresses.

"Shall we get a little more comfortable over there?" she said, pointing towards the Super King sized bed.

Declan smiled and followed Maggie as she got up from the sofa and he followed her closely towards the bed where she turned him around to face her and pushed him back down on to the covers and leapt on to join him with a shriek.

The girl knocked at the door, "Room service!" the voice announced.

"Aye, alright, I'm coming," said Declan as he pushed back the bed covers and hastily pulled a hotel robe from the floor. He padded over to the door, pausing to check his hair in the dressing table mirror first.

He let the teenager in at the door and she picked her way through scattered clothes and underwear that littered the carpet. The tray was placed on the dressing table alongside a blonde wig on a stand, the owner of which lay on the bed on her front.

"Come here Maggie, breakfast's up!" Declan gestured, grease from a piece of hastily grabbed bacon glistening on his mouth.

"Oh God, Declan, I don't know how you can," she said whilst stirring, "eat up and be on your way, I'm off out at 10."

"I could stick around and help you to err . . . prepare for the day if you like," he said, whilst moving on to the fried soda bread.

"Nah, absence makes the heart grow stronger Dec and I'm sure you've got a lot on today yourself," she said sleepily.

Declan finished the breakfast greedily.

"You'll not mind me having a shower before I go though," he said whilst licking his fingers free of grease individually.

"If it gets you on your way, then feel free," she said, sitting up and reaching for her packet of cigarettes from the bedside table. She took one out of the packet and lit it, inhaling deeply and pulled up the duvet to cover her naked form.

"You're not joining me then?" Declan asked, undoing his dressing gown and moving towards the bathroom door.

"Only in your dreams," she replied, blowing out a plume of smoke in his direction.

The sound of the shower spurred her into action. She hurriedly stubbed out her cigarette, threw back the bed covers and pulled on her own discarded robe from the floor. Moving swiftly to the dressing table, she opened a drawer and removed a brown padded envelope that was inside. She pulled out the contents that comprised of a small bundle of papers and carefully took off the top, faded sheet.

From the same dressing table drawer she took out another bundle of papers and placed the faded sheet from the first set on top and replaced this altered bundle back in the padded envelope and then back inside the drawer.

As the sound of the shower began to stop, Maggie moved quickly across to the curtains that were leaking daylight into the room and quickly picked at a pre-prepared space in-between the curtain and the lining, into which she placed the original paper bundle.

Just as Maggie stood up from her work at floor level, Declan opened the bathroom door, rubbing his wiry dark hair with a towel. The curtain swayed slightly to and fro as he walked into the room and Maggie reached out slowly to steady it with a hand whilst facing towards Declan.

"You really are wanting me gone aren't you?" he asked, padding over to a pair of discarded boxer shorts on the floor. "What are you up to?"

Maggie laughed, walked slowly over to Declan, grabbed the boxers out of his hand and pushed him once more on to the bed, her purposefully girlish shrieks and movements masking her cold, dead eyes. Maggie, forever the actress, providing peerless performances on demand.

Whilst Maggie wowed her audience of one, Kelly surveyed the scene of devastation in the place that until a few days ago had been his home.

The investigation teams had gone, windows had been boarded up, the stench of stale smoke and dampness filled the air so that it was almost visible against the glare from Kelly's torch as it tried to reach the depths of the far wall in the room.

In the space that had formerly been a study, the feeble light found an old bureau, perfectly grained and gleaming with damp on one side, black and as brittle as charcoal on the other.

With great care, Kelly opened the top drawer to reveal blackened papers and loose photographs streaked with clinging soot.

Kelly picked out a photo of his father – or at least he knew that this had once been a photo of his father, for blisters and dirt on the surface now obscured the once clear image.

Almost all of the photographs were the same, semi-visible, darkened, burnt and decayed and Kelly felt a sense of loss as he prised apart the damp paper. Memories of holidays, parties, Christmas, all now clouded with each blackened image.

Kelly's father had left when Kelly was 15. He had felt betrayed by this and was left caring for an ever-weeping mother who couldn't cope with her angry son.

Exams had to be faced whilst watching his mother grow bitter, his lack of outward recognition of her emotional state leaving him bound in a straightjacket of frustration and self pity.

He felt guilty if his friends asked him to go and see a film or to get a pizza at the weekend. If he went, he had an escape from the suffocation at home and if he thought of his mother and stayed, his resentment of his mother grew as she once again guessed about the details of the woman his father had gone to.

The last time Kelly had seen his father, he had just returned home from his job at the 'Belfast Reporter' where he was picture editor.

Kelly was still up quite late and he remembered the tune his father had whistled as he walked into the sitting room. Kelly hadn't looked up from the television set, simply muttering 'Alright Dad' before concentrating back on the programme.

Kelly's mother walked into the room and ignored her spouse – something she always did when he came home late and another dinner had been 'ruined'.

"Damn," his father had said, "I've left those negatives at work, I'm going to have to go back and get them for tomorrow morning."

"What do you mean, where are you tomorrow morning," his mother had demanded.

"Bangor, I'm meeting that publisher about the book."

Kelly's father had been putting a book together for years – a collection of photos and first hand accounts documenting the descent into the chaos of the 60's and 70's when he had been a freelance photographer. He had time and time again looked for a publisher but no one seemed to want to invest in the project – 'too raw', 'people don't want to be reminded of this' or 'we're not the right people for this one' being the usual responses to his impassioned pitch.

"John, it's ten o'clock, go back in the morning, early."

"No, can't, the meeting's at 8.30 – the chaps going on to Dublin afterwards for a lunch meeting," he replied, grabbing his keys from the hall table, "I'll be back within the hour," he'd said and he never came back.

Kelly had come down to breakfast the next morning wholly oblivious to the bombshell in paper form of a letter that his mother had found on the doormat when she woke that day to find that her husband had not returned to their bed.

It wasn't unusual for him to stay out all night sometimes, even when he promised to be back within the hour. Jean knew that he couldn't resist the lure of 'a quick drink' if a work colleague stopped him in his tracks at the office. In fact so regularly had this happened recently that she had insisted that he slept in the spare room on his return in the early hours so as not to wake her up.

Kelly had stumbled into the kitchen expecting cereal, toast, orange juice to be laid out on the table just as it was every other morning. Instead, he saw his mother sitting at the table still undressed, a single sheet of paper on the mat in front of her. She had obviously been crying and had a numb look to her face, staring at nothing but her hands clenched on the tabletop.

"Everything alright Mum?" Kelly had said but his mother said nothing, did not move for what seemed to Kelly like minutes. Then, slowly, she pushed the letter towards her son.

Kelly remembered the buzzing sensation in his head as he read the letter. The room had retreated into the background as he heard his father's words in the script before him.

'Darling Jean,' it had begun, 'this is the most difficult thing I have ever done in my life – I couldn't face you, couldn't see your face as you understand what I am going to explain.'

Chapter Four

7.45pm, the Piano Bar of The Europa Hotel in Belfast. Kelly sat in an easy chair listening to the live jazz singer and pianist entertain the great and the good of the city as they drank cocktails and pints of Guinness, a juxtaposition mirrored by the surrounding glitz of The Europa, yet on the street below, viewed through the large first floor windows, a down and out in front of The Crown Liquor Saloon coaxed his dogs into a performance for passers by who continued to push past the bicycle, the plastic bags and the blankets.

Kelly had already finished his pint and had been waiting for Kathleen since 7.15 when she said she would meet him in the bar.

Diners had made their way in twos and fours to dinner and Kelly, fed up of waiting, had made his way down the sweeping circular staircase that affords a view of reception on the ground floor.

As he did this, he caught sight of Kathleen and had been about to shout out her name until he saw that she was talking to a man with dark hair and wearing a smart dark grey suit.

Kelly felt as if he was intruding on what was obviously someone she knew well and he had quickly pulled his head back from over the balcony and made his way back to his table and its view of the street.

The fairy lights in the branches of the trees outside swayed in the dry wind that was racing between the buildings.

The man with the dogs and the bicycle had found an audience, two tourists who were taking photos. They tried to move on but the man made it clear that he wanted some recompense for the show he had delivered and gently blocked their path. The audience of two handed over some coins and quickly walked on in the direction they had originally intended before they were 'encouraged' to watch an encore.

The jazz music ceased with a mild ripple of applause from the drinkers and as it petered out, Kathleen arrived at Kelly's table.

"So sorry I'm late, you must have thought I wasn't coming – how are you?" said Kathleen, sitting down and looking quickly around the room in front of her.

"Grand, grand, don't worry, I've had a pint as you can see, have you had a bad journey in, or?"

"Well actually I was running a bit late anyway and then I bumped into a friend downstairs, completely lost track of time. Now can I get you another drink?"

"No, no, I'll get you one – what'll you have?"

"G&T please, thanks, if you are sure?"

"Not a problem. Have you eaten?"

"Well no, but if you have already, then . . ."

"No, err, we can get something later in you like?"

"Well yes, we could, yes okay that would be great, thanks."

Kelly had known Kathleen since he was a teenager. She was in her mid forties now and had been in her mid twenties when she had first met Kelly. He had been an interested teenager of fourteen who had had an attraction her to then and still had one now. She was still attractive, with glossy black hair that made her appear younger than her years. Her eyes always had a sparkle in them and her mouth was always wearing a smile.

The year before Kelly's father had left, the neighbours next door had moved out. The couple had been nice enough, conversations over the hedge, Christmas cards exchanged and always a card for Kelly's birthday but apart from that they had kept themselves to themselves, politely apart from the social scene in Marino.

Then, one day, a card had dropped through the letterbox. 'Just to let you know that we are moving,' it said and detailed an address on the north coast in Antrim. Kelly's mother never saw the couple actually leave but had noticed the removal van being packed with 'surprisingly little'.

So when Kathleen moved in next door with her parents, both Kelly and his mother had a lot to notice next door. New furniture, curtains and carpets arriving by the van load, enough to make Kelly's mother comment, 'not short of a bob or two there.'

Kelly's interest was only in the daughter. Every time Kathleen returned home from work, Kelly would notice her out of the front window where he thought he wouldn't be noticed but probably always was.

When Kelly's father had left the note saying that he would not be back, Kathleen's mother was the first to come around to see if everything was alright due to the curtains remaining closed all that morning. Jean never left her curtains closed past 8 a.m. and Kathleen's mother Mary was on the scene fast enough to relieve a thankful Kelly in the care of his broken hearted mother.

This was around the first time Kelly had properly spoken to Kathleen. She became sort of an older sister to him, taking him out to the cinema and coming around to watch TV in the few weeks before his father's departure. Kelly, of course, was both flattered and embarrassed by her attention but enough of a teenager to tell his friends at school that he was seeing an older woman. It was whilst trying to convince one of his friends that he had seen a film with Kathleen that his friend said 'What is she really though Kelly, like a sister?' that it dawned on Kelly that Kathleen may just have been kind, a considerate friend and a surrogate sibling.

This realisation, his subsequent red face and nervous silence only added to Kelly's untenable position with his friends. He never mentioned Kathleen again after that and was not so eager to please when Kathleen next called at the front door.

"So how about it Kelly – you get a comfortable roof over your head whilst the house is being sorted out and I get a house sitter whilst I am away, c'mon, it is the least that I can do after what has happened to you," stated Kathleen, moving her hand to cover Kelly's.

"Oh, I don't know, I'm okay at the bed and breakfast and it's not far form the house." Kelly had been staying at 'The Bramwell' B&B since the house fire. "I couldn't just stay at yours – I'd have to pay, I get some allowance from the insurance . . ."

"I won't hear of it – you'll need your money when you move back in to your house and get sorted out. I'll send you an invoice for the insurance company if it's going to make you feel better about it though. How long will the house be now?" asked Kathleen, her eyes wandering over to the spiral stairs leading up to the piano bar as she spotted her friend from earlier that evening.

Kelly expected her to acknowledge the man he saw with Kathleen in reception but she seemed to look through the guy as he walked straight past her to the bar.

"Oh, a couple of months, well maybe six weeks they're saying," explained Kelly, taking an increased interest in the dark haired man at the bar.

"Well, there you go," said Kathleen, grabbing Kelly's hand and bringing his gaze back to her. "I'm away from the end of this week and won't be around for six weeks minimum."

Kathleen had told Kelly some time before that she had a job with a pharmaceutical company and often worked overseas. "Take this spare key now – it's yours from Saturday – I'll even put a pint of milk in the fridge for you."

Kathleen's house was on Whitepark Road in Ballycastle, built about four years ago by a local developer with fantastic views of

Mull and Jura on a good day and sheltered from the sea winds by banks of robust green grass topped with the coconut aroma and piercing thorns of yellow gorse.

Kelly looked out of the window through the soft drizzle beginning to bead on the panes of glass and blurring the fairy lights in the trees swaying past the glass in the breeze.

"Well if you are sure, that will be brilliant, thank you so much Kathleen." Kelly said, "It'll be good to get out of the city for a while, it's been an age since I've been to the coast too. Maybe I'll take some shots over there."

Kelly worked as a freelance photographer, something he never thought he'd end up doing as his father had started out on the photo desk of the local paper and had become photo editor.

After Kelly realised his father wasn't coming home again he'd picked up the photographic equipment from the back room and had decided to put it away or even to sell it but instead, his curiosity encouraged him to start taking a few pictures, in fact he took pictures of everything over the following weeks in an unconscious link to his absent father. Samson and Goliath, the Lagan Bridge, City Hall, all ended up captured on celluloid and were the foundation of his first portfolio.

The rest of the evening in the bar passed with reminiscences of past times, recollections of past desires and the crushing realisation of present reality.

Chapter Five

Bright sunshine flooded Kelly's room at 'The Bramwell' B&B. He looked across to his alarm clock through half closed eyes and turned over for a few moments, but the lure of the day ahead was too much and he was coaxed out of bed by the sunlight seeping in through the thin curtains at the window.

He showered and pulled on a pair of faded jeans before picking out a clean t-shirt from the pine chest of drawers. The t-shirt was one of his last clean ones and was a colour that he didn't really like, plus it gaped at the neck, but after he had pulled on his favourite beaten up trainers he made his way down the creaky stairs to the breakfast room, crick, squeak, scrick.

The tables were covered with paper tablecloths and a 1970's brown plastic menu card huddled together next to a bottle of brown sauce and stainless steel salt and pepper pots for company.

'The Bramwell' was old fashioned, somewhat shabby, rarely full and in need of 'TLC' but their breakfasts made up for any lack of sophistication in Kelly's eyes.

Mary McCullogh brought out Kelly's order, an Ulster fry with toasted wheaten bread, orange juice, coffee.

"Oh, it's a shame you are moving on, it really is," said Mary as she cleared the plates from a neighbouring table.

Mary had been coming in to do the breakfasts at the B&B for as long as anyone could remember. Her plump figure, nylon tabard and florid complexion were timeless and ageless and reminded Kelly of his own grandmother.

"I know, Mary, but I am looking forward to my own place again for a while, but I'll miss these breakfasts and you of course."

"Well, you know where we are, you come back again now, won't you!" Mary shuffled back to the kitchen with her cargo of crockery.

Kelly stood up, pushed his chair under the table and climbed back up the stairs two at a time, keen to get on the road.

He cleared out the drawers and the wardrobe in his room, packed his sponge bag and sat on the bed for a while listening to the tap dripping in the bathroom and the faint hum of traffic on the road nearby. With a deep breath, he stood up, gathered his bags and headed down the stairs again.

The sunlight outside seemed to be so appropriate, a new beginning, almost a cliché.

Kelly rammed his bags into the boot of his car and joined the traffic heading about the city centre.

Heading on to the M5, Kelly caught sight of the flat expanse of Belfast Lough, sunshine bouncing off every wavelet to his right as he headed towards Carrickfergus.

Through the leafy suburbs of Whiteabbey and Greenisland the A2 took Kelly along the coast until he saw a Louis McNeice poem opening before his eyes as he surveyed the Norman keep and dark harbour of Carrickfergus.

The Borough Council had seen fit to adorn the castle entrance with a sign inviting you to 'catch the wave in Carrickfergus', its startling blue logo shouting out loudly from the cold grey stones of the castle walls.

Street lamps like anorexic lollipops, all stick and no top, marched down the sea defences and urbanised the keep and santitised the harbour setting.

The traffic moved on and drew Kelly on past Eden, next to the gasworks.

At Whitehead, the road left the outer coastline of The Gobbins and Island Magee and headed northwards to Larne.

On reaching the town centre, Kelly decided to stop and buy a newspaper from a shop just off the main road. Spotting a space for the car just outside another selling decorating supplies, he quickly pulled in. As he did so, a silver Audi swerved out to avoid the rear of Kelly's car. "Christ, that was close," Kelly muttered, stepping out into the pavement next to a window full of draped wallpaper pinned out from the corners of the window to the centre akin to a fabric display. Terracotta red, white, cream, silver with black bamboo.

He hadn't been in Larne for many years and the main street seemed unchanged apart from a new department store with wooden cladding showing up the older stores clustering around its base.

"Hello son," he heard as an elderly woman shuffled past him on the pavement. "Hello, how are you?" He answered back, something familiar about her triggering a memory in his mind. Then, as she shuffled along, Kelly recognised the big coat, the arthritic frame and his mind was taken back to the station at Great Victoria St and the woman asking for train times to Larne.

He didn't go after her immediately but wondered if she was just saying hello or if she actually remembered him from that fateful trip home that ended in a bloody mess in Bangor. He automatically rubbed his hair where he had been hit that day and started down the road after her with mixed emotions, happy that the old girl had reached her intended destination, but pained by the recollection of events that had taken place later that same day. Shaking his head, he thought better of having the conversation, bought his newspaper and strolled back towards the car, once again passing the window festooned with future colours of rooms yet to see a makeover.

Kelly started the car, rejoined the main road and further up, past Ballygalley, Scawt Hill rose out of the sea in a tumble of rocks and buttresses, grass and determined vegetation clinging to ever steeper cliffs that climbed on out of eyesight.

The road hugged the coast again, twisting back and forth, spring water flowing down the rocky walls and splashing across the road underneath the car tyres before meeting and merging with the welcoming sea.

Bladderwrack and saline pools caught the sun as the road cut through a rock archway, blue sky and smoke white clouds framed by its random decent seaward.

Antrim glens surge down to Glenarm and Carnlough before Larne defers to Moyle at Garron Point. At Glen Ariff, Kelly passed a car parked at the side of the road, the driver catching his eye in his wing mirror.

The silver Audi started to pull out onto the road behind Kelly, a passenger now visible too in the rear view mirror. The car reached the road in a sudden scramble of loose chippings before matching Kelly's speed as they passed through Cushendall.

Having had little company on the road out of Larne, Kelly kept checking his mirrors, wondering if the silver Audi was the one that swerved violently out of the way when he had stopped for his newspaper. Thoughts of 'road rage' clouded his concentration and Kelly nearly hit the kerb at the side of the road in his efforts to peer back into the other car.

The following car slowed down as Kelly skewed back towards the centre of the carriageway, 'almost as if it is following me,' he thought, laughing at himself and the self-created moment of drama.

The car continued to pull back though as if it wanted to be less visible. A farm truck then joined the road behind Kelly's car from Glenaan and obscured his view of the Audi. Expecting nothing behind him except for the truck, Kelly was suddenly aware of a car engine accelerating purposefully behind him. His mirrors told him that the Audi had overtaken the lumbering truck and regained its precise distance behind him.

Intrigued once more, Kelly noticed the road to the right to Cushenden, quickly indicated and raced across the road in third gear. He kept looking in his rear view mirror for signs of the following car but it had gone. He decided to pull over in the village though just in case the car had decided to wait in a lay-by further up the main road.

The wind caught Kelly's door as he opened it and he reached over for his jacket from the passenger seat. Facing into the wind to close the door, he turned his back on it to pull on his coat.

The beach at Cushendun is topped by marrom-covered sand dunes, a footpath from the beach leading up to the small Victorian church. There wasn't a soul to be seen although a couple of small boats bobbed around in the river mouth near the bridge and seagulls hovered overhead, stationary in the brisk wind, their legs dangling behind and adjusting to the breeze.

Kelly sat down at the base of a dune, gaining some shelter. The sun still shone brightly, but its warmth was been carried away on the wind. His dark hair was whipped around and lifted away from his face.

A woman then walked on to the beach, letting off a chocolate Labrador as she did so. The dog raced along the beach, stopping at the shoreline and it placed two paws in to the sea. It turned to face his owner and gave a bark and Kelly watched this scene for a few minutes, his eyes following the dog chasing after a piece of driftwood the woman threw into the air.

Standing up and dusting the sand from his clothes, Kelly walked back along the beach and headed for the car. As he reached the seafront car park, he noticed that in the corner, a car had parked up, its driver and passenger sat inside. It was the same silver Audi.

Maggie was now fully dressed, over-dressed in fact for a Tuesday morning in Belfast. Blonde tresses cascaded from her head and fell on to the shoulders of her designer suit. Accessories clashed together as she paced around the room, "C'mon, c'mon, c'mon, ring will you!" she said to her mobile, perched on the dressing table amidst the lipsticks, creams, blushers.

A sharp ring made her jump and she scrambled for the 'phone, false nails tapping along the tabletop.

"Yes, uh-huh, fifteen minutes, twenty max., uh-huh, uh-huh, right." This was the call she had been eagerly waiting for and provided enough information to send her on her way and she grabbed a long coat and dark sunglasses plus her set of car keys as she exited the room.

Meeting nobody between her bedroom and the lift she descended to reception, checking the accuracy of her make up in the mirrored lift interior as she travelled.

She passed by the reception desk with purpose but the Duty Manager spotted an opportunity and raced over to her side.

"Not now please, I'm in a rush," blurted Maggie, not slowing her pace.

"I'm sorry Miss Haugh, but you did say that you would settle your bill two days ago now and we must ask that . . ."

"Yes, yes, you'll get your money, I'll be back with it this afternoon," she added. Maggie had been asked to settle her account after staying in the hotel this time for more than a week. The credit card she had offered had been refused but then so had the debit card and the cheque taken from the crumpled cheque book hidden in the deeper recesses of her bag.

"We will need it later please Miss Haugh," stated the Manager, finally stopping his pursuit of one of his least favourite regulars. Awareness of her benefactor led the Manager to stop short of ensuring her departure through blocking her room key.

Maggie exited the lobby and walked down to the car park. Her cabriolet Mercedes was parked across two spaces at an angle, her usual parking style. She flung her coat off and on to the passenger seat, checked her make up again in the rear view mirror and surged up on to the main road.

She made her way quickly along to Alfred Street near to St Malachy's church and parked the car illegally before approaching a property fronted by a closed plain door and an intercom buzzer. Pressing it awkwardly with a fingernail, a voice announced, "Come on up," and she pushed open the door and made her way up the staircase in front of her.

Tommy MacGuire opened the heavy door at the top of the stairs a crack on the chain and made sure that Maggie was on her own.

"Declan not with you then?" he questioned as her opened the door wider.

"Oh no, he's busy just now, I'm dealing with this one," replied Maggie casually, sitting herself down on an ancient sofa.

Tommy MacGuire was a slight man of maybe eighty. The years had not been kind to him and even those who knew him well thought he was a good ten years older. He had certainly being doing what he was doing for as long as anyone in his circle could remember, outliving glamorous crooks and infamous charlatans. He had seen many 'customers' end up inside a number of times as new found freedom had gone to their heads, turning quickly to boredom and when the only thing keeping them satisfyingly occupied was the activity that put them inside in the first place.

Tommy took off his pair of black, wide framed glasses. His eyes were surrounded by deep wrinkles and bristling grey eyebrows but the eyes themselves were as bright as they had ever been. He rubbed the glasses on the front of his grey woollen jumper and replaced them on his face.

"Will ye be wanting a drink or something?" Tommy asked, picking up a bottle of cheap own brand whiskey from the 1960's sideboard and pouring himself a generous measure into a blue Tupperware beaker.

"Err, no, I don't think I will Tommy thank you, I really just want to leave these with you," Maggie replied, reaching in to her bag.

Tommy was a sometime forger, a fraudster, a thief, basically whatever would provide him with cash income and an easy life. Not that there were any signs of wealth immediately apparent in the near squalid flat and certainly not in his clothes which displayed the traces of many a meal, the smell of many a cigarette and the remnants of tots of whiskey dribbled down from his wrinkled mouth.

Condensation ran slowly down the window in the room, framed by russet velvet curtains, black with mildew at their base.

The smell of stale cooking fat seeped into the room from the kitchen and reminded Maggie not to stay too long in the type of place she had once had to endure herself.

Tommy took hold of the packet of papers that Maggie handed across and made his way over to an old bureau across the room. Papers were stacked on top of it and a film of dust coated what little wood remained visible.

He opened the top of the furniture though to display a pristine working space within, the forgers' tools filled the letter racks and the drawers were all neatly filled and immaculate.

He switched on an aged angle poise lamp and its light shone down on to the open desk and he took up the first of the bundle of papers, a small magnifying glass grasped in his other hand.

"How did you come by this Maggie?" he asked, continuing his slow analysis.

"Oh, I've had them a long time Tommy, got them from a friend," she replied, looking vacantly towards the window.

"Oh right," he said, "that friend would be Declan Doyle would it, only he's mentioned bringing me some papers like this recently too."

"Er, well, he knows well enough that I'm bringing them over to you, but I'd rather keep this between us for now Tommy. I'll, er, make it worth your while if you come to me before you go to Declan once you've completed things," she added, looking directly at him.

"Doesn't much matter to me whose they are Maggie, so long as I get my pay," he said with a small grin, returning to the bundle of papers.

The papers were all similar and comprised of lists of numbers in seemingly random sequences. Each sheet was carefully typed out and numbered individually at the top.

Tommy was well known to be good with detail, whether it was for his photographic memory of passbook signatures or his ability to piece together financial treasure trails in pursuit of the hidden spoils of criminal activity. In another life he would have been a top detective, darling of the fraud squad. Instead, he lined his pockets with stolen cash and maintained his position within his peer group by knowing just enough about everyone and everything to keep himself safe and little enough to ensure he wasn't a target himself.

"I'll ring you when I'm done Maggie," he said, placing the papers neatly in a bureau drawer.

"You think you can work it out Tommy?" Maggie enquired, trying to conceal her fervent interest.

"As I say, I'll ring you when I'm done," he replied quietly, locking the front of the cabinet. He stood there for a moment, mouth slightly open, his shallow breaths betraying the damage to his aged lungs.

"I'll be hearing from you soon then." Maggie said, trying to gain an idea of a timescale from him.

Tommy didn't answer but did escort Maggie to the door before he closed it softly behind her, turned the lock, put on the chain and returned to the yellow whiskey in the blue plastic cup.

Chapter Six

Kelly stood in the car park for a while watching the silver Audi. He pondered on the chances of it being there simply through coincidence but remembered the near miss in Larne and the second meeting on the A2. He recollected that as he'd pulled off the main road to head into Cushendun, the Audi had sped along the A2 travelling north but must have double backed or come via Glendun and down from where the road switches back.

Either way it seemed odd to Kelly to see the car there again where he had had little other company during his stop.

He took his time getting back into his own car, trying to peer over to the driver and passenger in the silver car. The driver though was holding up a newspaper, obscuring Kelly's view and the passenger seemed to be searching for something in the glove compartment.

Kelly had visited Cushendun before – it being a popular scenic stop off for holiday makers heading along the coast, or at least was before the troubles in the cities scared away many families and their tourist pounds. He remembered that there was another road out of the village around the majestic Carnanmore and Torr head. It was more of a track really than a road, steep, precarious and only just accessible still, due to landslides.

The nagging uncertainty about the other car convinced Kelly to take the road around the cliff top. He set off from the car park, keeping his eyes on the rear view mirror for any movement from the other car. Just as he began to think that the other car wouldn't follow, the Audi made a move too.

As Kelly reached the junction where the road heads up the hill to Runabay Head, he turned off and urged the car to go as quickly as he could up the steep road, the engine racing between the gears.

'That's done it,' thought Kelly, 'it won't follow me up here.'

Before he had too much time to think about the other car though, he saw a sign in front of him saying 'Road Closed Ahead'. He slowed down and paused, wondering whether to go back to the main road but his peripheral vision noticed the silver Audi creeping slowly, almost silently up the hill behind him, its roof visible through the bracken on the switchback bend below.

'This is just a joke,' thought Kelly, perspiration beginning to bead on his forehead as nerves began to kick in, certain now that the car was following him, but unable to fathom why. His brain told him that maybe the car driver was annoyed about the near miss in Larne but he couldn't understand why the driver hadn't taken the opportunity to confront him in the car park.

Doubt began to creep in to his mind about his chances on a remote hillside road if the driver and passenger really did mean to tackle him. Kelly put the car back into gear and pushed his way around the road closed sign, his driver's side wheels skidding in the loose chippings at the road edge.

His heart raced, a mixture of fear building in his mind about the following car and the anticipation of what the road ahead would bring and whether there would be a way through at all. He tried to bring his eyes onto the road ahead whilst still looking in to his rear view mirror for the Audi. He drove on, the engine whining again as he pushed as much as he could out of it between gear changes.

The road ahead looked clear and Kelly relaxed just a little, noticing the sea stretching away down to his right hand side.

Gulls hovered in the air, wings dipping this way and that in the off-shore breeze. The bright sun hit the tops of the white waves and sanitised the power of the sea beneath them.

Kelly slowed the car down and took a deep breath and decided that the following car must have had second thoughts about the road and turned back at the road closed sign.

He neared Torr Head, his car finding all the pot-holes in the road and slowed the car down further, aware that he couldn't see the road direction up ahead, presuming that it might drop into a dip.

As he edged the car forward he realised why he couldn't see the road, the bank of the left hand side had slipped down, scattering a tumble of earth, bracken and stones across the single track road.

"Shit," Kelly spat out, foot pressing down firmly on the brake pedal.

Something about the seemingly hopeless route ahead forced his mind to focus. "He thought 'I've got to turn around, car or no car,' as he looked over his shoulder and out of the rear window.

Gulls circled again in the gusting breeze, letting out complaining calls as they were buffeted up and down towards the cliff edge. Kelly put his hand on the gear stick and was just about to put the car into reverse when behind him, the noise of its engine drowned out by the birds' cries, the Audi neared its target, edging forward towards Kelly's car.

No further expletive tumbled from his mouth although his lips moved silently, shock and unease growing and numbing his senses.

In a split second more, he rammed the car into first gear and launched it at the rubble-strewn road ahead.

Wheels spinning, the car skated over the mud and sent a myriad of stones scattering seaward. The tyres crunched over the random surface with a crack and a pop as the rubber bit into the surface.

The car skewed this way and that, providing Kelly with an unwanted close up view of the cliff edge. His mind was telling him that he was mad to even try risking pushing through, knowing that he could just stop, ask the other car what it wanted, but something told him that he had to carry on.

His front tyres spun again, trying to get traction. "C'mon!" he shouted, changing gear and pushing the accelerator down harder.

Thankfully it worked, the car flew forward and reached clear tarmac again. Risking a glance over his shoulder, he could see that the Audi wasn't giving up, the Quattro four-wheel drive enabling it to take its chance more easily now that it had seen Kelly get through.

He sped on, trying to build a gap between them but he could see the other car reach the tarmac again too and could see it trying to close the gap. Kelly changed gear and stamped his foot on the accelerator again, determined to make ground.

He rounded a sharp bend, struggling to keep the car on the road as it skated wide.

Up ahead, he spotted a chance to escape from the chase as he saw a small track on the left leading away from the cliff, the other heading for Torr Head. He took the track and forced the car on over the un-metaled road.

Behind him, the Audi reached the same sharp bend and slowed before it reached the fork in the road. Unable to see Kelly's car ahead it had to take just one route and it made its choice of road and pushed on.

A girl walked down past an old school building to the sand dunes that divided the base of the cliffs from the wide sandy beach at its base. The girl was barefoot, relishing the feel of the sun warmed, dry sand beneath her toes.

Light breezes combed the grass-topped dunes, imperceptibly moving thousands of grains of sand and building new mounds around and over any shoreline imperfection.

The sky was bright, pulling the girl onwards towards the shore. As she climbed the last dune the muffled sound of the sea focused in her ear to produce a windborne cacophony of crashing waves and rolling breakers.

She stood there for a moment with her eyes closed, absorbing the sounds, the smell and the sensation of the soft air and rising heat from the sand.

Opening her eyes she saw she was absolutely alone on the beach. She kneeled down on the sand, resting on her heels. Her bare arms moved slowly in the sand, pushing her hands back and forth through the warm grains.

The sea sizzled as it pulled back from the shore, then raced forward, gaining ground every few waves, moving ever closer to the girl.

The girl had come home. She had lived here at Whitepark Bay all the time she grew up and all of that time she longed to escape the solitude, to leave behind the wide-open expanses and surround herself with buildings and cars and noise and people.

The opportunity came to escape when her cousin in London visited and filled her head with glamour and excitement.

Having just left school, the girl begged her cousin to take her back with her and much to the despair of her ageing grandparents and mother, her cousin agreed to the move as long as she got a job to pay her way.

The job was menial, the hours un-social and the flat in Tower Hamlets was noisy, cramped and damp.

Four years later, the novelty had truly worn off, her cousin had moved out of the rented flat and Sophie's grandmother was dying at home in Ballintoy and called her granddaughter home.

Sophie grabbed the chance to escape again and leave her city exile and took the next flight with the rent money for the flat, back to the north coast, back to her childhood.

She sat on the beach, watching the waves, watching her childhood return with the tide.

Chapter Seven

Nothing followed Kelly on to the A2 at Ballyvoy. He spent more time looking in his rear view mirror than he did at the road ahead as he drove down to Ballycastle, gaining reassurance from familiar buildings and the presence of holidaymakers walking along the front.

He took the road up out of town onto Whitepark Road, passing under a number of anniversary banners detailing political casualties, sons now departed, a reminder of troubled times.

He began to relax as the car climbed the road and out into the countryside again until, near the brow of a hill, he saw Kathleen's house, all white render with a tower enclosing the staircase. He drove carefully over the stony track leading up to it, bounded by great flat stones on each side topped by gorse.

The sun warmed him as he stepped out of the car and he paused to admire the views out to Rathlin Island. It was too late in the day to see all the way to Scotland as haze covered the horizon to his right.

Below him, a donkey brayed its greeting, making Kelly smile as he remembered waking up in a guest room when he visited Kathleen before to the same donkey making its presence felt.

"You've still got a lot to say for yourself," said Kelly and moved back to the car. He unpacked his bags and took them into the house, leaving them at the base of the stairs.

He made himself a cup of tea – black, as he realised that there was no milk in the fridge. He pulled his face as he swallowed the bitter brew and gazed out of the windows along the side of the house facing the sea.

Relaxing more by the minute, he kicked off his shoes and rested his head back on the soft cushions of the waiting sofa. His eyes narrowed, then closed, the peace of his surroundings lulling him into early slumber.

It was the donkey that woke him again, as walking near to the house it let out a long bray. Kelly's eyes jerked open and he wondered momentarily where he was. The time surprised him and the setting sun flamed in the distance and attracted his lazy gaze.

He returned to the kitchen to check on supplies. He had intended to shop for provisions before the evening but his unplanned sleep had prevented his excursion.

Checking the cupboards and the fridge, he was disappointed to find only various condiments including vinegar, flour, sugar plus the tea bags of course. He then spotted a lonely tin of tuna at the back of a cupboard and half a pack of wholewheat pasta in another next to a packet of cornflakes.

Kelly was a good cook, he enjoyed a challenge and being inventive with ingredients but even he was challenged by the lack of items before him. The lack of food reminded him of when his father had left, when his mother's depression had begun. He often had arrived home to find her sitting in front of the television where she didn't move to greet or acknowledge her son and seldom cooked in the way she had before. Then, with no husband to cater for, she had filled the freezer with cheap burgers, frozen oven chips and brightly coated fish.

Some weekends though, Kelly got to do the supermarket shop and he started to try recipes he found on Ceefax or in his mother's newspaper supplement. His mother didn't seem to mind that he had taken over in the kitchen, in fact it gave her more time to watch the old films being shown on BBC2 in the afternoons, gave her more time to escape from the memories of her life at home with her husband.

Kelly's thoughts had snapped back to the present and he closed the cupboards with their meagre rations and took instead the stairs in the circular tower up to the bedroom that Kathleen had prepared for him – last on the right.

The floorboards creaked as he walked along the corridor until pushing open the bedroom door, he saw a pleasant room before him complete with French windows opening out on to a metal balcony.

Kathleen had had the house renovated some years before. It had been a farmhouse but when her parents had both died, she had invested their financial legacy in the property and had been able to extend it, building the staircase tower and adding balconies to the upstairs rooms on the seaward side.

Kelly undressed, showered and pulled on his only smart pair of trousers, teaming them with a blue check shirt.

He moved back downstairs and got into the car, enjoying the breeze that was rushing out to sea. Putting the car headlights on, he swung out along the drive and back down Whitepark Road into Ballycastle. He stopped the car at the bank to get cash and noticed a restaurant in the triangle there, down a small flight of steps. He got the cash and locked the car up.

The restaurant had about ten tables, arranged in booths and using old furniture which gave the place a homely and welcoming feel. Kelly relaxed in the dim light and ordered a drink from the barman.

With his drink came the dinner menu and he realised that it must be weeks since he had a chance to be relaxed. He wanted to clear his mind and put the last few weeks behind him, to move forward, but still knew that until he could get home to a re-furbished home, he'd still be in an uncertain limbo, in an 'in-between' state, waiting for normality to enter his life again.

A car pulled up outside and Kelly's thoughts returned to the journey along the coast and his apparent pursuers and he checked nervously that it wasn't the same silver Audi.

He shook his head, almost ashamed of himself for being so nervous and looked down the menu, deciding on crispy duck pancakes to start, recommended by the waiter. To follow he would have ice fish topped with a crab crust. After this, he finished his second small glass of wine, ordered a coffee and checked the time.

It neared eleven before he paid his bill and wandered back up the steps to street level to reclaim his car.

After the two glasses of wine and the good food, he felt relaxed again as he drove up the road, out of town and back to the house.

He didn't pass another car for the whole journey back and only saw an old man walking a greyhound, the dog struggling to match the pace of his owner who was heavily reliant on a walking stick. The dog kept trotting on a few feet then would stop and look back at his master, encouraging him on.

Nearing the brow of a hill, Kelly indicated left and pulled into the drive to the house. As he did so he had to instinctively slam on the brakes as a figure darted in front of the car. A girl shrieked and threw her body back in fear as she tried, panicked, to resume her original route, her hands scrabbling at the edge of the bonnet.

Kelly could see that the girl was distressed, as tears and mascara streamed down her face. She stopped at the side of the track and her back slid down the side of the stone flanked banks of the driveway. She sat on the ground, her legs useless as shock set in.

Kelly's heart raced but in a few seconds he managed to think and he pulled the handbrake on, left the engine running and got out of the car to admonish the girl for her stupidity.

"What the hell do you think you are doing, I could have killed you," he berated, walking over to the figure now sobbing at the side. Before he waited for an answer, he could see just how distressed she was and realised this couldn't just be from the near miss. He saw again in his mind the look of horror on the girl's face as it was caught in the headlights, before she even realised the car was there.

"Are you alright?" he asked, moving nearer to see her face that was still turned half away from him. The girl was still fighting against the wracking sobs but then calmed slightly and Sophie turned her face towards him. This was the same girl that had only that afternoon been enjoying the warm sands at Whitepark Bay and she looked up at him, hand outstretched to another human being, a childlike plea for security that couldn't mask a cowering fear in its trembling advance.

Tommy MacGuire felt the sense of satisfaction that he always felt when he knew he was 'on to something'.

Since Maggie left him with the papers, he had been studying them hour after hour, trying to analyse the columns of figures, looking for sense in the sequences.

It was the numbers in the corners of the pages that gave Tommy his lead, whilst the columns of numbers on each sheet were seemingly random, the numbers in the top right corners only varied so many times. The first sheet had '05' at the top of it, the next '08' and the next '20'. The numbers continued in this seemingly random nature until the last sheet, which was numbered '80'.

Tommy put down his magnifying glass on to the desk and decided to pour himself a drink of his favourite whiskey, not that he wasn't used to having a constant supply at hand, but his numerical discovery gave him cause for celebration, a reason to indulge himself further.

He carried the plastic tumbler through from the kitchen, placed it down on the side and opened a new packet of golden crunch biscuits. Tommy's diet hardly varied, consisting of a cup of tea and biscuits in the morning before fried egg, bacon, and potato scone to follow.

Lunch was usually a cold sausage roll and a bag of crisps from the shop on the corner and dinner was chips accompanied by whatever took his fancy from the illuminated, foil lined heated cabinet at the local takeaway that lured him with its welcoming warmth on cold nights.

Friday was always fish cakes. Sometimes on a Saturday he would go further along the road and buy a portion of fried rice from the 'Beijing Palace'. There, he would always come across couples waiting for their orders and rowdy groups walking along the pavement outside and felt the buzz of life that was missing from his own flat.

He returned to the living room and flicked on the television to view the snooker. He'd never played the game but he enjoyed watching the frames, the restrained battles between the stars of yesterday and the new kids playing the game today. Tommy thought that there was something very dignified about snooker – it was the green baize, the referee's white gloves, the waistcoats, the bow ties. You didn't get that with any other sport.

Tommy's tumbler rested on the greasy arm of the once red sofa. He flicked away a few biscuit crumbs from the side of his mouth, catching some inadvertently on his sweater, adding to the culinary mixture captured within its welcoming fibres.

He rested his head back on the cushion, peered at the TV screen down his nose, mouth slightly open, until his eyes flickered and closed.

Tommy started awake as he heard a rapid knocking at the door downstairs. Spilling the dregs of his whiskey accidentally down a trouser leg, he got up from the sofa and mumbled "Oh Christ," as he brushed away the liquid.

"You in Tommy?" questioned the visitor through the door, lifting up the flap of the letterbox to do so.

"Aye, I'm coming, I'm coming," Tommy complained, fumbling with the chain whilst peering through the spy hole.

"Oh, Declan, it's you – come on in, come on in," he said, moving to the side to allow his guest through.

Declan's eye was drawn to the wet stain on Tommy's trousers and hoped inwardly that he would never grow old.

"Will you be wanting a drink Declan?" Tommy asked, bending down slowly to pick up the blue tumbler.

"Ah no I'll not, Tommy," Declan replied, looking around the room to pick up any signs of other visitors to the flat.

"You on your own?" he asked, sitting himself down in the single armchair.

"Oh yes, quite on my own," his host replied, his eyes beginning to twinkle as he added, "so, what can I be doing for you Declan?"

"Well, I just thought I would call in and see how things were going, you know, if you've got lots on at the moment," he asked, trying not to too readily give away his fervent interest.

"Oh you know Declan, doing this and that, this and that," Tommy replied as he sank back into the sofa.

"Anything in particular keeping you busy Tommy, anything you might like to tell me about? Declan asked, sitting forward in his armchair.

"I wouldn't want to bore you with all my comings and goings Declan. There could be something particular but I'm not sure I'd be able to let you have all of the details, I have a confidence to keep you see."

"You know I'm always good to you Tommy, but God help me, if you're thinking of taking me on, I'll . . ."

"Declan, Declan, please calm yourself," Tommy stated, "we've known each other too long to start any unpleasantness," he continued, getting up slowly from the sofa and moving towards the desk. "Whatever's troubling you I'm sure we can clear it up Declan," he added, slowly closing the desk cover and turning the key clockwise before dropping it into his trouser pocket.

Declan paused for a moment, ready to berate the small old man opposite to him but also highly aware that the same small old man still had a lot of friends in the city – a lot of friends that wouldn't think twice about 'calming Declan down' if that is what Tommy desired.

Tommy still had respect because he knew the right people, he knew information that could put most of his contacts away, but more importantly, people still needed Tommy's talent. So, for now, until someone else could fill his shoes, he needn't fear his visitors too much and treated them all with the same polite civility.

Tommy picked up his packet of cigarettes and offered one to his guest who declined before lighting one for himself between yellow fingers.

He exhaled slowly, filling the air with death's miasma.

"Sorry Tommy, it's just that the job I had lined up for you seems to have gone missing along with the papers I was expecting, Kenny Slater has disappeared but not before he was seen with my Maggie."

"You and Maggie aren't having any trouble are you," Tommy asked, "if so that's a shame, you seem so well . . . matched."

Declan's face reddened as he struggled to contain his frustration.

"Me and Maggie are just fine," he replied, "but you and I know that she sometimes, well, forgets who pays for her little extravagancies. I sometimes need to remind her of that and sometimes hear about her trying to do a bit of her own business and I won't have it, particularly when I'm owed that bit of business."

"So shouldn't you be speaking to her then Declan and not me, lovely though it is to have you call in," suggested Tommy, who then inhaled heavily on the cigarette.

"You and I both know that if that job has turned up, it's you that the papers will come to Tommy and I'd just like to 'refresh' your memory about whose papers they are," Declan replied.

"Well you've certainly been clear there Declan, I'm in no doubt that if any papers show up here when you've gone, I'll be sure to let you know about it."

"Thank you Tommy, we seem to be understanding each other nicely," Declan acknowledged and pulled himself out of the armchair, "and another thing, if you see Maggie around, or you hear of her, you be sure to give me a call now, you hear?"

"I hear you Declan, I hear you," replied Tommy, as he pulled himself out of the sofa, his other hand still clutching his favourite paper and ash confection.

Declan didn't wait for his host to show him the door but pulled it to sharply after himself before Tommy put back on the chain and the dead locks, flicked the Yale lock and returned to the seductive snooker.

Chapter Eight

Maggie walked into The Spire's shopping centre just as the bells started their melodious chimes. She was killing time, waiting to meet a contact.

She had the air of someone who doesn't want to be seen, turning to peer through the shop windows when shoppers passed by through the central walkway.

She found herself reading posters in the window of a music store, concerts at the Waterfront Hall, shows at the Opera House.

She checked her watch again and moved with determination further into the mall and headed to the coffee shop.

People looked up when she entered the café, the bright blonde locks that framed her face drew the eye nearly as much as the leopard print coat she sported.

She took a seat at the first table and waited to be served. A few minutes ticked by before the woman behind the counter nervously stated, 'We've no waitress on today, I'm very sorry."

Maggie reddened slightly with annoyance, drumming her nails on the table top whilst replying, "Coffee please, I'll have a white coffee."

With other customers, the woman would have left the coffee on the counter but something in the look and manner of Maggie brought her out from behind her scones and over to Maggie's table.

"That'll be £2.70 please," holding her hand out in expectation.

"£2.70?" Maggie retorted, eyeing the coffee to find hidden qualities, "For one cup of coffee?"

"We do a complimentary top up Madam if you'd like that," said the woman, still holding out her hand.

Maggie fumbled in her handbag for her loose change, which she generally tossed into the depths of it when she actually had any, which was rare as she hasn't been used to paying for anything herself of late. She did find a £2 coin though and gathering up an assortment of ten and twenty pence pieces, she thrust them into the waiting palm.

"Will you be wanting anything to eat?" the woman enquired half-heartedly whilst taking a step away from the table.

"Oh no," Maggie replied, "I don't think I shall," as she rolled her eyes and forced a smile, inwardly wishing she had never set foot in the place.

"Oh I am sorry," continued the woman, I've forgotten to give you your complimentary biscuit," and placed a thin caramel café biscuit on the edge of the table before retreating once more behind her counter.

Maggie ignored the biscuit and its cellophane wrapper and played with the sugar bowl until her coffee cooled.

Faint music played in the background, hushed voices talked quietly of holidays, of family weddings. Inane chatter amidst the chintz.

Maggie certainly felt out of place, her presence and attitude too large for the small table she sat at.

More comfortable after dark, a night owl in nightclubs and bars she preferred a champagne glass to the plain white cup with the tiny handle her nails grappled with now. Bubbles and fizz more energising than overheated coffee and yesterday's milk.

She continued to stir the coffee round and round, her fingers missing the cigarettes she always used to take with her drinks, her mind missing the calming certainty of warming nicotine.

Once the coffee had finally cooled she drained the cup and stood up, pushing the chair back with a scrape. She grasped her bag from the table and moved towards the door of the coffee shop, just managing to mainly step over the carelessly left shopping bags at the next table. As she did so, a woman sat at the table frowned at her as Maggie's heel crushed the corner of one of the bags. The woman was about to remonstrate with Maggie but as she made eye contact, she thought better of it, understanding in an instant that her protest would only go one way and she turned her head away quickly in a gesture of compliance.

Maggie moved out into The Spires again and exited into Howard Street, walking along to College Green.

She sat down at a bench on the green facing the Technical College. This seat was as near a seat of learning that Maggie had ever been – an absentee from school in her later years, the world of education became something for others, for the kind of people Maggie grew to despise, thinking that they 'had it easy'.

Given the choice, she wouldn't have changed her lot, but she had a consistent childlike curiosity of things she did not understand, deriding the learned lives she occasionally came across.

Maggie checked her watch and reached down into her bag for her cigarettes and her lighter.

The flame leapt up from the lighter fluid, coming dangerously close to igniting the blonde hair spilling over her bag as she leant over to light the cigarette in the gusting breeze. Inhaling deeply on the comforting smoke, she felt more herself than she did in the coffee shop, her nerves becoming dulled to the anxiety gnawing away inside of her.

She surveyed the passing traffic moving along College Square, picking out the changes in the speed and direction of the cars and halfway through the cigarette she spotted a black Mondeo flashing its headlights as it drew to a stop alongside the kerb. As it did so, it drew an angry blast from a lorry's air horn as it is forced to swerve out sharply to avoid hitting the slowing car from behind. It mercifully found a gap in the traffic to squeeze in to.

Maggie was already on her feet and threw down the cigarette as she grabbed the passenger door handle of the car. As soon as she was seated, it accelerated and threw her back into the seat.

"What's the hurry?" she complained, pulling down the visor mirror to check her appearance.

"You ask me to pick you up on one of the busiest streets in the city, in broad daylight and ask me what's the hurry?" the driver complained, turning into Divis Street, "You don't exactly merge into the background either do you," he continued, eyeing up the hair and the leopard print coat, "I thought we were trying to keep a low profile."

"I'm not the one scared to death to be spotted though am I," she retorted, putting the visor back with a snap.

Along the Falls Road and turning right into Northumberland Street, Kenny Slater headed for the Shankhill Road, checking his rear view mirror as he went.

He scratched his dark, unshaven chin and pulled the car off the road along from the Argyle Business Centre. He turned off the engine, undid his seatbelt and turned his head close to his passenger and said, "Let's get to business, Maggie."

Tommy was studying the racing pages looking for the horses that he'd put a few bob on later that day. He circled the likely contenders with a stubby pencil whilst pursing his lips together to form an 'o'. Every time he followed this ritual, his inner addict was excited by the prospect of the race that he'd watch in the turf accountants along the road. He's stand there looking up at the televisions, shouting 'C'mon' in encouragement to his chosen steed, his mind visualising the moment of victory.

The last time Tommy was in the shop he had had a winner, his first in weeks.

'Artolli' had been given to him as a tip by an acquaintance he'd done a favour for and he'd doubled his usual bet from a fiver to a tenner. His hand had passed the stake over slowly at the window, stalling the moment that he would have to let go.

He had paced nervously outside until the race was due to start. Normally, he didn't trust tips, or tipsters to be more precise, but Brian McClure had always been straight with him and he took the chance.

3.40 and the race started. Tommy's mouth formed its characteristic 'o' as he squinted up at the TV screen until it widened into a quiet grin as his horse came home.

'Artolli' gave him just short of £500. He had counted the money again at the window and said 'Just right' ignoring the tuts and mumbled complaints from his fellow winners waiting for their own payout.

Most of the money followed the rest of his savings into a battered red biscuit tin that he kept hidden between the wardrobe and the wall in his bedroom when he got home, the gap covered by curtains on one side and his bed on the other. If he sat up in bed and carefully reached down he could touch the tin and satisfy himself that all was still secure.

He folded up the newspaper to leave the page he had circled on top and picked up his old tweed coat from the sofa, checking that the bureau was locked as he always did before leaving the flat. He unlocked the door and was about to go out but he stopped for a moment and went back to the bureau and unlocking it, he took out Maggie's lists of numbers.

Something in the numbers began to trigger a memory and he looked down again at the pages of his newspaper and looked across again at Maggie's pages.

His eyes flitted back and forth between the two, finding something that began to unlock further memories, something that might just hold a key to the patterns of spaces and digits neatly typed across each sheet.

Realising though that he needed to get back to the bookmakers, he locked the bureau again and headed out, his eyes glassy with concentration and his mouth fixed in an 'o'.

Later on, a fiver down, Tommy headed back towards home past the shops he rarely visited, his head down but with his mind racing, now able to concentrate on the puzzling numbers in the bureau waiting for his attention.

As he walked past one of the remaining houses that was complete and not sub-divided into bedsits, a front door opened and a woman shook out a door mat, small remnants of accumulated visitors scattering grittily to the pavement.

Some of the dust caught in Tommy's throat and blinking, he stopped in his tracks for a moment to rub his eye before walking on. His face broke into a mellow smile as he went, the scene of domesticity triggering a long forgotten scene from many years ago.

He remembered back to a time when he must have been six or seven, picturing his mother shaking out their doormat at home every day. She always used the event as an opportunity to rid the house of the children in the mornings, sending them off to school with tired but neat uniforms and a biscuit in their pockets for breaktime.

One morning, his mother lay in bed ill, suffering from the early stages of a chest complaint that would take her away for good in the years to come.

Between rasping, gasping breaths she had made Tommy promise to shake out the doormat before he left for school. Tommy did just as he was told, little understanding at a young age that his mother was not so concerned with the accumulation of another day's sooty detritus, but more concerned about the neighbours who would see that no matter what, she ran a good, clean home, the mat being shaken out as a show of domestic routine and harmony.

Later on, his mother would still stand at the door, shaking the mat even though it aggravated her chest and she was left shaking as she clutched on to the door frame, racking coughs doubling her up as she retreated back into the house.

Tommy was there when she died. His mother lay in her bed, suffocating and suffering but still keen to check on which household chores had been done, who had cleaned the grate, who had swept the yard and washed the windows.

The morning she went she had been unusually calm, the fight seemed to have left her. Her breath was still shallow and rasping but she didn't try to raise her head from her pillow. She had instead asked Tommy to draw back the curtains in the room, complaining that she couldn't see him properly and he had gone obediently to the window, pulled back the already open curtains a little further and turned back to his mother's bedside.

When he looked back at his mother, her eyes were staring back at him glassily from the pillow, the last drop of life had left her when his back was turned.

Chapter Nine

Sophie sat on a sofa opposite Kelly, one of his coats draped around her shoulders. She held a paper tissue in her left hand and clutched her stomach with the other.

"C'mon, try a cup of tea, it'll make you feel better," Kelly said gently.

Sophie didn't acknowledge the statement.

Earlier, he had had no difficulty in helping the sobbing girl who had obstructed his driveway into the house. She had clearly suffered a shock but seemed to appreciate the security the house offered compared to the darkness outside.

Kelly had asked her what was wrong and asked if he could get in touch with a friend of hers or the police perhaps, but she had stayed resolutely silent after the sobbing had stopped, replaced with a frozen posture, her head bent down, tousled hair falling over her face.

He looked at his watch and seeing that it was now 11.05 p.m., he realised that he would have to do something and he tried one last time to get through to the girl, to get her to start to talk.

"C'mon," he said, standing up and moving towards her, "I'd best get you home."

The words resulted in Sophie recoiling away from Kelly and her face was screwed up in anguish.

"Look, I don't want to upset you, I want to help you," he said, "but you've got to help me to understand what's wrong. If something has happened at home, I can get someone to call around or I'll go back with you if you like," he added, instantly regretting the offer as he knew nobody close by who could call around and didn't relish the thought of having the silent girl as a car passenger for an unknown length of time.

"Can't go back," she replied quietly, "you can't make me go back there."

"How far away do you live?" he asked gently, sitting back down on the edge of the armchair, "You'll need your things from there wherever you end up going."

"Won't go back there, not now," she stressed, tears stuck in her throat, "can I stay here?"

Noticing Kelly's shocked face she added, "I'll go in the morning, I promise. I won't give you any trouble, I've genuinely got nowhere else to go to."

"I don't think that that is a good idea, the house isn't even mine," he said, "perhaps we can get you to somewhere in the town, a B&B maybe, I'll even take you down there."

"Please, please, don't make me go," she pleaded, "I really won't be any trouble, I will go first thing in the morning, I'll just sleep on this sofa."

Kelly pondered his options. He didn't want the risk of a complete stranger in Kathleen's house and yet he could tell that the girl had had a terrible time that night and the alternative was to force her to leave the house into goodness knows what danger.

"Look, I'll get you a duvet, you can stay down here but I think in the morning that you'll let me take you to somebody you know or let me get you into town."

Kelly knew that the girl seemed to have nothing with her, wearing just a thin dress and pumps, with no handbag or purse, no mobile 'phone, nothing that said she had expected to leave wherever it was she had come from. He didn't know how she would actually manage in the town without anything, but felt that was the right thing to do and wanted to help her somehow, his recent experience at Bangor station having mellowed his attitude to strangers.

His mind recollected the sense of feeling like a criminal, being on the end of abuse himself and having been left to find his own way home alone from the hospital. That all left him feeling that he should trust the girl, to at least give her a chance to show him that she needed help and had no ulterior motive.

Trust is built from past experience. Most of us start out trusting everyone around us, because that is all we are able to do. Our early years' vulnerability though soon toughens into cautiousness and uncertainty. We experience unfairness, unkindness and start to feel a once solid sense of security fade as independent reality encroaches into our inner selves.

This imperceptible cycle proceeds through adulthood reducing our dependence on others until later in life, when we progress from being the carers for others to being the ones being cared for as we travel backwards to re-experience our juvenile emotions in old age.

Kelly felt well and truly out of his depth. Here he was, trusting that the girl on the sofa was not going to take his wallet in the night or turn out to be in some way psychologically unbalanced. He could visualise himself being interviewed by the police in the future, 'Why didn't you call the police service Sir – did you know the girl' and so on.

He went through to the kitchen, drew a glass of water from the tap and placed it along with two biscuits on to the table next to the sofa. "You'd probably best try and get some rest," he said, "the bathroom is just at the top of the stairs, I'll get that duvet for you."

Taking a duvet from one of the spare bedrooms, he returned downstairs to see Sophie lying on the sofa, her feet curled under her and her head resting on the cushioned arm.

Putting the bedding down softly next to her, he said, "I'll see you in the morning, we'll get this sorted out then, just have a think please about who I can take you to in the morning."

Kelly wished that he was back home in Marino, able to ask a neighbour to come in, to get another opinion about what he could do. He thought about who he could ring but he stopped short of making a call, hearing the disbelief from the receiver of the call when he would describe how he had allowed an unknown young girl in a state of shock to sleep on a sofa in a house not his own.

Later, he lay awake in bed, waiting to hear a sound from downstairs. Concentration prevented him from finding sleep as he strained to notice some imperceptible noise in the silence.

As he lay there, images flashed through his mind; the coast road, green topped cliffs towering above the craggy shoreline, sun glinting off the water as it shallows over white sands, a pair of headlights catching a frightened girl in their path.

Kelly threw back the duvet and let out a sigh. He looked at his watch which frustratingly displayed 3.40 a.m. He sat up, swung his legs to the floor and walked quietly to the window. Drawing back the curtains he looked out into the moonlit night and the heavy black sea topped with bright peaks, the tide pulling the water seaward.

A distant boat appeared on the horizon heading east towards the salt jetty down the coast. Looking out further in the same direction he strained to see signs of the west coast of Scotland that he knew would hover into view in the morning, deceptive Jura looking near enough to get to in a few moments sail.

Feeling his eyes grow heavy, he moved back to the bed and climbed in, pulling the duvet back over himself and tried to find a comfortable position. He finally drifted off to sleep with the sea still moving in his mind, a chink of dark light from between the curtains reflected in the mirrored wardrobe door at the foot of his bed.

He woke up with heavy eyes, vaguely aware of a noise downstairs that focused his senses.

Last night's events flooded suddenly back into his mind and he stopped breathing for a moment as he listened for a recognisable sound.

After a few seconds, he got out of bed and moved quietly across the room to pick up a pair of jeans from a chair at the side of the window and pulled them on and as he did so, he heard the keys turn in the lock of the front door.

Kelly had left the keys hanging from the lock, perhaps hoping that the girl would disappear silently in the night, but the early morning brought a new level of curiosity to him and he was determined to find out who the girl was.

He suddenly remembered that his car keys were also hanging from the same bunch of keys and panicked by the thought that the girl might take his car, he flung the bedroom door open and dashed along the landing to the window overlooking the driveway.

He could see that Sophie wasn't at the car and wondered where she had gone, listening for a crunch of gravel to betray the direction that she had taken.

He quickly returned to the bedroom and found a t-shirt to pull over his head as he made his way down the tower staircase.

At the front door, he shoved on a pair of trainers and blinked in the early light as he stepped out through the door into the morning.

A haze sat out at sea, blurring the boundaries between the land and the now placid water. A gentle onshore breeze began to pick up and drew Kelly across the gravel driveway to a gap between the huge stones holding back the fields and cascading gorse.

Through the gap lay countless souls, victims of the shameful famine of 1845/6 that triggered such an exodus from Ireland's shores and subsequently triggered revolutionary upheaval.

The Fenian leaders of the new Ireland across the Atlantic, passionate about the bitter memories of famine and the loss of a third of Ireland's people overseas, encouraged the rebellion that stirred Britain to disestablish the church and to carry the Land Act.

The simple dependence of millions on the very soil and limited crops of Ireland led to the formidable movement against wider British rule, all for the want of employment, sustenance and identity.

No gravestones marked the resting places of the dead, instead meadow topped the burial place, bordered by scrubby field walls and ragged gorse.

In one corner, Sophie sat pondering over the events of the night before, trying to reconcile the scene she had witnessed in the dark.

Kelly walked up to her slowly, saying, "Hello there, are you okay, I noticed the front door opening."

"Yeh, okay thanks and thanks for last night, I'm really sorry for the trouble I've caused you," she replied, looking into Kelly's eyes for the first time since they had met.

He could see that she had not had much sleep either, dark circles just visible under the young, blue eyes.

The breeze picked up, lifting Sophie's fringe and making her squint her eyes together, a shiver passing through her body.

"Come on back to the house, and let's get some breakfast, you look like you need some," Kelly suggested, holding out his hand towards the building.

"Thanks, it's a bit cold out here, I just wanted to come and look at the sea," she said, turning towards the coast.

"I know, I could look at it for hours," Kelly replied, letting silence reign for a moment.

"Don't you get used to it, living here?" Sophie asked, turning back towards him.

"No, I mean, it's not my house, I live in Belfast," he answered, "I'm just looking after it for a friend."

Sophie's gaze turned to the ground and Kelly tracked her eyes downwards.

"I'm just going to go now if that's okay, I've caused you enough trouble," said Sophie, lifting up her face before adding,

"I didn't know what I was doing last night, I just ran along the road, sorry you nearly crashed into me."

"Hey, don't you apologise, I'm the one who nearly hit you."

"All the same, I'm okay now and I'd best go before your friend comes back," she added, standing up and taking a tentative step forward.

"Oh, don't worry about that, Kathleen's left me on my own here," but as these words came out of his mouth a voice in his head asked 'what if she doesn't go now, what if she wants to stay?' so he quickly added, "I mean she could come along at any time I suppose."

"Don't worry, I need to go now as I said, I'm going to walk to the main road – it's not that far home from there and it's a lot better now that it is light," Sophie said, as she started to regain the drive.

"Oh hey, it's the least I can do to give you a lift, c'mon, I'll take you now, unless you want that breakfast," he added with a smile.

"No, I'm going to walk, I want to be in the air, I hope you don't mind and thanks for everything that you've done, I really am very grateful," she stated, touching him on the arm as she walked past.

Kelly watched her as she negotiated the gravel drive, arms folded and head down as she re-traced her steps of the night before, back out to the drive entrance and the main road, back out to face the light.

Kenny and Maggie stepped out of the car at the Argyle Business Centre having first checked that nobody else was hanging around to see them.

Maggie's heels went 'click, clack' as she forged ahead to the premises of 'Robyns and Sons, Building and Joinery'.

The sound of a circular saw buzzed away in the workshop next door as she pushed open the front door, leaving it to slam in Kenny's face as he tried to follow her through it.

The receptionist looked up from the tired, teak desk in front of her and asked, "Can I help you?"

Maggie though was already on her way up the staircase next to the desk, Kenny in hot pursuit.

"We've got an appointment with Gerry Collins," Kenny explained, looking back at the girl who was starting to move from behind her desk.

Instead of following them though, she sat down and started to ring through to her employer's office, hurriedly explaining to him that a man and a woman were about to arrive without an appointment that she was aware of.

Gerry Collins placed down the telephone receiver as Maggie and Kenny entered the room without knocking.

"Well, well," he said, "Kenny Slater and if I'm not mistaken, you've brought along Declan's err . . . 'partner' as well, how delightful."

"We need to talk to you Gerry," said Kenny.

"Most people make an appointment Kenny, even you know that," Gerry stated firmly, raising his voice. "I'm busy just now, so I suggest you both go back downstairs, see Lisa and arrange a convenient time."

"Look, I haven't got time to come back Mr. Collins," replied Maggie on their behalf, "I understood that you knew Kenny well, but if I'm mistaken . . ."

"Maggie is it?" questioned Collins and not waiting for her to confirm or deny this stated, "Kenny and I go back a long way but I am surprised to see him out and about, especially in the full light of day and would much have preferred any meeting we would have had to take place well away from here."

"Gerry, I'm sorry, I couldn't risk waiting, I sort of owe Maggie here a favour, we only need a few minutes, honestly!"

Realising that getting rid of the pair could take longer than speaking to them, Gerry picked up the 'phone again, "Lisa, pop up with some coffee for our guests would you and let Danny know that I may be a little late."

'Danny' was Gerry's agreed codeword with Lisa, it meant to put a few of the workshop lads on notice that their presence might be needed in the event of any unpleasantness in the building from uninvited guests.

"So what couldn't wait Kenny?" Gerry asked, leaning back in his office chair, audible groans rising from its base as it strained to counterbalance the builder's bulk.

"I couldn't wait Mr. Collins," replied Maggie who leant forward and rested a hand on the desk, "I need your help with something, just a bit of information really."

"Ah, we get there," he smiled, "but what's Kenny here got to do with any of this," he smiled as he swivelled the chair around to directly face Maggie, "I wasn't aware that the two of you were acquainted."

"Oh, we go back a little way Mr. Collins, we have an area of erm, mutual interest, one that could interest you too I think," explained Maggie.

"Mmm, I don't think that anything you've got to tell me is going to interest me Maggie. Don't get me wrong, Declan is always welcome here but seeing as he isn't with you, I won't be able to help you at this time. Ah, Lisa is here with the coffee," Gerry noted and passed Kenny a china cup and saucer.

Kenny handled the cup gingerly, wondering how his finger was going to fit through the overly small handle.

Maggie bit her tongue as coffee was passed over to her. She paused for a few moments to let the coffee ritual pass and allowed Gerry to take a mouthful of his milky brew before saying, "You'll have heard of Shane O'Neill, Mr. Collins?"

"I take it that you are referring to the bookmaker Maggie and not the historical figure," questioned Gerry, a patronising smile creeping across his flaccid face.

Maggie had no knowledge of historical Ireland and the O'Neills or the Desmond Geraldines might have been any family from the South, but she was too much of a pro at improvisation to let her ignorance show, too competitive to let a builder from the Shankhill Road gain a psychological point at her expense.

"If you want to talk history Gerry, we can talk about some of the deals that you've done with Declan over the years and talk about the tax you've avoided and the regulations that you've ignored and the bribes that have been given and received to help to line your own pockets."

Maggie's words were slow and deliberate and left Gerry in no doubt that Maggie was not just an accessory of Declan's but that she knew enough about him for him to listen to her.

"C'mon Maggie, you've got my attention," Gerry replied quietly, placing his coffee down on to the desk and leaning forward to engage with the blonde in the fake fur who leant back in her own chair, crossed her legs and said, "So, you've heard of Shane O'Neill, well listen up Gerry, listen up."

Chapter Ten

The day before the meeting with the builder, Tommy had phoned Maggie, incensed by Declan's visit to his home. He had no real interest in helping Maggie above Declan or vice versa but Tommy was not used to being threatened.

Whether Declan benefitted from the papers or Maggie, it was all the same to Tommy, he expect to get paid a fair price for deciphering the codes and columns of figures.

Something in Declan's manner had unsettled him. Maybe it was because he'd come into his home, interrupted the snooker, forgotten the help that Tommy had give to him over the years.

As he stared at the numbers, Tommy began to feel a sense of deja vu, something was making links in his brain. One of the number sequences was familiar. Tommy had been asked to do a job by a bookmaker some years before by the name of O'Neill.

O'Neill had been very particular about Tommy's need to remember a sequence as it would form part of a later job.

Tommy had a head suited to numbers, he memorised the form of racehorses from the paper week-to-week and year-to-year and seldom failed to recall the chaotic patterns that equine form could take.

He had phoned Maggie and told her that she needed to find one of the associates of Shane O'Neill as he was sure that the papers had been his.

Maggie was surprised to find Tommy so readily candid and open, he usually said little and left one wondering just how loyal he was to your own cause or in fact to any others. Not aware of

Declan's visit, Maggie had privately congratulated herself on her powers of charm and persuasion.

She had heard of O'Neill, Declan had mentioned him a few times over the years and Kenny Slater would know who to speak to about him.

Shane had died though two years before, a victim of a lone gunman who had knocked on his front door, brushed his teenage daughter out of the way enough to take a fatally good aim at her father coming down the hall towards the door.

O'Neill's life had ebbed away from the hole in his chest as his daughter screamed her anguished lament.

"How d'ye get on Maggie," asked Tommy, hands rammed low in the pockets of his black coat, wisps of grey/white hair sweeping upwards from his face in the biting breeze, "did you find him?"

Maggie struggled to light her cigarette in the wind, her mouth pouting and grasping it in a vice like grip. Tommy tried to provide some shelter, placing his back to the wind as Maggie stooped down to his level, furiously rolling the flint on her lighter. It finally caught and Maggie sucked for all she was worth until her lungs had enough smoke in them to exhale out in an ecstatic release of toxic vapour.

"Good Tommy, good, he was only too pleased to help in the end," she said, smoothing her own hair back with her spare hand.

The shop they stood in front of was shuttered, the trading day finished some hours before. The road behind Castle Street wasn't exactly busy in the daytime, garish shop front signs at street level leading your eye away from the decaying fabric of the upper storeys. Now, as the light was failing fast the odd passer-by strolled along en route elsewhere, otherwise the pair were quite alone.

The shutters in front of the shop window offered a glimpse of the goods inside – green rugby shirts, posters of Georgian doors, fridge magnets pretending to be glasses of foaming stout – tourist fayre.

The windows either side offered no such glimpses, barricaded as they were with roll down blinds of metal giving most of the street the look of a war zone, soulless, empty, waiting for the next attack on the once thronging thoroughfare.

"So is he the guy we want Maggie?" Tommy asked.

"Oh yes, he's one of the trustees alright although he was mighty suspicious when he realised the answers that I was looking for," she replied, letting flaking ash peel off in the wind.

"D'ye think he'll speak to Declan, Maggie?" he questioned quietly, moving a step closer to her.

"I don't think so, he knows that I know enough about him to make things difficult if I wanted to, but he'll want his share Tommy."

"Don't underestimate Declan, Maggie, he gets to hear most of what's going on," he replied, scanning the street to make sure that nobody else had ventured near to them.

"Aye and when he does, I'll deal with it, there's too much at stake here to let him spoil this one. You don't worry yourself, he'll not know that you're involved – I'll tell him that Kenny was behind it."

Tommy knew that Declan would never believe that Kenny was capable of pulling all of the pieces of this puzzle together. He also knew that he'd come knocking at his door again to question him further just as soon as he got wind of it. Tommy would have to call in some favours, call in the guys above Declan in the pecking order of illegality.

He suddenly felt his own vulnerability though, he hadn't been careful enough this time, he'd allowed himself to get in-between Declan and Maggie. He was though, the catalyst that could fuel a destructive meltdown of the fragile balance of power and contacts that existed in the backstreets and lock-ups, warehouses and store places of tax-free goods and guilty secrets.

He knew, standing there, that he didn't want to take these risks anymore, knew that he wanted the security of the racing pages and the decaying cocoon that passed for a home.

"So what's next Maggie," he asked, stamping his feet to ward off the chill that was building in his bones.

"We need Kath Bruce involved, need her to get some more information," she replied, "I'm going to call on her tomorrow so I'll be out of town for a day or so – she lives up on the North coast these days, just out at Ballycastle."

Tommy's stomach churned at the knowledge that Kath would need to be involved, she was trouble in his mind, a dangerous reminder of the dark days of the seventies.

"We're not playing with too much fire Maggie?" he queried, his hands perspiring in the depths of his coat pockets.

"Too late for that now Tommy, you're in with me on this one and I'm not letting this one go." Maggie pulled the cigarette stub out of her mouth and crushed it underfoot on the pavement. "I'll call on you in a couple of days," she said, turning on her heels and headed off in the direction of the taxi rank at the corner of Bridge Street.

Tommy stood there, shivering slightly in the wind before sighing deeply as he began to walk south.

A taxi driver eyed up his passenger in his windscreen mirror as his car entered Ballycastle.

He had tried to engage in conversation with her as they had left the rank in Belfast but it was clear that this passenger wasn't for making conversation.

Maggie sat in the back of the cab, sunglasses shielding the made up eyes from the coastal glare. She didn't like being out of the City, everything seemed too small to her and the roads lacked the bustle that she favoured.

No tall office blocks here containing businessmen who liked

to entertain, no modern malls containing the textile armour she donned before conducting her 'business' battles.

The taxi swung left up the main street leaving the grass buffer between road and shoreline behind it.

Newsagents and gift shops moved past the windows as Maggie stared out. Dying for a cigarette she silently cursed the no smoking sign that the driver had pointed out to her before accepting the fare this far north.

At the triangle, the road swept uphill to the right and the driver turned around to ask for directions.

"Along here, take a left at the junction – Whitepark Road," Maggie replied, tapping her lighter impatiently against the cigarette packet on her thigh.

The car continued to climb up the road, glimpses of the blue sea once again coming into view. On to the white house it pulled onto the drive and crunched slowly over the sharp gravel.

"Don't wait, I'll find another cab later," Maggie snapped as she passed over a wad of notes to cover the fare from Belfast.

The driver gave her one of those looks that meant, 'No chance of me waiting here anyway', as he checked the money and purposely took a long time to find the £3 change he eventually passed over to her.

She took a good look around her before walking up to the front door, she knocked and lit the much-anticipated cigarette in her hand, exhaling the first delicious mouthful of carcinogenic smoke as the door opened.

Kelly was faced with the 'full works' Maggie as the cloud of smoke cleared, brash blonde hair framing the spotlessly, overly made up face.

"Kath not here yet? she asked, gazing through Kelly to the hallway. "Kathleen? Is she coming, here? I haven't heard from her in a few days," said Kelly, trying to hide his surprise.

"I've phoned, she's on the way – I'll come in and wait,"

Maggie replied, her forward motion forcing Kelly to clear a path for her to enter the house.

"She didn't mention that you'd be here," Maggie stated, making her own way through to the sitting room.

Kelly closed the front door and followed Maggie through to the room and observed her flicking ash into the remains of his cup of tea.

"So you're a friend of Kathleen's then?" he asked, sitting opposite the visitor.

"Oh, we go back a long way," Maggie replied, her gaze focused lazily on the sea view surrounding the property on this side until she was brought back into the room by the ash growing larger again at the end of her cigarette.

She dropped the ash and the filter into the mug. "Kath used to smoke as much as me but I see you've not got an ash tray in the place."

She turned her head back into the room and faced Kelly square on for the first time.

He took in the perfect lipstick as her tongue moved slowly across her teeth, attempting to clear off the taste of the smoke.

"You visiting Kath then are you?" she asked, half heartedly trying to make conversation.

"Sort of, she's letting me stay here whilst my house is being repaired, there was a fire and . . ."

"Oh, a fire, imagine that, hope nobody got hurt," she commented as easily as if she was discussing the weather.

"Err, no, thankfully I was out at the time, but it made a real mess of the place," he added, hoping that Kathleen would walk through the door at any moment.

Maggie got up from the sofa and walked over to the mantlepiece, her heels sinking into the carpet as she went. She picked up a framed photograph from the top and a faint smile crossed her face.

"That was taken a while ago," Kelly said, "Kathleen and her father."

"Oh yes, I remember Jim well enough," she replied before asking, "did you know him?"

"Lived next door then, my father took the photograph," Kelly smiled, the faint memory of the day coming back to him. It had been a hot, sunny day, one of the few where a cloudless sky lasted from dawn until dusk. Kids played on the streets, cars were washed in driveways, people sat on their fold out chairs on freshly mown lawns.

Kathleen's father, Jim, had come home in a new car, the paintwork gleaming in the bright sunlight. Kathleen had stood with him in the driveway, her bright smile matching the paintwork, hand in jeans pockets, taking in the aroma of the British Leyland velour.

Kelly's father John was taking photos of the summer scene, capturing shots for a feature in the Belfast Telegraph. He had been heading back to the house and was distracted by the gleaming car next door, Jim and Kathleen both leaning in to examine the dashboard.

"That would make a nice shot," John had called out cheekily, lifting the camera up to capture the rear ends of father and daughter but as they heard John approaching, they both turned their heads around at the same moment, the shutter clicked and a picture was taken that captured the summer mood of the day.

John dropped off an office copy after the shot appeared alongside others in the next night's paper to his neighbours.

"Hey look at that," Jim had stated, "it'll look great in a frame, I'm going to get one for it."

So Jim and Kathleen continued to smile out from the mantlepiece as Maggie re-positioned them to gaze on from their 2D world. She turned back to look out of the window again, her hair turned into bleached candyfloss in the strong sunlight.

Gravel crunching and cracking announced another visitor, Kathleen.

Kelly's unease with his visitor suddenly dissipated as the Vauxhall stopped in front of the field walls of gorse and rock.

He walked quickly to the front door, determined to beat Maggie to greet her but Maggie just walked back to the sofa and sat back down, crossing her legs, her aloft foot kicking rhythmically up and down.

At the door, Kathleen greeted Kelly with her mantlepiece smile, somewhat older, less elastic, a little lipstick bleeding out into the fine lines around it, but the same smile all the same.

"Kathleen, lovely to see you, we've got a visitor here," he stated, his eyes flashing momentarily toward the sitting room door.

"Has Maggie come by already?" she replied airily, taking off her jacket and wiping her feet on the interior mat, "I was hoping to get here before her so as not to trouble you Kelly – how are you getting on anyway?"

Kelly's mostly relaxed tenure of her home ended at that moment with the return of its doyenne.

"Just fine," he replied and followed her along the hall.

"How's the work going back at home?" she asked whilst looking back over her shoulder as they both entered the sitting room.

"Oh yes, I think they'll be able to finish quite soon thanks, hopefully I can get out of your hair before too long," he said, trying to make it sound that he wasn't too bothered either way although he was, in reality, not sure that he was looking forward to returning home to the house he last saw as a burnt out shell.

The two women smiled at each other as Maggie stood up, "Maggie, how are you?"

"Kathleen, great to see you again, how are you keeping?"

"Now come on, let's sit down and catch up," Kathleen said as she directed her two guests to the sofa.

"Oh, I don't want to intrude, I'm sure that you'll have things to talk about without having me hanging around," stated Kelly, ready to spring back out of his seat.

"Oh no, you're fine," Kathleen replied, but Kelly sensed the women might want some time so insisted he was busy with some paperwork for the house insurance claim and quickly excused himself from the room, secreting himself away from the pair in his room upstairs.

He opened the long floor length windows in his room and breathed in the fresh, salt laden air. The intense sunlight picked out some of the detail on the nearby headland.

The cliff tops shimmered in the heat as Kelly absorbed the warmth on his body, his eyes shut serenely, his hair moving slightly in the breeze.

His ears strained to pick up any vestige of audible conversation from the room below but could only register the low hum of a discreet conversation.

A sound from down below on the ground re-focused his concentration. A black and white collie walked slowly along, its head facing straight ahead but consciously low, trying to skulk by unseen.

The breeze ruffled the dog's fur and a nervous eye peered up towards Kelly, the collie's paws tentatively continuing to reach silently forward.

Kelly knew that the dog would race ahead if he moved too quickly himself and the dog was ready to do so if it sensed a flicker of movement from the window above. His eyes followed the intruder's progress until the dog stopped just by the field wall opposite the window, turned around and lay down on the ground, its gaze conscious still of Kelly but facing more towards the sitting room window.

"What's your business here boy," Kelly said under his breath, "why aren't you at home?"

Chapter Eleven

For the five days following Kathleen's visit to meet with Maggie, Kelly chased his builders daily, feeling that the time had come for him to move on, to move back to Marino where he would feel at home again.

On the sixth day of chasing, the workmen confirmed that the plastering was finished, the electricity re-connected and the house was (just about) habitable again.

Kelly 'phoned Kathleen to thank her for her kindness at Ballycastle the same afternoon. She didn't hide her shock that Kelly wanted to return to a half finished home and insisted that he should stay at her home for a longer period, or at least until the following weekend to allow more to be done.

He had looked out of the window that afternoon at the distant shores and rolling fields and whilst on the telephone, agreed that he would stay until the weekend, giving him another couple of days at the coast. Kathleen ended their call at that stage quite abruptly, saying that a client had just come into her office and Kelly put the 'phone down with some satisfaction that he had made a decision to leave and walked down to the sea front, stopping off for a newspaper on the way back.

Two teenagers were playing tennis on the sea-front courts as he went by, their explosive energy in stark contrast with the sedentary pensioners sitting with their sandwiches on the regulation municipal benches.

Kelly felt like a holiday was coming to an end, the remaining hours and days would accelerate until he would be back home in the house he had known since childhood.

He longed to return the more he thought about it but was fearful of needing to enter into routine again, the need to get back into work hovering in the wings of his mind, ready to carry him away from the wide skies and glorious beaches of the north coast.

His mind took him back to Bangor, to the train carriage, to the embarrassment of the attack that stopped his life where it was and left him feeling vulnerable for the first time since his father had walked out of the family home.

The fire seemed surreal, the house someone else's, the scene part of a gritty television drama. He remembered the smell for real though, the scent of the blackened, sodden remains of his life to date that had lain amidst the charred walls and strewn amongst the damp ashes of his home. The attack on his physical environment was more devastating than the effect of the wound now healing up on his head.

He felt the scar in his hair, the new skin feeling smooth between the hair growing back around it. Not knowing who had attacked him made him angry yet it was not knowing 'why' that troubled him more – the whole incivility of it.

He'd start work again soon, back to the photography, capturing delicious moments in time in his ravenous camera lens.

Initially he'd resisted photography, being his father's profession. What had started as a hobby built out of an admiration for his father's work was instantly put aside after his father's departure. Passed down equipment, quality lenses and developing materials were all consigned to the back of a wardrobe, hidden away from his mother, out of reach of curious temptation.

High school turned into college and a passion for writing developed in him but Belfast didn't need any more scribes charting shocking scenes of sadness. A photo though, depicting anguish, terror, the clouds of dust following a blast – these were ever present elements readily consumed.

Years of being sent out on assignments brought in a steady income but Kelly always knew that he would go it alone, re-focusing his lenses on static scenes, vistas, faces and a wider perspective that the streets of the capital city could not offer.

Successful exhibitions set him up for a while, collaborations on literary spreads produced regular income and one such coffee table volume had just been completed before the fateful train journey from Belfast that had forced him to lay aside his camera, to look inward rather than outward for a period through his usual window on the world.

His eye framed the tennis players in one shot, the pensioners eating sandwiches from plastic bags in another, hearing the shutter's click in his mind.

The elderly couple next to him had shaken out the carrier bag they had nursed once it was emptied of its contents and this immediately attracted the attention of the waiting gulls. The sound of the bickering birds forced Kelly to move off towards the hotel situated on the front and his eventual walk back up towards the house.

He passed neat gardens fronting Victorian houses; holiday homes from another era now harbouring the hospital worker, the council officer, the banker and the barmaid, social cohesion courtesy of the brick built remnants of another age.

Once back along Whitepark Road, he turned into the gravel drive and walked to the front door.

As he passed his parked car, he noticed that a bag had been placed between the planter next to the front door and the house step. Taped on to the top of the gift bag was an envelope with two words written on the front of it, 'Take care'.

He picked up the bag and turned his key in the lock, walking into the kitchen where he put down his newspaper and his keys on the worksurface. He pulled the envelope away from the bag and opened it.

No note was inside the envelope, it had simply been stuck down and attached to the bag, so Kelly pulled open the bag and peered into it expectantly. He pulled out a woollen scarf and as he unraveled the unexpected gift, out onto the worktop fell a battered handgun with a metallic clatter.

In Marino, a torch flickered into a beam that lit up the empty sitting room of Kelly's house.

Bare, newly plastered walls showed patches where they were still drying out. The replaced skirting boards topped the old floorboards at the edges of the room where new had replaced the sodden timbers in the middle. Dark in colour and paint spotted, the old boards gave away their age and told a story of past colour schemes.

In a corner, one of the floorboards was slightly shorter than the rest and the owner of the torch bent down and scraped years of detritus from receded screw heads and took out a screwdriver from a pocket.

Needing to place the torch on its end to enable a better grip that would loosen the resisting screws, slow, deliberate turns took out each screw which were left in turn on their ends on the floorboards nearby.

The now loose board was lifted up and out of the floor. Underneath were two black metal boxes, slightly bigger than cash boxes, with one caught in the torch's focused glare. A gloved hand lifted out the top box from its dusty chamber and it was placed in a large black rucksack, the drawstring and clips quietly closed after it. Replacing the floorboard and the screws, the figure picked up the rucksack and moved back out into the kitchen at the back of the house and in turn out of the back door.

Kelly packed the last of his belongings at the house into bags. He walked over to the bedroom window and drew back the curtains to reveal the morning light.

Large white clouds swept across the sky, a gusty wind rattled the windows along with the stiff gorse topping the banks around the house. Kelly wanted to get out into the fresh morning as soon as he could so he turned back to his luggage, lifted the first bag onto his shoulder and picked up the second. He walked down the spiral staircase, intending to go through the front door and out to the car but as he reached for the keys which were usually in the lock of the door, he noticed that they weren't there and were instead placed neatly on the hall table alongside.

Picking them up with some curiosity, he went back to the door and tried the handle. The door opened easily and a stiff breeze gusted it open further into the house. Kelly was certain that he had locked the door the night before.

He stood there motionless for a moment before vocalising a thought in his mind and he shouted out, "Kathleen – are you back?"

His ears strained for a reply but only picked up the noise the wind was making outside. He looked across to where his car was parked, to check if Kathleen's car was there alongside and its absence curtailed his breathing as he wondered once more how the house was left open. His body tensed and his stomach tightened, momentarily paralysing any further movement as the gun left in the gift bag flashed back into his mind.

Unsure whether to go back into the house or to move further towards the car, he wheeled around with fright as he heard a pane of glass shatter at the back of the house.

He dropped his bags onto the gravel and slowly edged his way round to the side of the house, peering slowly around the corner.

Seeing nothing, he started to move as silently as possible along the house wall, feeling the render to maintain contact with the house for some type of 'security' and to steady himself. He remembered though that he had left his car keys with the house keys at the front door and whispered, 'Shit' to himself, placing his back to rest against the wall as he realised he may be trapped there with no means of escape.

Deciding that he needed the car to be available to him, he started to edge his way back around to the front of the house.

As he reached the corner, he stopped as he could hear footsteps on the gravel nearby. He paused again, hearing only the sound of his own heartbeat pounding a fast rhythm.

The footsteps crunched closer and Kelly was transfixed into inaction until he heard a voice say, 'C'mon Michael, we've got what we need," followed shortly afterwards by the roar of a motorcycle as it tore out of the drive.

A cold sweat trickled down Kelly's back as he started to regain his composure. Still mindful of potential danger, he made his way slowly back to the front of the house and seeing his bags still there, felt completely at a loss as to what was going on.

A slight nausea was still hanging over him as he stepped back into the house, intent on finding out the reason for the visit. He made his way into the kitchen and saw the cause of the shattered glass in the open doorway. One of the large stones from the walls surrounding the house had been heaved through the back door to create access to the lock.

A cupboard door in a unit by the back door was left ajar, the panel at the back of it removed and this was lying flat on the tiled floor. He took in the scene and his mind began to wonder how he would begin to tell Kathleen when he remembered the open front door. The door had been open all night and yet the guys on the motorbike clearly weren't the cause of this as they had clumsily forced their way in through the back.

Kelly thought for a while about what to do first – to 'phone the Police or Kathleen. He made the choice to ring Kathleen as he thought it might look strange to be present in a house that wasn't his where there had been a break-in, particularly with his packed bags lying on the gravel outside.

Kathleen answered the 'phone straight away and gave Kelly the number of an odd job man who could come by quickly and replace the glass. Kelly explained to her why he had called her first before the Police and she asked him if he was alright as the whole experience must have been a shock.

He explained that he was okay, that strange things seemed to be happening to him all the time at the moment and that if it was still okay with her, he would wait for the Police to come, wait for the odd job man and then return to Belfast.

Kathleen empathised and said that she was sorry he'd had to go through this, but not to go and trouble the Police.

"Not trouble the Police?" Kelly asked incredulously, "You've just been broken in to and a cupboard ransacked, plus the front door had been left open this morning."

"Oh, I'm just thinking of you," replied Kathleen in her most soothing tones, "you're supposed to be getting a rest after all that's happened to you."

"All the same, the Police need to be called," he stated, amazed at her cool reaction.

"No, really, I don't want a fuss, I don't need you to call them thank you," she replied, a note of urgency conspicuous in her voice.

"Not call them? You're happy to come back to a house not knowing who has broken in, or why, or what for?" Kelly's mind began to wonder what they had found in the cupboard and he waited for Kathleen's reply.

"Look, I've got a lot on just now, believe me, it'll be fine. I'll tell the Police about it over the next couple of days when I get back there," she stated, leaving Kelly to retort, "So you've been burgled but you're happy that nothing happens about it?"

"I'm surprised that you're still there anyway," she replied, "I thought you were leaving early this morning."

"Kathleen, what's going on?" he asked. "This isn't right, I'm meant to be looking after your place and burglars have got away with goodness knows what and you want me to do nothing about it?"

Kathleen's tone changed. "I'm just thinking of you, I really am," she said soothingly, "I'll get a colleague to cover for me and I'll be there later today – just do me a favour and leave the Police to me would you? Do say that you will, I really, really don't want them coming around when I'm not there."

"Well, if that's what you want Kathleen, but I think you're mad. It's your house though but are you sure you don't want me to stay?"

"Quite sure," she said, "quite sure."

Chapter Twelve

Spices drifted on the air as Tommy walked back home past the fast food takeaways and curry houses en route, each jostling for position and calling out for custom with their extractor fan outputs of deliciousness.

The pavement was littered with chip cartons and plastered with discarded chewing gum. Tommy shuffled along in his thick overcoat, head down but acutely aware of the late night revellers congregating outside the brightly lit caverns of ghastly gastronomy.

He had a packet in his hands, passed over to him in a quiet spot outside 'The Gasworks' at the end of Cromac Street.

Maggie knew Tommy wanted more data, more clues to enable him to piece together and solve the riddle of the lists of numbers and had managed to get more to him through various contacts.

Kenny had come up with a name to contact after the meeting with Gerry Collins. Kath Bruce knew about Shane O'Neill and about who had taken possession of the trustee information Tommy needed and she had known how to get it.

Tommy hated the fact that Kath was involved, of all the shady contacts he had come across, he simply could not work her out, couldn't categorise her into his typical character profile boxes.

Tommy knew how to assess the risks in his contact points but Kath defied his usual assessment.

He also didn't like how many people were now involved in

this process. What had started as Maggie and Tommy had quickly grown to include Declan, Kenny, Gerry Collins and now Kath Bruce too. Too many participants in this paper trail, too many players reaching for the same prize.

A girl shrieked as she was hauled up onto the shoulder of her boyfriend who then ran down the street with her, both tipsy on nocturnal temptation.

Taxis vied for passing trade before their late night club pick ups would begin, flashing headlights and blaring horns filling the air and on the wet carriageway, tyres sprayed out the earlier rains.

Tommy kept to the inside of the pavement, occasionally weaving out of the way of an overflowing rubbish bin or groups of lads devouring messy kebabs, the superfluous salad leaking out of the bottom along with the spicy sauce to further adorn the pavement.

Once Tommy rounded the corner, the noise became more distant, punctuated by the occasional noisy accelerator from distant boy racers.

He got home, placing the packet onto the bureau, ready to set to work. His coat was hung up next to a pile of fading racing newspapers and an ancient vacuum cleaner, unused since the sockets changed many years before.

He moved into the kitchen and shook the watery dregs out of his blue plastic tumbler. He then went back to the coat hook in the corner near to the front door and reached down into the deep pockets for half a bottle of convenience store whiskey.

He took the bottle across to the worktop to join the tumbler but didn't open the bottle – not yet.

An incentive waiting for the breakthrough result that he determined was on the way with the data.

He flicked on the angle poise lamp, took out his magnifying glass, his mouth formed into an 'o' and he set to work.

* * *

Maggie was on the 'phone. Declan stood behind the bathroom door of their hotel room, the door slightly ajar as he strained to pick out information from the hushed tones coming from the bedside 'phone being used.

Maggie was talking to Tommy but she suddenly stopped as she became aware that Declan's shower had stopped – she strained her ears until she was sure that he was moving around again in the bathroom.

Declan, aware that Maggie was listening, continued to dry himself with a large white bath towel before wrapping it around his waist, checking his hair in the steamy bathroom mirror before striding out into the room just in time to hear Maggie say, "I'll see you later."

"I thought you were coming out with me later on Maggie," Declan stated.

"Play your cards right and I might," she replied, turning her head to face him, "unless I get a better offer first."

Declan thought on his feet.

"Right then, I'd best get you to come out right now hadn't I, no time like the present."

Maggie smiled a broad grin and replied, "I might just make you wait until later on Declan Doyle, a girl has things to do you know."

"What are you up to Maggie Haugh?" Declan asked, a note of insistence being betrayed in his voice.

Maggie, ever astute, noticed he was clearly curious, suspicious even and decided to tread carefully. "Declan, do you not trust me or something?" she said, thinking that he would avoid conflict at this point.

"I've never trusted you Maggie, I'd be a fool to," he replied, sitting on the edge of the bed, effectively trapping Maggie in next to him, "so what's going on?"

He said the last two words slowly, deliberately, moving closer to her and leaving his left arm down on the bed, restricting her escape from next to him.

She paused for a moment before launching herself into his imprisoning arms, Declan landing on top of her with a surprised grunt as his arm gave way under him.

She made a calculating move and kissed him furiously, then reaching down to his towel, undid it, pulled it away and Declan unquestioningly responded just as she expected.

Declan lay next to Maggie, perspiration beading on his forehead, his dark hair plastered flat to his temples.

"Ah Maggie, I'm going to have to have that shower again now all over again," he said, swinging his legs onto the floor from the bed and standing up to reach down for the towel left on the floor.

"Oh, go on with you," she said playfully, slapping his naked backside as he bent down.

Declan leapt out of the way with a laugh and headed back into the bathroom, closing the door behind him.

Maggie seized the opportunity and leapt out of bed as quietly as she could and running across to the wardrobe, pulled out a low cut dress from a hanger and quickly pulled it over her head. She glanced into the dressing table mirror to quickly adjust her blonde tresses and stepped into a pair of high heels.

She dashed back to the bed and shoved some change and her 'phone into the pockets of her coat along with Declan's wallet which was conveniently situated on the bedside table. She grabbed her handbag and paused for a moment to check on the noise coming from the bathroom. The shower was being turned off.

Maggie glanced back to the table and grabbed Declan's car keys too, but in doing so, knocked an empty wine glass to the floor. It broke with a crash as it fell against the side table.

Declan's ears picked up the sound from the bathroom and he reached out for the handle of the bathroom door to check on Maggie.

He opened the door just as Maggie was carefully opening the bedroom door to exit the room.

"Hey! Where do you think you are off to!" he shouted out.

"I'll see you later," she cried, "someone to see!"

Declan paused for a moment before suspicion and a growing sense of rage filled his chest and he flared his nostrils as he took in a deliberate gasp of air.

He ran out of the bathroom and flew over to his suit trousers and pulled them on over wet legs and raced to the wardrobe for a shirt. He fumbled with the buttons as he tried to hurry the process, wet hair dripping on to the cloth. He dashed over to the bedside table to grab his car keys and his shoes and as he did so, he stepped on to the broken glass and screamed out with pain as the jagged stem dug deep into his foot.

He raged as he drew the glass back out of his foot but had to accept defeat as blood began to pour from the wound. He hopped over to the discarded towel and wrapped it about his foot, crying out, "Bitch, bitch, bitch!"

Chapter Thirteen

Tommy, hard at work over the lists and the codes supplied by Maggie, suddenly sat up straight, his eyes focused on an empty space in front of him as his mind focused on the mismatch on the pages before him.

Tommy had been so sure that the data from Maggie had been the last link he needed but the numbers from her were clearly designed to deceive.

He hadn't needed much confirmation to complete the picture and had hungrily poured over the new jigsaw pieces, tumbler of whiskey at hand to toast his own success.

Earlier that evening he had taken a risk and called Maggie, his usual careful reserve and patience caught up in the realisation that he was nearly there, that he could produce the whereabouts of the money that Maggie wanted so badly.

Now, he realised that someone knew what he and Maggie were doing in their quest, were aware of how close they were to completion and had purposefully provided obviously incorrect information to make this point blatantly clear.

He looked down at the numbers again but this only confirmed what he realised from first review. The colour drained from his face and his hands turned cold and clammy. Wanting to remove the papers from his sight, he had slammed the bureau shut, staggered across to the musty sofa and fell back into the chair, closing his eyes and rubbing his wrinkled forehead with his craggy hand.

He sat there motionless, waiting for Maggie to arrive, he knew she was arriving expecting the best of news, knew that she would be able to leave Declan behind in her wake as she would have the means to break free but knew now that she had nothing at all. Tommy was only providing an empty gift to her with his reckless 'phone call.

Tommy's heart missed a beat as the doorbell rang. He'd been sitting on the sofa, waiting for the minutes to pass by until Maggie arrived, thinking of what he would say, replaying it over and over in his mind.

Thinking of who he could contact to ward off Declan when he came calling in search of Maggie, thinking of past jobs, past successes, humbling failures.

Something at the core of Tommy surfaced for the first time in many years, the desire for maternal protection, for the cocoon that he had inhabited for his very first years before he had been left to live with relatives, cold, unaffectionate relatives, after his mother had passed away.

He felt nauseous as he opened the door, feeling his years as he fumbled with the Yale lock.

"We're going to have to be quick," Maggie said, pushing the door closed behind herself, "I've left Declan at the hotel but he's going to be coming after me, he knows I'm on to something."

"Maggie, I need to tell you . . ." Tommy started but didn't get chance to finish.

"I've taken the car, so we should have time – have you got the lists for me?" she asked, finally pausing to look at him.

What's happened to you," she asked moving her head down to Tommy's level to read the furrowed brow, "you look like you've seen a ghost."

"You'd best sit down Maggie," Tommy said, motioning weakly to the sofa.

Maggie blinked slowly a couple of times, her own brow forming into a furrow, "You have got the lists for me haven't you Tommy, you told me you'd finished the list and locations."

"They're the wrong numbers Maggie, you've been given the wrong numbers, someone knows what we're up to," Tommy replied, surprising himself with his ability to sound calm.

Maggie's mouth formed to speak but her jaw just jutted forward, her mouth frozen open as the enormity of the news hit home. Unsure what to do whilst her mind raced, she sat down on the sofa after all and said, "Christ Tommy, get me a drink for God's sake."

Tommy moved to the kitchen to find a clean glass but could only find an old, thick glass tumbler in the cupboard, dust and dried deposits lining its dull interior. He rinsed the glass out under the tap and dried it on his jumper sleeve after shaking out the excess water.

Maggie had already found the half bottle of whiskey though and was taking a swig from it as Tommy re-entered the room with the glass.

Screwing the top back on the bottle she said, "Tommy, tell me what you know and tell me everything," her lips moist from the whiskey. "Have you any idea what we've got mixed up in here Tommy, any idea who we're mixed up with?"

"Oh Maggie," he replied, I'm too old for all of this, I should never have taken the task on, I wish to God I hadn't, I really do."

"Tell me how you know they're fake lists, how do you know its not just your mistake Tommy?" she said, stabbing her finger in the air in his direction, but as the words come out, she knew that this man didn't make mistakes – if he knew that the clues were wrong, then they were wrong.

"Maggie, I'm telling you as it is, whoever gave you that information has planted duff information within it, knowing it will be of no use and knowing that we're going to realise it. Someone is watching what we're up to and they are steps ahead of us Maggie, steps ahead." Tommy explained whilst beginning to cough as an amount of phlegm caught in his throat.

Maggie raised her eyes towards the ceiling, letting the words sink in as she sadly took in the wrinkled and peeling wallcovering at the top of the walls and the spots of black mildew eating up the paper in the corners of the room.

"But how can you be sure Tommy, for all we know, we might just be missing something, you know, like last time," Maggie replied, her pleading eyes looking up at him, wanting him to soften his fixed glare.

"No Maggie, whoever gave you the last information knows we are on to something and has purposefully given us the wrong information. There's no doubt in my mind, the figures aren't just different than I was expecting, they're written to look like the others but the sequences are all wrong. The only question I have in my mind is who gave you these and how long ago." Tommy stared at the bottle of whiskey, still resting in the grip of Maggie's manicured hands.

"I've just run out on Declan, Tommy, you said you'd finished, that we were there, why in God's name did you have to ring me if you weren't sure of the location?" Maggie implored, her words beginning to slur a little as she paused to take another mouthful of the distilled fire water in her hand.

"Whoever gave you the data gave me just enough to make me certain, but I knew as I finished it off that something wasn't right with the answer I'd come up with. Someone clearly knows the way I work Maggie. You're going to have to tell me where you got it, either that or you and I aren't going to be able to stay around here much longer."

Maggie finished off the whiskey and dropped the empty bottle on the floor.

"Kath Bruce told me who to contact to get it, she gave me the contact."

"I told you we shouldn't get involved with Kath, Maggie – there's just too much history there, too many people have got burnt before." Tommy stooped down and picked up the discarded bottle, setting it upright on the sideboard. "Who did Kath put you on to Maggie?"

"Oh God, no one I knew, some number out in Armagh, some lads said they knew how to get the information," Maggie replied, her head then resting decisively back on the grease stained backrest of the sofa, a permanent reminder of the chair's usual occupant.

"Oh Maggie, why didn't you let me find out more about them before you got them involved?" Tommy questioned, a note of despair entering his voice. "We've got to find out who is behind this and quickly, before they know that I've worked this out – that is, unless it is too late already."

Maggie's eyes opened wide, "I'll go and see Kath, she'll help us surely."

"Maggie what are you saying, why do you think we can trust her? How do you know that she hasn't set us up herself?" asked Tommy, his arms outstretched to stress his point.

"Kath wouldn't do it to us, I'd know, Tommy. Someone else is behind this," she paused for a moment before her voice raised to say, "oh Christ Tommy, what if it's Declan?" She sat bolt upright in the chair and continued, "He's been asking questions and been asking about you too."

"Whoever it is, we have got to find out Maggie. Who else knows that you had the information?"

"Just Kath and Kenny of course, but he's alright. Oh, and Gerry Collins knew we were digging around. But what if it is Declan, he will kill me for sure," she stressed, looking sorrowfully across at the empty bottle on the side, "in fact, he'll kill us both!"

"I don't think we just have to worry about Declan, Maggie. I can deal with Declan to some extent but we have to work out if Kath or Kenny or Gerry has been tipping someone off – even all three of them – so how do we start to find out? I'm not doing any more for you on my own."

Conscious of the potential danger looming over them both, sniffing around someone else's hidden proceeds of crime,

Tommy realised they had few options. "You're just going to have to contact Kath, see what she knows – but I'm not going to be there Maggie."

He let the words sink in, waiting to see if she picked up on his self preservation strategy.

"I'll get her to come here, show her what we know, show all our cards so we can see her reaction Tommy. I'll ring her now," she says excitedly, reaching for her mobile from the replica Prada bag at her side.

"No Maggie, not here. She'll be suspicious enough if she's involved in the deception, she'll never come here. No, meet her somewhere public, somewhere you can see her reactions, that way she still doesn't have to know that I'm involved does she Maggie. I mean, you've not told her I'm involved surely?"

"No, God no, but I'm telling you one thing. We're in this together so don't think for one minute that you're leaving me to deal with this on my own because if you do, I'll make sure she knows you're involved!"

Maggie's usual bravado started to return as she regained her composure and felt a little more in control.

"Maggie, if it is Kath we've got to worry about, I don't doubt that she'll already have worked out it's me, so just don't go giving away information until we have to – keep her guessing and all that. We've got to be the ones in control here," he said, pausing to rub his creased brow with his hand. "What'll you do about Declan, Maggie?" he asked quietly after a moment, the realisation that he was still a current problem coming back to the forefront of his mind.

Maggie didn't get a chance to reply. At that moment there was a heavy pounding at the front door, the thin wood shaking violently inward.

Declan's voice screamed out into the flat, "Maggie! Maggie, I know you're in there you WHORE!"

* * *

Kelly turned the key in the new front door. The door that had been replaced following the one the fire brigade had smashed in to bring the earlier fire under control.

The downstairs of the house had been largely gutted by the fire, with only a few items of furniture relatively untouched by the damaging smoke and flames. The entrance hall had been completely wrecked along with the stairs and landing where the other rooms had showed varying degrees of blackened walls where the heat had forced its way through gaps in between door and their frames but had broadly survived.

These few furniture survivors had all been grouped together in the least affected room, the sitting room, but sheets had been draped over them to protect them from the new plasterboard and skim that had replaced the old walls.

As he opened the door, he was faced with two tone plaster walls, some still showing signs of drying out, displaying darker wet between the lighter sandy colours.

The decorators had started to paint, including the base coats on the skirting boards but Kelly had asked them to go to another job for a few days, saying he wanted a little time to get used to being back in the house without other people around.

He breathed in the heady mixture of new gloss and undercoat, mixed in with the reek of drying plaster. He walked over the plaster-spattered floorboards, sighing as his shoes went crunch, crunch over the gritty mixture.

For all the newness, for all the smells, all the mess, he was still glad to be home.

He made his way upstairs, back in to the house he knew so well. Apart from the landing, they had managed to contain the fire downstairs before it had scrabbled its way up into the bedrooms.

He looked across to where the new plaster skim ended, spread as it was across the torn off remnants of wallpaper on the sound wall alongside. He tutted as he felt the uneven edge where the builders had messily finished their work, plaster and paper mixed together.

He continued into his own bedroom and opening the door, was relieved to see that much of it was just as before apart from the strong smell from the fire that has oozed its way into everything.

He dropped his bag on the floor and lay down on the bed, letting the events of the past few weeks lock themselves away somewhere in his brain. He wanted and needed to move on, to leave that whole chapter behind him in another place, one that no longer existed.

Sitting up, he looked at his watch, which showed 5pm. He pulled one of his bags towards him and took out his laptop. Powering it up, he waited for the desktop to load impatiently.

Picking 'photos' from the toolbar he surveyed the photographic work he'd recently stored there. He also had many scanned images of his father's work in there too, all taken before he went away.

He clicked on a few of the recent images and started to edit the ones that he had taken whilst in Ballycastle. He clicked on a photo of the famine graveyard taken early one morning when the cool mist rising from the ground seemed to suggest the countless, nameless spirits of the souls buried beneath.

He clicked on another, a broad spreading tree near the clifftops, the windswept boughs permanently whipped upwards by the seemingly unceasing breeze. He zoomed in on some of the lower branches and spied a cat sitting amongst the tattered leaves, watching Kelly as he unknowingly had watched it.

In another, he smiled at a donkey peering over thorny yellow gorse and random broken rocks.

He clicked now on another folder and selected a photo of himself. Pictures taken in an introspective moment, black and white self-portraits, a study of a man behind the lens with the aid of a timer.

He zoomed in and peered into the dark hair standing up from the unwrinkled forehead. He stared into the large, inky eyes, past the small nose and then past the even teeth visible between parted lips. The picture was full of contrast and was sharply focused, highlighting every pore of his skin and each hair of the stubble defining the line of his chin and stretching down his neck.

He clicked on another folder and stared into his father's face. He paused, perhaps seeing for the first time the similarities in their faces, this image though betraying more years than Kelly's, his father's face etched with furrows, his stubble taken over at the chin with white. Kelly wondered if this is what he would look like in the future and then remembered that his father would now look much older than the photo, wondering if he would even recognise him if he saw him in the street.

He decided that his father's mouth was wider than his, his eyes duller, his hair thinner and felt uncomfortable with the memories the detail in the picture brought back to him.

Searching through the other scanned photos taken by his father, he spotted one of an Army Land Rover amidst broken glass and broken people. Windows being blown out of a store in another, spraying dust, brick and smoke across an empty street.

In another, a shot taken of his father, grinning ear to ear as he was caught falling backwards from the end of a bed, arms outstretched, grasping the air for invisible and absent support.

Kelly clicked off the shot but as the picture closed, something caught his eye. He clicked back on to the image, something else was in the shot.

He zoomed in behind his father's shoulder to focus on the floor length mirror on the wall near the head of the bed. As the software cleared the image his eye caught the reason for his puzzlement. He stared and stared at the image caught by the mirror of the person taking the photo of his unrobed father.

He stared again, completely bemused by the image he could see of the scantily clad photographer inadvertently captured in the reflection, for the person he could see with the camera lifted to their face, wearing nothing but knickers, was none other than Kathleen. A young Kath Bruce in the same bedroom as his father.

Chapter Fourteen

Kath's 'phone had rung a number of times. She had purposefully missed the calls, letting the phone buzz away on silent without checking the screen to see who was calling.

Kath rarely answered a call when she wasn't expecting one, preferring to be the instigator of a call, preferring to be in control.

She scrolled down the screen to see who the calls were from and saw Maggie's number first, followed by Kelly's. Pausing for a moment, she selected Kelly's number, conscious that he had planned to move out of the house at Ballycastle earlier that day.

Kelly answered straight away with a reserved 'Hello'.

"How are you getting on John? I noticed a missed call from you there," she prompted whilst sitting down to listen to his reply, expecting the call to take a while.

"Kathleen, we need to meet up, I need to talk to you," he stated.

"Good heavens, is there anything wrong over there," she quizzed, "not something with the house again?"

"It's nothing to do with the house Kathleen, I need to see you to talk through something, where are you now?"

"Well you can't just leave it like that, c'mon, what's on your mind, I'm not sure I like the sound of this, something is clearly bothering you?" she replied, trying to gain an explanation from him.

"It's about my father Kathleen, I need to see you to talk about my father."

Kath paused, letting the situation sink in, wondering why Kelly was bringing up his father at this point in time, after all of the years that had passed in-between.

She presumed Kelly wanted to reminisce maybe, that he was simply looking to re-live the happy years when she had lived next door to him. Simpler times, before the hardening years had taken their toll.

"Well," she replied slowly, "shall we meet for a coffee in a day or two – my treat?"

"Kathleen, I need to make myself clear, I want to see you now," he stated, "not tomorrow, not the next day, just now please."

Kath realised that she wasn't going to end this call easily so looked at her watch and said simply, "I'll come to you then, say fifteen minutes?"

She ended the call and breathed shallowly, trying to second-guess what Kelly wanted to know.

Many images and recollections crowded her thoughts as she left the apartment and reached her car.

Once there, she sat inside and picked up a voicemail from the second missed call. Thinking it might be from Kelly, she dialled to listen to it wondering whether it would give her any clue about the conversation they had just had. Instead a voice sobbed over the loudspeaker, "Kath, . . . Kath, if this is you behind all this I swear I'll . . ." but the voice then broke down before resuming, "I need to see you, we need to talk," then silence for a moment before Maggie continued, "Oh Christ!!" and the line went dead.

Kath let the words sink in, let Maggie's pleading words wash over her and then she calmly started the car's engine and turned out into the road in the direction of Kelly's home.

Declan ran out of the hotel and into the street desperately following Maggie. His open shirt and bare, bloodied feet attracted more than a passing interest from passers by unused to scenes like this on a weekday morning.

When he realised that the car had been taken along with his keys, his choice expletives could be heard some distance away.

He raced back upstairs from the street to his hotel room and thrust his painful feet into the nearest pair of shoes and grabbed his jacket.

He had a hunch where Maggie would be as he'd thought he had recognised Tommy's voice in the background of the telephone conversation she'd had as he had come back out of the bathroom and disturbed her.

He reached the street again and jumped into the first taxi he could find and shouted at the driver to take him to Tommy's address.

Suddenly conscious that he didn't have any money as Maggie had taken his wallet, he told the driver that he was picking up someone at Tommy's address and then they would go back into the City centre.

As they pulled up in front of Tommy's, Declan told the driver that he would just ring the doorbell for his friend and be straight back. It had been a quiet day for the driver and he sat there quietly whilst Declan ran up the steps to the flat.

He pounded on the door, taking out all of his frustration on it.

"Maggie!! Maggie, I know you are in there you whore!" he screamed, continuing to hammer on the door as it bounced on its very hinges.

Inside the flat, Maggie sat bolt upright on hearing Declan arrive whilst the colour quickly drained away from Tommy's face.

Maggie roused herself into action and grabbed her handbag, dashing into the kitchen area. As she went, she fumbled with her bag to reach her mobile 'phone.

The noise at the door went 'wham, wham' again as the door strained with the force on one side of it that threatened to weaken the aged hinges and locks.

Tommy shouted out, his own voice tight and strained, "Declan, Declan, what are you doing man, c'mon Declan, leave it alone!"

"I know she's in there Tommy, I swear to God . . ."

Tommy thought quickly and risked, "She's not here Dec, she was here but she's already left."

Declan screamed out, "Don't take me for a fool Tommy you old bastard, my bloody car's outside your fucking front door!"

Maggie managed to dial Kath Bruce's number on her mobile, her false nails clattering on the keys as she tried to steady her hands enough to dial the number.

She left a message for Kath hoping that she would have answered, maybe even given her an idea of who it was that they needed to watch out for, needing to know if she had to calm Declan down or run for her life in the opposite direction.

As she left Kath the urgent request for contact, Declan kicked and kicked the door with all his strength, unconscious of building pain in his knee and his feet as he did so. One last attempt and the door flew inwards and he flew into the flat as the metal chain on the door snapped and scattered across the room in pieces.

Hearing what seemed to be an explosion happening in the sitting room, Maggie let out, "Oh Christ!" in fright before dropping the 'phone to the floor from her shaking fingers, inadvertently cutting off the call as she did so.

Declan glanced around the sitting room before quickly moving into the kitchen, sweat dripping down his temples, his face maroon with anger.

Maggie opened her mouth, a mouth where the lipstick that had already smudged on the neck of the whiskey bottle was beginning to look patchy at best. She tried to speak, to pretend that there was nothing unusual in her being in Tommy's flat, only having taken Declan's car, his wallet, his very dignity.

Words raced around her head but sentences didn't form. All that would come out between her lips was a faint, "Don't . . .".

Now close to her, Declan slapped Maggie full in the face with all his remaining might, sending her hurtling to the floor and on to her side as she fell.

He paused just long enough to watch her try to get up, her blonde hair all flung over to one side, trails of spit oozing from her rapidly reddening mouth.

He launched his arm back to send another blow her way, towards the pitiful sight that sickened him to the pit of his stomach, but Tommy got in the way.

He had come into the room after Declan, hoping to somehow prevent what had already happened, to tell him a fabricated tale to explain away the meeting, anything to just get him out of the flat.

This second, even heavier blow struck Tommy as he had got in-between Maggie and Declan. It hit the side of his head but although a mainly glancing blow, not intended for him, it sent him sideways and his old legs struggled to move quickly enough to prevent his fall.

He tottered, almost in slow motion until his foot caught in a loose piece of greasy lino and he went down, his head striking the corner of the kitchen worktop with a load 'crack' as he fell.

Maggie saw her chance and scrambled to her feet, dashing past Declan who was still shocked by the blood pooling out of Tommy's head wound on to the tacky kitchen floor.

Declan came to his senses and gave chase after Maggie who had reached the door. She hurtled down the steps to the street where the taxi driver was still waiting, mesmerised by the activity happening in front of his as Declan had forced his way into the flat.

She pulled at the door of the taxi but the door was locked shut. The taxi driver stared open mouthed at Maggie, her hair piece barely still attached to her head, makeup streaked down her face as she screamed, "Let me in, let me in," to the driver, hammering on the window as she did so.

Declan had reached the steps and the taxi driver saw the state he was in, dripping with sweat and what looked very much like blood on his hands, the result of him trying to hurriedly drag Tommy back upright.

"Let me in!" screamed Maggie again and the taxi driver did as he was told. He opened the door and waited just long enough for Maggie's feet to get into the car before accelerating off down the street leaving Declan there yelling obscenities in the street behind them.

Kathleen pulled up outside Kelly's house and stared into the front room, the window absent of curtains, clearly displaying Kelly pacing the floor back and forth.

Kelly looked up and saw Kathleen. She raised her hand as if to wave but he had already left the room and was walking down the hall to open the front door.

He was aware of his heart beating faster as he held open the door for Kathleen as she made her way into the house. Neither of them spoke, no friendly greeting, both knowing that a conversation neither of them wanted to have was about to take place.

As Kathleen brushed past him, he muttered, "Thanks for coming," under his breath.

He took her through to the new kitchen, the units and worktops completed but as yet no tiles sanitised the walls, no floor covering underfoot, just the gritty remains of dried plaster.

Vacant spaces lined the room where appliances would go but for now, the gaps were cluttered with dangling wires and the last kitchen's wallcovering which the builders knew wouldn't show.

Kelly rested against the granite worktop and Kathleen did the same, placing her handbag down before saying, "So what's this all about, are things okay?"

Kelly let her tone of innocence sink in for a moment before replying, "I need to talk to you about my father."

Kathleen stared at Kelly's face, her lips pursed together, holding back the immediate response she wanted to give of, 'Goodness, what on earth for,' and instead asked, "What do you want to know?"

Kelly didn't expect her frank approach and looked towards the window, in which he could see Kath's face, the same one that he could still see reflected back in the photograph etched into his mind.

"When did you last see my father?" Kelly asked, his voice betraying the suppressed emotions swirling around in his mind.

"When do you think I last saw him John?" Kathleen asked, looking straight into Kelly's eyes.

He broke the visual contact, breathed shallowly and replied, "Just tell me when you last saw him please."

Kath paused again, considering how much Kelly might know, how much she could afford to give away.

"Your father, I last saw about five years ago John," Kath stated, ensuring that she met Kelly's gaze full on before letting the confession leave her mouth.

Kelly struggled to speak. His father had walked out on his mother and him twenty years before with nothing other than a note to his mother at the time. No other contact was made, no 'phone calls, no birthday cards, nothing.

The only confirmation that Kelly had that his father had been alive was in the form of money regularly deposited in the old joint bank account each month. Kelly's mother knew intuitively that he was with another woman, but took the money each month, seeing it as her right, his duty, the very least he could do, to look after his wife and son even though from afar.

"Five years ago?" he said, emphasising the 'five'. "You saw my father five years ago and you never even thought to tell me he was alive? Not once in all those years?" Kelly wiped the spit from his mouth as his emotions welled up inside his core. He choked back tears that refused to let Kathleen see and rubbed his hand over his face, the look of incredulity failing to shame Kath's impassive face.

"You wouldn't have understood if I had," she replied.

Kelly snorted with incredulity, his watery eyes hardening as his brows knitted together, trying to reconcile Kathleen's comment.

"Wouldn't have understood! I wouldn't have understood, well thank you Kathleen, thank you for your caring approach. You are just unbelievable. What was there for me to understand for God's sake?"

"Leave it, John, before I tell you things you don't want to hear," said Kathleen, picking up her car keys.

"You shack up with my father, who for all I knew had been dead for years and expect me to just take it, as if it was something that happened every day?"

Kelly moved towards the door to block Kathleen's exit.

"I think we're done here, John, at least until you calm down and can be civilised," she replied, pushing him to one side.

As she did, Kelly blocked her path again, breathing heavily with the frustration inside him, his arms outstretched in a show of defiance that their conversation was not yet over.

"So where is he? Where's my fabulous father who left us to play out his mid-life crisis with the girl next door?"

Kath paused, looking down at the floor. She took a heavy breath and said, "This isn't the way you should have to find out, not the way it should be."

"Find out, find out what?"Your filthy secret has been discovered now Kathleen, you can surely do no worse," Kelly said, "what is it, is he now shacked up with someone else, did he get bored of you? Has he got another family, three kids in tow or what?"

"No, none of that," she said quietly.

"He's lying low somewhere then, too ashamed to face his family?" he said, irony in his voice.

"John, I just don't know," she paused, "I'm really sorry but your father moved away five years ago, that's why he's not around here to do any of those things. I have absolutely no idea where he is now, but he made it very clear that he wanted to escape from his old life completely." She looked up into his face as she said the words, watching each blow land and register, demolishing his defences, leaving only the dry dust of despair behind as his hope crumbled inside.

Chapter Fifteen

The tap dripped slowly into the kitchen sink of Tommy's flat, the sound of each drop echoing around the otherwise silent room.

It was dusk; the fading light was retreating from the day, carving shadows out of the furniture onto the walls.

The linoleum floor still held enough of the light to pick out the sticky blood oozing from the wound in Tommy's head. He lay on his side, his glasses twisted and broken so that one arm stuck out sideways from his face.

His lank hair was mixed with the blood on the floor, his right arm trapped under his body, the fingers of his right hand a deep blue, immobile after he had failed to get up following Declan's unsuccessful attempt to place him back on his feet.

Rasping breaths rattled out of his lungs between his drying lips. His eyes stared blankly across the room to the printed 1970's wallpaper but were unable to focus on the pattern.

In the silence, Tommy could hear his own heartbeat as it struggled to keep a steady rhythm.

His head felt very light and he felt very tired.

His eyelids began to close slowly until they left narrow slits, just enough for him to catch the last of the daylight as it left the room.

Tommy's eyes closed fully now and he allowed himself to welcome sleep.

"Where do I drop you?" asked the taxi driver, his eyes glancing up to look at Maggie in his rear view mirror.

The figure in the back was slumped in a corner behind the driver's seat, her head resting on the glass of the side window and swaying slightly as the car manoeuvred through the busy streets.

"What?" replied Maggie hazily, lifting her head away from the window as she did so.

"Where'd I drop you love, I'm sorry, but I've got a booked fare to pick up," the driver stressed, looking up again into the mirror.

Maggie caught his eye and he looked embarrassed and he quickly looked back towards the road ahead.

Maggie knew that he probably didn't have a booked fare to pick up, knew that he probably wanted rid of his passenger after the scene outside Tommy's flat.

She played along with him though, looking hurriedly out of the window saying, "Oh that's fine, you can just drop me off along here. I can be on my way from here, no problem."

As the driver pulled in, Maggie took out her compact from her bag and her lipstick. With shaking hands, she flipped open the mirror and took in her swollen jaw and lips where Declan's blow had landed heavily.

She sucked in air through her teeth as she skillfully applied powder to her face and lipstick on top of her throbbing lips.

"That'll be £14.90 then please love," the driver said, suddenly feeling guilty as he took in the scene, Maggie trying to regain her dignity, trying to cover up what had happened, applying another mask of make-up.

As she opened her purse, the coins she wanted fell down into the foot-well and out of reach. Maggie stared down at the floor for a moment, saying, "Oh shit," before taking out a £20 note and saying, "keep the change, it's fine."

"Do you not want the money you've dropped, I . . .," Maggie cut him off with, "leave it, just . . . leave it."

The car had stopped along Oxford Street, the bright lights of the Waterfront Hall reflected in the Lagan alongside.

Maggie opened the car door and stepped out unsteadily onto the pavement, slamming it shut behind her. As she did so, she caught sight of herself reflected in the window of the door.

Her eyes opened wide as she took in the rapidly worsening swelling around one side of her face. Just as she did, the taxi driver moved off into the traffic in the direction of May Street.

She looked around her, unsure what to do now, where to go – failing to stop a growing sense of bewilderment.

Walking along the Laganside walk, she was greeted by the 'Beacon of Hope' who held out her hoop to Maggie before the blonde carried on and stopped to stare at the 'Big Fish' sculpture now in her path.

She focused in on the ceramic tiles, seeing adverts for 'The Royal Manufactory of Linen and Damask', another for 'William Sloan, All Kinds of Ornamental Wrought Iron Work'. Hotels advertised, the 'Belfast Royal Hotel' in Donegall Place,

the 'Belgravia Hotel Ltd' in Ulsterville Avenue.

'Cowan's celebrated whiskies', 'McBurney's', 'Inglis & Co biscuits', 'Kincaid Bros for Curled Hair, Wool and Flock'.

Finally she looked at one for Messrs.' R Morrow's 'Trenia Irish Beauty Soap', seeing the fresh face of a Victorian beauty staring back at her. Maggie felt acutely aware of her own inner feelings, of despair, of uncertainty. Her eyes focussed again on the woman's face and she turned into the pixellated dots she was made up of and was no longer whole.

Maggie broke free from her gaze and opened her bag, scrabbling about for her cigarettes and lighter. With shaking hands she managed to catch the stick of trembling tobacco in the roaring flame from her throwaway lighter.

Turning her back on the stone lion leaping from its portico on the Custom House building and the languid waters flowing towards Queen's bridge, she waited for a gap in the traffic and crossed to the City centre side of Oxford Street near the Obel Tower.

Seeing a few more passers-by here, she flung her bag confidently over her shoulder but kept her head instinctively down as she headed past the bright lights of the Victoria Square shopping centre.

Uncomfortable though of walking in this revealing glare, she cut back down Montgomery Street and turned into May Street, heading for hopeful anonymity amongst the bustle of Donegall Square.

High heeled hutzpah masking her loneliness, high gloss covering internalised structural cracks, she wandered onward, battered and bruised but already plotting her next bravura performance.

Kathleen walked away from Kelly's house to her car. He'd told her to, "Just go," and she had seen that it was either choosing between departure or facing hours of emotional questioning from the broken man. She chose the easiest option and fled the scene she had created some years before.

She opened her car door and plugged her mobile 'phone in to charge.

As she did so, she remembered the missed call and message from Maggie and dialed her number.

The 'phone wasn't answered and Kath decided to listen to the voicemail message again.

She sat there silently, unemotionally, as she listened to the scene that unfolded at Tommy's flat before the line went dead.

A small flicker of her eyelids betrayed her solid stoicism as she took in the blow that struck Maggie and sent her 'phone to the floor, cutting off the call.

Kathleen pressed '3' to delete the message and calmly drove away from the house, turning on the radio to drown out the evening's events.

The wind built as she drove along and the trees of the leafy suburbs waved frantically at her as she passed by, the light from street lamps flickered as it was hidden and then revealed once more by the branches.

She knew where she needed to go now and what she needed to do. She looked ahead, past the immediate street scene and knew that her road ahead was clear.

Kelly heard the front door close behind Kathleen as she left the house, left him behind to face the devastating news that had stemmed his newly found hope of reconciliation.

All the years of friendship that he felt had now been betrayed flooded back and mingled with the images of his father in his younger years still present in his mind. A slide show presentation of the past running on until the screen turned blank with the bright white light of nothingness, leaving him feeling empty and very alone.

After a few minutes spent listening to his own breathing return to normal, he stood up and closed the kitchen blind, shutting out anything that would encroach on his insular introspection.

He looked across at the worktops and saw the printed photo of his father and Kathleen he'd left out to show her, intending to share the damning evidence.

He walked over to it, considering whether to rip it up, to tear it apart, to tear 'them' apart. He looked at his father's laughing face and let himself smile a little as he picked it up.

He walked slowly through to the sitting room with it, intending to close the curtains as he has done thousands of times before, but as he entered the room he took in the windows bereft of their hangings, nothing left there after the fire and building works.

As he turned to walk back out of the room he dropped the photo and it wafted down into the corner of the room.

He walked over to it and bent down to pick it up. As he did so, he noticed that the floorboards here were screwed down. Full of curiosity, he ran his fingers over the shiny screw heads, drawing them back suddenly as they caught on the tiny shards of metal filings flaked up as the long in place screws had been hurriedly forced to turn by a visitor a few days before.

He crouched down there for a moment, wondering why the boards had been screwed down when all the others were simply nailed.

He got up, turned off the bare bulb hanging shabbily from the centre of the ceiling and resolved to find a screwdriver in the morning.

Outside the house, parked against the kerb, the driver and passenger of a silver Audi watched the light being switched off in the front room of the house and waited.

Chapter Sixteen

After Declan had pursued Maggie to the taxi with Tommy's blood on his hands and after he'd seen her escape from him in the retreating car, he returned to the flat.

Seeing Tommy still lying there, propped up against the kitchen units where he had left him, he went back over to the old man full of anger and frustration having seen Maggie get away.

He wanted to hit him again, to vent more frustration but the figure before him, once so full of a confident reserve, just looked pathetic and childlike in his helpless state.

He stood there looking at Tommy for a while, waiting for him to recover, to get back up so that he could interrogate him about the documents he'd been working on but Tommy just stayed there where Declan had put him.

Declan went over to the sink to wash the blood from his hands, struggling to get it out of his nails where it had started to dry and harden.

As he wiped his hands on a stained tea towel, he suddenly heard Tommy speak. Quietly at first, but then more audibly, he said, "Drink, a little drink Declan please," the words struggling to leave his dry lips.

Declan looked over to him, minded to ignore him, to start the search of the flat to get the information back that he wanted. Something though told him that he might be able to use the situation to help his cause.

"What are you after Tommy, a little whiskey perhaps?"

Tommy's eyes opened a crack and he replied, "Oh yes Declan, a little whiskey would be grand."

"Well, let's help each other then shall we Tommy, you tell me what I want to know and you get to have your whiskey," Declan said, looking around for a bottle.

Tommy's face did not betray his inner thoughts as he replied, "I'll be just fine with a little whiskey, just what I need to get me back on my feet again."

Declan looked about for the bottle of spirit he knew would be there but only found the bottle that Maggie had drained earlier in the evening.

He went back over to the sink and found Tommy's favourite blue plastic tumbler. He drew some water from the tap into it as quietly as he could and turned back to Tommy.

"So Tommy, where are my documents?" he asked, showing him the tumbler.

"A sip Declan, a sip please, it'll help me to tell you."

"You get the drink when you tell me where the documents are Tommy and not before you old fool," Declan replied, putting the tumbler back on the worktop, out of reach of Tommy's gaze.

"They're not finished Declan, not finished," Tommy replied quietly, his eyes closing once more.

Declan strode over to the old man and shook his shoulder harshly, saying, "Wake up, c'mon, wake up, tell me where the papers are Tommy and I'll get someone back here to help you."

"Help me Declan?" Tommy questioned with surprising volume, "Who's going to help me? Kathleen?"

"Kathleen? Has Kathleen got the papers Tommy?" Declan coaxed, "Can I get them from her then?"

Tommy didn't reply for a while, his breathing beginning to labour again but eventually he said, "Need Kathleen, she knew where to get the information . . . someone in Armagh . . . brothers in Armagh."

Declan took up the tumbler and held it close to Tommy, brushing it against his hand.

Tommy responded by slowly grasping for the drink but Declan held it just far enough away for it to stay out of reach.

"Need the right figures Declan . . . given the wrong ones . . . Kath knows . . ." Tommy slurred out.

Deciding to look in the flat for the information he knew must be there, he asked Tommy, "Papers in your desk are they?" lifting the tumbler up again towards the man's lips.

Tommy took a tiny sip of the water and a smile crept across his grey face. "Ahh, that's better Declan . . . whiskey does the trick."

Content in the mistaken knowledge that he had just tasted whiskey in his favourite blue tumbler, Tommy rested his eyes again, leaving Declan to go into the sitting room and to the bureau.

When there, he tried to lift down the flap but it was locked. He looked around for a moment for a key on the top or nearby but he couldn't see one.

An old brass toasting fork hung on the wall near to the desk and he picked it up and forced one end into the small space between the lid and the desk itself and used it as a lever, scratching the polished surface.

The top opened with a loud crack.

Declan was momentarily surprised by the neatness of the interior, by the neatly stacked papers, the bottle of ink, the pens, paper clips in a pot, eraser and pencils alongside.

He went back to the kitchen to make sure that the forced lock hadn't roused Tommy.

It hadn't. Tommy was either asleep or unconscious, the tumbler still in his hand but at an angle, with the contents spilling out gently on to the kitchen floor.

Declan saw a supermarket carrier bag on the side and picked it up, emptying out the contents of the racing pages and an unopened bar of fruit and nut chocolate.

Taking the bag back in to the other room, Declan filled it with all the papers he could get from the desk.

He didn't go back into the kitchen, didn't return to check on the man sitting on the floor, blood oozing from his head wound.

Instead, he took up the carrier bag and left through the front door, slamming it closed as best he could behind him.

Back in the kitchen, Tommy slid sideways on to the floor, on to his outstretched arm that held the blue plastic tumbler, which then rolled away from his grasp.

Maggie stared at the Georgian perfection of The Mall as she drove her hire car along the planned streets of Armagh. The former racecourse was luxuriant with early summer verdant greenery, tall trees standing proudly in front of stately buildings.

The gaol of 1780 at one end of The Mall and the courthouse of 1806 at the other balanced the space and created something formal and rarely seen in the rest of the country, a sense of order and solidity, a torpid tranquility.

Richard Robinson was created Archbishop of Armagh and Primate of Ireland in 1765 and did more than any other at the time to change the face of the city.

The Royal School, the Observatory, the Archbishop's Palace, Charlemont Place's refined terrace overlooking The Mall all combined to advise the visitor that this place was important, still is important as a place of learning and one where the Protestant and Catholic churches share the city, jointly recognising its role in the development of Christian Ireland.

From the Church of Ireland's ancient St Patrick's atop Ard Macha you can clearly see across on Sandy Hill, the twin spires of St Patrick's Catholic cathedral soaring skyward, piercing the sky with Armagh limestone.

Maggie was there in search of the two brothers who provided the last set of information to her and Tommy.

No message back from Kathleen told Maggie that she didn't want to help; that perhaps she was in even deeper than she first thought, after all, Tommy was seldom wrong.

Maggie stopped the car and her mind turned for a moment to Tommy and Declan, to the scene in the kitchen. Her mind blocked out the terror she felt when Declan had come into the flat and she cursed herself for leaving the papers vulnerable to Declan's 'thieving hands'. She hoped that Tommy could hold back the truth and give her enough time to track down the brothers before Declan worked anything else out.

Two girls walked past the car wearing orange Armagh GAA jerseys, their giggles and girlish closeness making Maggie feel old.

She pulled down the sun visor to check her makeup in the mirror. Somewhere under the camouflage, under the mask of foundation, mascara and lipstick, lurked the innocence long since consigned to history by Maggie's adolescent rejection of social authority and lack of conformance to accepted norms.

With time to kill, Maggie got out of the car, cursing the strong breeze that threatened to detach her blonde hairpiece. She held one hand to the side of her head to anchor her hair in position and locked the car, struggling to put the keys away with one hand into her handbag amidst the makeup counter contents.

She struggled up the hill towards the Observatory, perched near to St Patrick's on Ard Macha, her heels digging defiantly into the paving slabs to steady her ascent.

Maggie paused when she reached the first corner of the library buildings and turned her back on the wind for a moment at the red pillar-box.

Sunlight gleamed in the twelve paned windows of the library as it also does from the expanse of glass shining out from St Patrick's RC cathedral as it rose above the descending rooftops of the incline. The wind caused the anemometer atop the

Observatory to whir around faster and faster as she reached the solidity of the railings outside it.

She leaned back against them to catch her breath and smiled a louche grin at a passing cleric. She then grinned inwardly to herself as she observed the reddening face and quickening steps of the retreating reverend.

Once he was out of sight, she allowed herself to look around, to search for signs of the man she was due to meet.

No one else entered the scene until a figure approached from her right, from behind a large specimen of Phormium tenax, its strap like leaves waving back and forth in the unceasing wind.

The figure didn't speak but gestured with a flick of his helmeted head that Maggie should follow him.

He led her silently up the hill to a parked motorbike.

"You happy to jump on the back?" Michael Flanagan asked, opening a pannier to produce a helmet that he passed to her.

Maggie stared at the helmet, looked down at her short skirt and coat and was about to protest, to demand another form of transport but Michael said, "C'mon, we've got to go."

Maggie pulled her handbag over her elbow and forced the helmet down over her helmet hair. She pulled her skirt up and clambered on behind Michael, her heels not really cut out for purchase but she rose above these difficulties and grabbed Michael firmly around the waist.

"You on then?" he asked, looking around and smiling under his helmet at the red face filling the helmet behind him.

Michael opened up the throttle and pulled away at speed. Two kids, trying to light the remnants of a cigarette they had picked up, looked up at the sound of the BMW engine to take in the expensive bike, to see its driver, clad in black leather and his passenger, who couldn't look more out of place if she had tried.

Maggie's legs were displayed for all to see, her head hunched down towards Michael's back and her handbag lifted up, suspended on gold and leather chain straps from her elbow's clutches as the speed increased.

One of the lads by the roadside gave a loud whistle and the other laughed until the wind carried the sound away.

Chapter Seventeen

Kelly was in the garage at home, rummaging around in an old fashioned tool box that sat on his father's old work bench, its ubiquitous black vice yawning away with its handle hanging straight down, gathering cobwebs as it waited for use once more.

His head brushed past the 1960's yellowed net curtains strung up at the window, suspended on an elasticated cord that deposited a quantity of dust onto him.

He grumbled and shook the collection of insect wings, desiccated moths and general detritus that the net had sucked up over the years, from his hair.

The garage had a damp smell to it as old garages do, cardboard boxes stacked on shelves on the end wall containing rusting tins of ¾ used emulsion paint and brushes caked with solidified gloss.

Kelly found the screwdriver that he went in for and reached to turn off the dangling light bulb.

Windblown leaves crunched underfoot as he left the garage by its roll up door. Once back in the house, he made for the sitting room and the corner where the floorboards had been screwed down.

He suspected that the builders had done a 'bodge-job' on something and needed to hide poor workmanship with an overly secured floorboard.

Ready to call them back in if he found a problem, he just managed to get the old screwdriver to bite in the screw heads and turned them slowly, feeling the bruising pressure from the wooden handle in his palm.

Once all the screws were out enough to lift the board up, he placed the plank to one side and shone his torch into the hole in exploration.

The light shone back from the top of a metal tin in the shallow hole.

Kelly stopped for a moment in surprise before lifting the tin out from its resting place and opening the lid, eager to discover what was secreted within.

The night was still and the starry sky seeped into the kitchen of Tommy's flat.

In the living room, the moonlight showed the splintered top of the bureau, its contents hurriedly removed from the neat interior by Declan in his haste to gather the papers that he knew stood between him and a potential financial windfall.

Tommy had nearly succeeded, he's cracked the code in the lists of numbers that Maggie had kept out of Declan's reach. He'd found the links, sorted the sequences and pieced these together with the information that Gerry Collin's had given under duress to Maggie.

Just as a jigsaw comes together piece by piece, the puzzle had been solved bit by bit by Tommy whilst he concentrated on the task between his daily racing pages routine.

He'd spent decades studying the form of the horses performing at many and varied racecourses, long enough to find the trends and signs the casual observer does not see.

Then, just as a puzzler searches the box for the inevitably missing jigsaw piece, Tommy had come up against a problem.

The picture had been clearing, the puzzle coming together to form a recognisable whole, but one of the final pieces did not fit.

Tommy had tried to force the information in the right way

into the puzzle, but squeeze the edges as he might, it would not slot in correctly.

Maggie thought that she had delivered that final piece, obtained from Kathleen from her contacts in Armagh and it was in response to Tommy's plea for the correct piece that had brought Maggie to his flat and also brought Declan after her.

Well before Maggie's hurried exit from the violence she had witnessed, Tommy had told her what he needed from Kathleen's contacts and more importantly, told her what this information meant and how it might lead to the wealth they were preparing to benefit from.

The months of work and Tommy's labours had cleared the fog in the lists of numbers. Each number represented a bank sorting code that in turn represented a specific town behind that number.

Some of the numbers appeared to be dead ends as the sort codes failed to tie up to any branch that existed today but Tommy's patience paid off when he found in his desk old bankers association books that listed all of the sort codes and branches before mergers and centralisation. He had hoarded these books years before when a bank branch had closed and a 'helpful' bank employee had passed on anything that might not be missed to him in thanks for keeping a loan shark and the repretational risk and bad press off his back.

So Tommy had forty branch locations and these forty locations he plotted carefully onto a map. From Ballyhackamore to Colraine, Lisburn to Portadown, all were placed to find a pattern.

One place caught his eye on the map as he was ready to plot the next location – 'Greenore'.

As a child he had dreamt of arriving at Greenore by steamer from Holyhead.

He imagined sailing through Carlingford Lough to arrive at the small port set amidst the ever-present stunning scenery.

He first saw the beauty of the place captured on a poster of 'London and North Western Railway' destinations. Tommy's father was employed by the railway whilst he had worked in the North West of England before the first war. He had returned to Ireland with little in his pockets after the war to end all wars except for a lightly folded scrap of railway poster showing some of the locations that the railway had served.

Set between watercolours of Lichfield Cathedral and the Liverpool waterfront was an inset scene entitled, 'Greenore, County Louth, Ireland'. It showed a majestic lough surrounded by the greenest of mountains and there, jutting out into it on the Cooley peninsular was the most wondrous hotel, part surrounded by the reflecting waters.

Gliding towards the fairytale scene was a ferry from Holyhead, about to dock at the Raj-like floating palace that was, in truth, a railway hotel sat amidst a commercial dock.

To Tommy's father though, this was his reminder of home. He had torn the bottom of the poster off when it was being replaced by another as he had felt both pangs of nostalgia at the stylised Irish scene and had also fostered an ambition to arrive one day at the hotel from the sea and mingle with wealthy guests and travellers.

Tommy's father never made it to Greenore but he passed his travel dream on to Tommy saying, "When we have the money son, we'll all go and stay at that hotel, oh I tell you, it's like a palace!"

Tommy visited Greenore himself in the fifties when working his way along the coast. By the time he had got there though, the steamers had long since stopped coming to the hotel and the verandah, originally served by uniformed waitresses which once looked out upon the tennis court and manicured lawns now looked out upon dock gates and fields of ballast. This was all accelerated by the last of the trains leaving the integral station soon after the second war.

He'd crept through what remained of the Edwardian gardens

and peered through the pallid panes of glass that looked out with sadness upon a much-changed world, the early glamour of the place now swallowed by port accretion.

Having adjusted his eyes to the gloom, he'd seen the soaring arch through which the staircase ascended, with remnants of heavy furniture and jardinières at its base.

His eyes took in the shabby reality whilst his ears strained to hear the string quartet his father had said would have played for the guests as they descended the stairs to dinner.

Tommy was glad that his father hadn't seen the place in his dying days and that he had retained his mythical view of the palace on the lough.

The visit did fuel though Tommy's natural yearning for finding patterns in places that others would not see.

At the hotel, which was one of the few buildings in that part of Ireland to be built from red brick, he'd been fascinated by the regular brick courses and the regimented dormers. He saw detail where others saw none and it was this ability that flourished into finding and connecting financial links in the lists of numbers that Maggie had procured.

Forty locations gave Tommy, over intervening time for consideration, forty addresses with numbers attached such as 43 High Street, 61 Bow Street, 32 Hill Street, 247 Upper Newtownards Road.

He had puzzled over the numbers for some time, unsure if they were a dead end, but something inside him – the same something that saw and remembered the patterns in the form of horses in his racing pages, persuaded him to persevere, to continue with his mathematical deliberations.

He ended up with six sets of two number groups, 43, 61 etc. and 28 numbers left in mainly ones and a few threes.

They seemed to go together.

The 28 numbers were plotted against the alphabet so number 4 High Street would be a D and so on. Tommy did this for all the numbers and letters and ended up with a jumble of vowels and consonants.

He had tried moving the sequence on by one so that the four was now an E or back one so that the four was a C, but the mist refused to lift.

He knew at that point that he needed more, that there would be a crucial code that would break the sequence and produce something tangible.

Were the three set numbers the key to cracking the single numbers and were the double number groups actually a group at all or part of the sequence?

He looked back at the original list of numbers – the bank sort codes – and looked for something that he had missed the first time around.

Initially, nothing seemed to stand out but a simple tick back of the street numbers in the bank branch addresses behind the sort codes showed that the codes were listed in order, so that the six groups of two number sets had come first, followed by the three number sets and finally the single numbers.

Tommy also noticed that something had been torn very neatly off the bottom of the sort code list. Under scrutiny and with the aid of his magnifying glass, he saw that the fibres of the torn paper edge were brighter than the rest of the paper itself – the tear had been recently made.

He knew that this piece of missing paper must hold the key and he determined to get it even if procuring it meant that others would know about their attempts to crack the code and avail themselves of the funds that lay at the end of the tortuous trail.

So Maggie had persuaded Gerry Collins to part with his long protected knowledge that led him to Kathleen Bruce. Maggie didn't know if Gerry truly felt worried by her threats to bring Declan into the equation or whether he was playing a game, but at the time she didn't care whether he became co-operative to avoid Declan Doyle or whether it was to 'get one over' on Kathleen. Gerry had ended up being compliant and that was all that mattered. Maybe he had been too keen to help.

Kathleen put Maggie in touch with the brothers from Armagh and they had obtained the extra information, the very missing section torn from the first list in Tommy's possession.

Tommy worked hard over the new data but the numbers just didn't turn into the letters that he expected, instead they remained an undoable puzzle, frustrating no matter which way he turned them about in his mind.

Doubting his own ability for a moment, he had reached for his blue tumbler and his bottle of whiskey. He'd recalled suddenly though the freshly torn edges at the bottom of the first list, re-visited through his magnifying glass.

Tommy had sat back in his favourite chair at this realisation and removed his glasses from his face, placing them down so that he could rest his tired head in his tired hands.

On the one hand he felt vindicated when he realised that the extra numbers might be intended to deceive – he hadn't after all lost his ability with patterns and numbers. On the other hand was the crushing realisation that whoever had supplied the missing piece was all too aware that someone had been trying to crack the code.

In addition and to cement Tommy's despair, the spoilers clearly had knowledge of the first set, knowing about the torn edge and it would only be a matter of time before they might come to ask questions to whoever was looking for the answers.

He'd sat there wondering what to do for hours, alternatives racing around in his mind as he contemplated leaving the flat for a while to let things die down.

He also had to face the admission to Maggie that he'd been unable to complete the code work after all and even tried to convince himself that the providers of the second sheet of numbers would be simply satisfied that they had provided fake information and that would be that.

Instead, filled with conflicting emotions and a sense of advancing fragility, he had 'phoned Maggie, 'phoned the one who had then brought the man to his flat who had left him bleeding on the floor of his own kitchen, struggling to cling on to life.

Declan walked back down the office stairs of Robyn & Sons builders at the Argyle Business Centre. It was after hours, the receptionist on the front desk had long since clocked off and there were no signs of the workmen who during working hours, created bespoke joinery in the adjoining workshed.

Declan walked casually to a car in the car park and clicked the button on the remote in his hand. The car responded with a flash of its lights and he sat into the driving seat.

As he took hold of the wheel, he winced in pain and he looked down at his reddening, swelling right hand. He gingerly started the engine and drove out of the car park. On the seat next to him he'd placed two recordable DVDs.

Back in Robyn & Sons, in the first floor office, the CCTV DVD recorder lay smashed on the floor, its disks now with the driver leaving the car park.

Situated opposite was the desk of Gerry Collins. Underneath the desk lay the groaning man himself where Declan's rain of blows had left him. The office chair base, weakened by years of strain to keep Gerry's corpulent frame aloft, had finally given way and collapsed down on itself, throwing the occupant to his resting place between his own desk drawers.

Gerry finally hauled himself onto his knees with a roar of effort, his red face betraying both the marks of Declan's fists and his over stressed blood pressure.

He couldn't help thinking to himself that if Declan had come over earlier in the day, he would have had the lads from the workshop bounding up the stairs in no time to eject an unwelcome visitor. Instead, Declan had planned ahead and waited for the last of the boys to knock off for the night, leaving Gerry alone with his paperwork.

Moving uneasily, Gerry lifted himself up with his elbows balanced on the desk top and tried to stand up straight, but the best that he could manage was a crooked stoop with the aid of support from the desk.

The petty cash lay on the top of the desk, the same as when Declan had entered the room. The visitor had not wanted cash but had wanted information. Gerry had tried to put up a fight, to resist the blows that flew across the desk, but Declan made it clear that Gerry had only got one option open to him – to tell him what he knew about the list of numbers that Maggie had obtained.

The impact of the blows alone would not have been enough to get Gerry talking, but the impact on Gerry's mind when Declan grabbed the framed picture of much loved teenage daughters from the office unit, describing in vivid detail what he would do to them if their father did not co-operate was enough to first anger him, then silence him into disbelief and finally to loosen his tongue.

Declan had not taken anything away with a monetary value from the office on his 'smash and grab' raid that evening, but Gerry had lost something he prized much more highly – he'd lost his dignity.

Kelly peered into the contents of the metal tin that he had retrieved from the space under the lifted floorboards.

Inside were mainly scraps of paper with faded writing on them that he recognised as his father's. He lifted these out and placed them down on the upturned lid.

Underneath were various documents including Building Society passbooks, cheque book stubs and folded statements.

He was ready to put these items back into the tin, presuming that they were put there by an over cautious parent but something just didn't add up in his mind.

He couldn't work out why his father would want to put the tin under the floorboards, and this in turn be covered in fitted carpet and furniture in the years before fire swept through the room much later on.

Kelly looked again at the papers and pulled out a laminated security pass, clearly much used from the scuffs and bends in the edges. He turned the pass over and looked at the picture. He didn't recognise the man looking out from the passport-sized photo. He didn't know that the man staring back at him was Kenny Slater. What Kelly did know is that the name on the card, the name of the owner of the card, working for 'JC Security', was his own name.

Kelly took a large breath in, conscious that he had stopped breathing as he tried to understand what was in his hands. He looked at the card again to check the details, to make sure that he wasn't mistaken, but he wasn't.

He looked more closely at the remaining papers and unfolded one of the statements, looking at the account holder name at the top. The name was again his own name.

The address on the statements was Kathleen's.

Kelly grasped at his forehead with his spare hand, his mind reeling, asking a hundred questions at the same time. He started to look through the rest of the paperwork.

Each time he looked further into the bottom of the tin, he found more items in his own name including a long expired credit card and finally another Building Society passbook, complete with a signature on the inside cover.

Kelly wondered inwardly if he was losing his own mind. He expected to wake up at any moment and find himself in his bedroom with the morning light creeping in through the curtains.

His body shuddered from a chill of shock whilst his forehead glistened with gathering beads of perspiration.

He sat down on the bare wooded floor with the tin between his outstretched feet and tried to make sense of what he might be staring at.

Turning away from the documents for a moment, he looked over to the curtainless window as a distraction and as he did so, his eyes met the glare of another pair of eyes at windowsill level staring in furtively through the glass. Kelly's heart skipped a beat at the same moment that the watcher at the window dropped from sight.

Kelly let what he was holding fall to the floor and leapt up, knocking over the tin with a clang. The figure outside the window was already getting up from his prone position and scurried over the front hedge as Kelly reached the window.

Kelly made a dash for the front door and once he had opened it, was just able to see that the car the figure had got into before it screeched off down the road, was the same silver Audi he'd seen before.

Kelly shouted down the road after it, "What do you want with me?" but the words were lost in the air by the sounds of the accelerating engine from the retreating car. He was left there once again in despair, not knowing which way to turn, whom to trust, how to move on.

Chapter Eighteen

Tommy, when just a toddler, had stood behind his mother's legs, peering shyly between those and the bars of a school gate to catch a glimpse of the boys streaming out from the classrooms.

He gave a broad smile as he caught sight of his brother Freddie walking towards the gate, a much repaired leather satchel slung over one shoulder.

Freddie's grey jumper had holes at the elbows and one starting at the neck. His boots were too big for him and were padded out with newspaper to try to make them a better fit and also to try and keep the damp out from the perished soles.

"Alright Tommy?" said Freddie as he caught sight of his little brother. Freddie then ruffled Tommy's blond curls and Tommy responded with a smile and clung to his mother's skirts as other boys started to come out noisily from the school yard.

An older boy with a threadbare jacket ran up to Freddie and cuffed him around the back of his head. "Is that your little brother Freddie? Doesn't say much does he," said the boy as he rushed past along the street.

Tommy clung tighter to his mother's legs and retreated behind her a little further.

"What you doing here Mam?" shouted Freddie amidst the din of the excited kids.

"Your Uncle Harry wants to see you, he's back in port for the night and we're going to your Aunty Kathy's for tea," she replied, reaching for Tommy's hand from the back of her skirt.

"Aw, I was going to go to Georgie's house, his brother's just got a motor bike . . ."

"You'll do no such thing today," his mother interrupted, Harry's only here for tonight and we are going over to Kathy's."

"Will Uncle Harry have a present for me Mam?" Freddie asked, realising that the visit might not be such a bad thing after all.

"Ah well, we'll have to see, now pick your feet up, I'll not have us late." She set off in the direction of her sister's house and Freddie fell into line beside his little brother who was staring ahead of him, intently focused on the regular symmetry of the paving slabs stretching out in front of him.

The sun was beating down, penetrating the calm sea and displaying dark seaweed clinging to rocks at the visible bottom, punctuated by flashes of bright turquoise where patches of clear sand reflected the intense light back up into the sky.

The cloudless sky was a pale grey blue that sat upon the inky blue sea at the horizon.

Slate grey rocks climbed out of the water creating random pools and continued upwards until these gave way to Thrift and other seashore staples. These in turn gave way to vertical columns of stone at the base of the ancient cliffs where seagulls cried into the gusting breeze.

Sophie sat on top of the cliff, looking down on to the scene below, her long blonde hair streaming back from her face in the early evening on-shore breeze.

She hugged her knees between her linked arms and shivered a little as the sun began to lose some of its daytime warmth.

She looked down on the white lichen covered rocks and gazed across the bay to focus on the white waves breaking up amidst the quickly filling rock pools.

Pebbles fizzed and popped as the tide washed over them down at the base of the cliff.

Sophie shook her hair and tied it up and stood on the edge, taking in deep breaths of the ozone rich air.

She walked away from the edge and reached into her bag for her mobile 'phone and scrolled down to a number she needed to call.

Moving down in alphabetical order, she came to her chosen number and pressed the green button on the screen. The number connected and was answered with an uncertain voice as she asked, "Kelly, we need to speak."

Tommy, a little older now, was sitting in a tin bath in the kitchen with his brother Freddie opposite him, chasing the soap around between his legs and the metal sides of the tub.

The kettle on the hearth began to steam and his mother stood by the table she made bread on, its marble top covered in a dusting of flour.

She took a look back at the recipe she was following in the 'Tit-Bits Cookery Book, 763 recipes and household hints – 3d'.

The scene on the front of the book mirrored the scene in the room, Tommy's mother in a floral apron standing in front of a large mixing bowl, drum of flour, rolling pin, spoon, cup and tin of 'Ideal' milk on top of the table.

She looked around at the boys and said, "Freddie, take that soap out of the water, you know not to leave it in there and whilst you are at it, you can get yourself and your brother out."

Freddie reached out for a towel warming on a rack by the hearth and placed the soap back in its dish.

He rubbed his hair vigorously with the towel to dry it and wrapped the towel around his shoulders as he lifted Tommy out and dried him with another towel from the rack.

A warm smell of baking wafted from the range door, the clock ticked the minutes away reassuringly on top of the mantlepiece and Tommy stood on the rag rug, its ribbons of cloth soft beneath his bare toes as he meticulously counted each one of the flowers adorning the wallpaper next to the bathtub.

Kelly looked at his watch. The minutes ticked slowly by as he waited atop the City walls of Londonderry.

Yesterday, Sophie's call had surprised him, adding yet another level of intrigue to the events that had unfolded that day with the earlier discovery of the box under the floorboards, with its cards and paperwork stashed within.

Sophie hadn't planned the conversation to be a long one but once Kelly had asked how Sophie was, he had started to ask her innumerable questions. He asked her what had happened after she had left that morning, where did she get the gun from, why did she leave it for him?

Kelly only got answers to the first couple of questions before Sophie said, "We need to meet, there's things you need to know."

Had Kelly not found the box and its contents that day he might have been tempted to play it safe, to allow his suspicions of Sophie's motives to outweigh the intrigue he felt and the desire he had to now meet with her.

He thought he heard honesty in her voice though and simply replied "Okay, when do we meet and where?" to her request to see him.

Kelly hadn't set foot in Derry for years. He remembered visiting a friend of his father's back in the 1980's though. He recalled being amazed by the murals and the flags of the Bogside despite the constant television and media coverage linking these images with countless acts of violence.

No strolling along the City walls that day, it had been all about family problems, kids and their issues at school, the increasingly wet weather, the strikes, politics. A plethora of aphoristic argument and boisterous bluster.

He'd watched the minutes tick by slowly that day too, sitting there as his father and Dougal Lynch relived their teenage rampages and how they had settled into sloth-like stupefaction.

Kelly looked again over the top of the walls to see if he could see the house he'd visited many years before but the murals had changed, the thin doors of the 1970's houses had been replaced and uPVC windows in a jumble of configurations and patterns had supplanted the previous local authority drab uniformity.

He strolled further along the stone walkway, passing an antique canon last used in the seventeenth century sieges and walked beneath the tall trees stretching upwards past the redundant bastions.

He paused again to look down upon the old city, picking out St Columb's Cathedral, the green-topped tower of the Guildhall and the copper dome of Austin's department store on its corner site on The Diamond, a product of Edwardian optimism.

A smattering of tourists loitered along the walls amongst the locals using the often broad walkways to make faster progress across parts of the city boundaries than the pattern of streets below allowed.

Kelly ceased his perambulations at the Bishop Gate, the designated meeting spot, and leant back against the wall, the stones cool behind his shirt. He checked his 'phone to ensure that he hadn't missed a call and whilst he was putting it back into a pocket, he became aware of a figure beside him.

"Hello Kelly, how are you doing?" greeted him as he looked up.

Before he replied, Sophie added, "C'mon, here's too public", and turned around, leading Kelly along the walkway. Kelly didn't attempt any small talk, he simply followed her, picking up on her defensive body language, understanding that she wasn't after conversation at that point.

Once down from the walls, she led him into the multi-storey car park of the 'Ferryside Shopping Centre' having walked through the mall itself.

Kelly struggled to keep up with her as she weaved in and out of lunchtime shoppers and bunking-off teens.

She took him up to one of the higher floors of the car park and opened the driver's door of an old VW Golf.

Reality clicked back into his mind and Kelly asked, "Err, where are we going?" suddenly conscious of the time running out on his own parking ticket.

"Just get in, we can talk inside," she replied, sitting in the driving seat and leaning across to pull up the knob to open the passenger door.

"No central locking then?" Kelly asked as he got in, instantly feeling foolish about asking such a lame question. Sophie however, didn't answer, her mind seemingly elsewhere.

As Kelly put on his seat belt, Sophie put the Golf into gear and looked over her shoulder to reverse out of the parking space.

Her bracelet jingled against the gear stick as she found first and drove along the deck of the car park towards the exit ramp.

As the car left the car park, Sophie relaxed a little and said, "Worried you're going to get a ticket? You should relax a little."

"I don't want a £25 fine thank very much, I haven't worked for weeks now as it is Sophie," he replied, then added, "sorry, that sounds ungrateful of me – how have you been doing?"

"I'm okay thanks. I hope you didn't mind me getting in touch like that, I just can't stop running things over and over in my mind and I figured I should tell you some of the things that I think you should know Kelly."

She indicated and turned the car off the road into a farm track and turned off the ignition.

"That sounds mysterious Sophie," he said, a nervous smile creeping across his previously serious face.

She smiled back, but it was more of a smile that you see on one in empathy with another, a pitying smile. As he witnessed this, Kelly's smile vanished and he readied himself for the encroaching silence to be broken.

"That night in Ballycastle," she began, when you nearly ran me over with your car . . ."

Kelly nodded, his mind reverting back to the figure caught in his headlights, the look of terror on her face etched in his mind.

"I was running from some people Kelly and to be honest, I'm still running from them. That night I'd told one of them that I was leaving, that I'd made a mistake in coming back home, but I know things that these people don't want me to know and now they're determined that I'm shut up," she continued, her watery eyes beginning to betray her otherwise combative exterior.

Kelly's stomach suddenly had an empty, sinking feeling as he automatically felt that he might be in danger, nervous anticipation resulting from an increasing level of adrenalin, fight or flight.

He instinctively looked around him, further out than the boundaries of the car windows, nerves jumping at the movement of the wind in the hedgerow next to the passenger window.

"Have you gone to the Police?" he asked, struggling to find the right tone for his question.

She let a small breath of muted laughter creep out of her mouth at the simplicity of the suggestion that Kelly suggested, reflecting on what a simple world other people live in in comparison with her own complicated existence.

"Sorry," said Kelly, "but don't you think that you need some level of help if someone is making threats to you?"

Sophie looked down for a moment and then let her eyes focus towards the far distance, outside of the car and the stilted conversation.

She took in a deep breath and continued, "These people Kelly, don't let things like that happen. Do you still have the present I left for you?" she asked.

Kelly's mind wandered for a moment, thinking of missed parcels, unopened post and then clarity came to him and he asked with an amazed gaze, "What, the gun?"

"Sure, the pistol was for you, well, more that I had to put it somewhere and I knew it would be safe with you." Her face betrayed far off thoughts again as she added, "Better for you to have it than for me. I couldn't be expected not to use it Kelly." She then examined his face, watching for a reaction.

Kelly turned towards her. "I'm struggling here Sophie, what are you trying to tell me? More importantly, why are you trying to tell ME?"

"Hey, I'll be straight with you," she replied, "I've been used for years, treated like I'm worthless, stupid, forced to do things that I didn't want to do and I decided it all had to stop, it all had to go away so that I could be myself for a change." She paused and then carried on, "You're being used yourself Kelly, do you know that? Do you see what you're involved in here?"

"Involved in?" he retorted, his eyebrows knitting together, "What am I supposed to be involved in?"

His thoughts quickly assessed the situation. Here was a girl he barely knew, who he had met in peculiar circumstances, telling him that he was being used and that he was involved in something that he had absolutely no knowledge of.

Images then formed in his mind of fake IDs, passbooks and the content of the box he'd found under the floorboards of his fire damaged home. Beads of sweat appeared on his forehead and seeing that her words had made an impact on him, she softened her tone a little.

"Why were you at that particular house in Ballycastle, Kelly?"

Thoughts raced around his mind. Struggling to understand her intended meaning.

"There was a fire at my house, a quite serious fire and I had nowhere else to stay and a friend suggested that I stay in her house," he explained. "She was going away, she didn't need it, you know, you saw me there didn't you?"

"Someone wanted you away from your house Kelly, away for long enough for them to be there themselves, uninterrupted."

She looked at his face closely again, looking for a sense of recognition in it, of pieces coming together to form the outer edges of a complicated puzzle.

"Do you know who would want to do that Sophie and why they would want to do that?" he enquired, looking at her and wondering what role she herself might have played, wondering why he was sat in a car down a farm track near Derry, miles from home, miles from the shell of his fire damaged home.

"This is just getting too weird," Kelly shook his head as the words came quickly out of his mouth.

"This whole thing is bigger than the two of us Kelly. I want to tell you where you fit in with it all but to be truthful I don't have all of the answers myself. What I do know is that you seem like a nice guy and I think that you should be ready to stand up for yourself when you need to, as the people that you're involved with like to make use of weaker people. They use them, drain what they can out of them and when there's nothing left and they become more of a liability to them, well, things happen." Sophie shifted in her seat, reached for her handbag in the foot well behind her seat and rummaged through the contents.

As she did, Kelly asked, "So just who is using me Sophie and why on earth have they picked me? I'm sorry to sound sceptical if I do, it's not that a lot of weird stuff hasn't been happening to me lately, but don't you think I'd know something about all of this?"

Sophie smiled, "That's just what I've been wondering too Kelly, since I left you in Ballycastle. I thought, 'this guy has got to know what he's caught up in', but over the weeks since, I've come to see that you are just a bystander in all of this. You're there but not there, things are happening to you but they're things that you don't seem to know anything about."

Kelly started to bite the dry skin on his lips between his top and bottom teeth. His mind turned over the first meeting with Sophie again, seeking to convince himself that he could trust her, that she's not just out to deceive him by draping a cloak of obfuscation over his already clouded mind.

"Why shouldn't I just go to the Police then? If what you're telling me is true, this 'someone' who wanted me out of the way, well, they should be up on a charge of battery and arson at the least."

Sophie raised her eyebrows and replied, "Go ahead Kelly, but you'll just accelerate the situation and put yourself and me for that matter at even more risk."

"But you'd be able to tell them what you know too, we can put a stop to whatever this is Sophie, here and now."

"Okay," she said, nodding her head with an air of sarcasm, "we'll go off to the Police and tell them everything we know and then when they send us home after our tea and a chat are you going to be able to sleep easy in your bed Kelly because I tell you this, Kathleen will not let that happen, no chance at all."

Kelly pictured Kath in his mind again, the picture where she was with his father, reflected back in the mirror, resplendent in his parent's bed. "What's Kathleen got to do with this Sophie?"

"Oh, only everything Kelly, just everything."

Chapter Nineteen

The sea was just beginning to slink its way back over the outermost rock pools of the foreshore at Bangor.

A child, now about seven or eight, was holding up a desiccated crab to show his brother and shouted, "Hey Freddie, see what I've got!"

The older brother looked up from the book he was reading and shouted back, "That's great Tommy, a dead crab, is that the best you can do?"

Tommy laughed and rooted around again in the bottom of a deeper rock pool, his stick lifting up the cover of small rocks to find out what lay beneath.

The sun was hot on his neck and he squinted as he looked back to see where the incoming tide had reached.

The water had crept closer, oozing slowly at first over the jagged rocks and then rushing onwards to re-fill waiting hollows and bring respite from the heat to drying urchins and rivets of limpets peppering the boulders.

Freddie shouted again, "C'mon Tommy, Mam'll kill me if you get wet again."

Tommy felt the danger as the tide began to encircle his position and he retreated a few steps closer to his brother. He felt guilty as his boots crushed sea snail and limpets alike beneath them, the cracks and pops just audible above the wind like roar of the invading waters.

"C'mon Tommy!" Freddy shouted again impatiently.

"I'm counting!" Tommy shouted back and went back to undertaking his impossible census of the languid limpets.

Mount Stewart shone in the late evening glow, basking in the remnants of the heat of the day, its low granite form holding on to the last sparkles of sunlight.

The last of the day-trippers and fervent horticulturalists had departed, leaving the small army of helpers and volunteers on the estate to finish off and lock up before opening the next day.

At the gravelled entrance courtyard, a figure stood motionless, obscured by a clipped Bay tree, observing the comings and goings, the routines of many that would culminate in the grounds falling silent overnight.

Lights were switched off in display cases, blinds were pulled, shutters closed and staff members drifted away to their car park to return to their suburban lives.

The portico in the middle of the façade sheltered a heavy wooden door leading into a cool entrance hall. The figure watched the process of closure and carefully checked the time on his watch.

After another few minutes the figure dashed noiselessly along the lawned edges of a low, balustraded wall facing the house and took advantage of the growing gloom to hug the house wall itself.

At this point, the figure stopped moving as the main door was closed and bolted shut.

Then, underneath a window at the corner of the façade, the figure peered carefully through the gap left open at the bottom of the sash.

Seeing nobody in there, the sash was slowly lifted, enabling the figure to drop into the apartment within.

As the figure looked about in the low natural light of the room, a voice cried out from the corner, "How do you do? How do you do?"

The figure started in surprise and backed into a table in shock, which in turn scraped along the hard floor with a chalk on blackboard shriek.

Along the corridor, a lady's voice shouted out, "Who's there?"

The figure looked around hurriedly, accustomed now to the poor light and headed quickly for a table in the corner of the room where the first voice had come from.

As he did so, the figure in the corner gave a croak like cry and said, "How do you do?"

Without any reply the figure grasped out for the side of the table and reached underneath, searching for something hidden underneath.

As his hand searched, it felt the strip of gaffer tape attached there and pulled it free of the underside of the table as the voice in the corner of the room cried, "Naughty boy!"

The second voice now responded, this time nearer than the last.

"If there's anyone there, I've already called the Police and they are on their way."

The figure froze for a moment and then checked the strip of gaffer tape. Stuck to the back of it was a key for a safe.

The figure quickly pocketed it and turned his back on the room, fleeing quickly out of the sash window once more and into the now evidently deepening dusk.

At that moment, the door into the room swung open and the light was switched on. The glow illuminated a large cage sat on the top of the table in the corner.

In the cage, a large parrot looked back at its owner and cried out again, "Naughty boy, naughty boy!"

The lady looked around the room and didn't notice that the table had moved slightly.

She made her way over to the window and pushed down the sash to close the window fully, grumbling to herself about the quality of staff these days.

Out in the grounds, sheltering under a giant leaf of Gunnera near the lake, the figure waited some time to ensure that no Police were on the way and once satisfied that nobody was coming, he slipped away along the edge of the main wall and eventually dropped over this and onto the main road back into Belfast and a waiting car.

Closing the door, the figure settled in to the seat and the silver Audi moved off into the night and the anonymity of the waiting city.

Chapter Twenty

Maggie shifted in the soft cushions of an over-used armchair, attempting to maintain an upright posture as best she could against challenging odds.

Once again she felt out of place as she looked around the room with its blown vinyl wallpaper and flatpack display cabinets showing a variety of pottery knick-knacks atop individual crocheted doilies.

The electric fire whirred away in the hearth, its coal effect 'glow' rotating to give the allusion of warming flame.

On top of the fireplace, a carriage clock ticked away the minutes as Maggie tapped away noiselessly with her nails on top of the arm of the chair.

"Michael will be back soon," said Moira Flanagan, her smile a little too fixed to be considered natural.

Moira had lived in the 'new' dormer bungalow for thirty-five years. The original house on the site that had been there for hundreds of years and seemed to be part of the very landscape was pulled down in an afternoon and the bungalow built to replace it.

The large picture windows afforded magnificent views of the countryside surrounding the house and they also made the house stand out in its setting rather than blend in as the old house had done.

Moira had liked that about the house when it was still new, being filled with pride as the previously scrubby boundaries had been replaced with concrete block walls and a tarmacadam sea that stretched out in all directions and cut the house off from the fields surrounding it.

Now though, as her years advanced and she was prone to reflect more on the past, she missed the solidity of the previously thick stone walls and the smell of a peat fire, even missing the cosy gloom created by small windows and fickle ventilation.

One corner of the asphalt surrounding the house had been hastily laid and the tar had barely made it up to the concrete edging stones.

Over the last few years, a gorse seedling had taken hold and had gradually grown up to fill the corner, its razor sharp arms reaching out as if it wanted to spear the house.

Michael had cursed the shrub last summer as his legs had been scraped and punctured by it as he had hauled a lawnmower past it on one of his 'helpful' visits to his mother's.

She had seen him advancing towards the gorse with a small saw in his hand, intent on destruction, but she had stopped him, asking him to 'leave it be'.

The old cottage with its whitewashed walls had also provided sanctuary for a gorse shrub in a similar corner and she was pleased that something had invaded the formality and modern lines of her home.

Michael had acquiesced although fully intended to return and complete the job the next time he was at the house and his mother out.

"Have you known my Michael for long then err . . . Maggie?" Moira asked, feigning a 'couldn't care either way' attitude that was far from reality.

"Not long," Maggie replied, shifting her gaze to the picture window to see if there was any sign of Michael's motorbike returning.

"Well it was a nice idea of his to drop you off here whilst he took care of some business, gives us a chance to have a chat and to get to know one another," Moira says, her eyes not quite meeting Maggie's limpid gaze.

"Oh yes, very nice," Maggie replied, forcing a fixed smile to form across her face but not quite hiding a note of sarcasm in her voice.

"Shall I get you another tea?" Moira enquired, looking for a reason to escape the tedium.

Maggie glanced down at her empty cup and pondered if she could stomach another of the strong milky tea, having had to force one down already.

On balance though she decided that another cup would be preferable to the present level of conversation and said, "Oh, yes, lovely thank you."

"Now my Michael has always liked those pink wafer biscuits, can I tempt you to one or two of those, I keep them in for his visits," Moira asked, relieved to be able to stand up with a purpose.

Before Maggie could respond though, their attentions were grabbed by the throb of a motorbike engine and the arrival of Michael himself.

"Thank Christ." Maggie said under her breath and stood up from the chair with some difficulty in order to greet Michael as he entered the house.

The front door opened and Michael entered the sitting room, placing his helmet down on a spare seat.

"You two been having fun whilst I've been gone?" he asked, stepping forward to give his mother a kiss on the cheek.

"I was just going to get Maggie here another tea," Moira stated.

Maggie's glance, shot across at Michael in an attempt to get him to leave sooner rather than later and to avoid the tea, was unnecessary as he stated, "No Mam, we'd best get going, there's things we need to be doing."

"Oh well, it was lovely to meet you Maggie, a pleasure, be sure to call in again now won't you?" Moira gushed, thankful that her visitor would soon be on her way.

After goodbyes, Maggie followed Michael out onto the lake of tarmac and he handed her a spare helmet from the pannier.

Maggie mischievously stopped and looked at him in the eye asking, "Pink wafer biscuits Michael?"

Michael reddened and was about to reply but Maggie's laughter drowned his intent.

Inside the bungalow, Moira's smile turned into a sneer as the pair sped away and she removed the lipstick-smeared teacup into the kitchen with distaste.

Tommy peered out between the tape stuck on to the inside of the windows of his mother's house to prevent flying glass in the event of a wartime blast.

He was keeping a careful watch on the street outside, waiting to see one figure amongst the many returning home from the munitions factory at the end of the street.

The tape had been on the windows for some time and was pulling away from the glass in a number of places.

Tommy's mind was taken back to when he and his brother were asked to lick what seemed like miles of the stuff by their mother before it was applied to the glass, all washed down with weak orange cordial.

Tommy was seventeen and the object of his affection was eighteen and walking past the house, her thick hair held back in place in a net.

Tommy pulled away hurriedly from the window, went quickly into the hall of the terraced house and pulled open the front door.

Gloria Byrne was already two houses further down the road heading for a house just like Tommy's in the next street.

"Gloria . . . Glo! Wait up!" shouted Tommy, narrowly avoiding a collision with a sturdily built woman pausing for breath on the pavement outside the house.

"Sorry," Tommy apologised, his voice trailing away as he headed for his quarry.

"You should watch where you're going Thomas McHugh. What's all the rush about?" retorted the woman, whilst steadying herself by grasping at the stone window surround of the terraced house.

"How've you been?" Tommy asked Gloria once he had caught up with her, his hands rammed into his jacket pockets, a brylcreamed strand of dark hair falling over his forehead as the gusting early May breeze worked hard to move anything it could manage.

Gloria was only nine months older than Tommy but the gap might as well have been nine years, as she refused to halt her homeward progress. She saw Tommy as an immature schoolboy who she remembered playing football in the street and made unfair comparisons between him and the handsome movie stars that Ada and she drooled over in the Gaumont on Saturday nights. Mustachioed men with twinkling eyes romancing celluloid girls, creating fairytale lives.

"Busy, Tommy and I've no time for you today," Gloria rattled out as she strode along, her gaze resolutely forward.

"I hear there's a big new order at the factory then?" stated Tommy, half rushing to keep alongside Gloria.

"I'm not allowed to say and even if I was, I've got better things to do than chat with you about it." Gloria answered, suddenly stopping dead in her tracks and forcing Tommy to scamper back to her.

She moved forward again a little more slowly this time and asked more politely, "How's your Ma doing?"

"Ah not so good, not so good," Tommy said, looking at his feet and the cracks in the pavement.

His quiet tone began to thaw Gloria's resolute defences as he continued, "She's not herself these days, that's what everyone is saying."

"Well you tell her that I was asking after her," Gloria added, looking at Tommy for the first time in today's conversation.

The mood had changed and Tommy no longer felt so keen to race along the pavement after Gloria. He looked back over his shoulder towards the house he had left which didn't go unnoticed by her.

"So I'll see you around then?" added Tommy, the same question he always left Gloria with, ever hoping, but not expecting a reply.

Today though was different. Today, Gloria replied, "Yes, see you around," before continuing her homeward march.

Tommy watched her go as he began to take a few steps back along the street. He turned his head around and was struck by the irregularity of the brick wall alongside the pavement.

One brick had become dislodged from the top and had fallen into a small front garden, leaving a toothless gap.

"Oh, only 148 there now," Tommy said to himself as he returned back towards home to dream of Gloria and his plans for them to walk out together.

His mind raced forward a few years to visualise their house together, their children, their dog, the life he wanted to create for them both.

All that was missing was the movie scene in-between where Tommy the hero finds Gloria falling in to his arms in a display of passion. Try though he might, he couldn't see how the scene would come about so instead he counted paving slabs out of the corner of his eye, looking for inspiration in their cracked irregularity.

Chapter Twenty One

"Hey Fanta pants!" cried a teenage girl to a passing schoolboy, his bright ginger hair aflame in the afternoon sun.

The girl turned to grin to her friend and both laughed, school jumpers pulled down over their hands and long fringes hiding pubescent pustules.

The boy's face reddened but he didn't turn around and continued to walk along the pavement, his worn schoolbag slung over his over-large blazer.

Kelly wanted to smile at the boy with a show of sympathy but thought better of it as his mind warned him that it might be misconstrued.

The girls were still giggling as Kelly walked by. The vocal girl let out a quiet wolf whistle as he went along which resulted in an even louder laugh then before.

His mind was taken back to a girl in his primary school who used to make him give her the chocolate biscuits Kelly's mother had sent him to school with most days. That girl was like this one, self confident, eager to score some points with her friends.

The primary school girl had towered over Kelly when they were ten but by the time secondary school had come along, she seemed to grow smaller as Kelly grew up past her.

One break time, years later and well after the chocolate biscuits had stopped being 'donated', her sidekick had come over to Kelly who was with a couple of friends.

"You know Janice," she asked, not waiting for a confirmatory answer, "will you go out with her?"

Kelly's friends had pushed their fists into his sides and cheered on a response from him.

"Don't think so," Kelly had said.

"Why not?" the messenger had enquired.

"Because she's ugly," he'd explained simply, not meaning a word of it but eager to show backbone with his friends.

Janice heard the response and instantly burst out crying and was consoled by her entourage who shouted playground obscenities across in his direction.

Suddenly the girl that Kelly had hated for years intrigued him and he had his first inkling of the complexity of juvenile emotions.

Janice ended up a teenage bride smoking 40 fags a day even in her wedding dress, three kids in tow and a husband who worked around the clock to make a dishonest buck.

Kelly once bumped into her at the station.

They both recognised each other but only made fleeting eye contact. She had looked angrily at her kids running about the platform before telling them to behave in the quietest way she knew. This though still managed to drown out the recorded announcement emanating from the overhead tannoy.

It announced the arrival of their train and a welcome cessation of their uneasy proximity.

Kelly wondered what would have happened if he had gone out with Janice all those years before.

Would those have been his own kids eating bags of crisps and depositing them on the floor of the carriage, his wife looking out of the window and ignoring the empty packets thrown to the floor?

Would they have been 'his' bullies, hassling the weaker kids at school to 'donate' their lunch money, his woman to collect the nightly takeaways and fill the never empty washing machine?

The giggling girls picked up their bags from the pavement and headed towards the Castle Court shopping centre, leaving

Kelly to walk on to the newspaper offices he frequented when employed on a job.

Having followed his father into photography with the newspaper, his freelance status took him back when time allowed, to consult the visual history nestling amid the columns of countless past editions.

He could always spot his father's work by the composition, the exposure just discernable through the pixellation.

He walked past reception offering a smile and a wave to the man on security who had become ensnared with a hapless delivery man in an over long discussion about over-running road works on the way into the city.

He also passed the desk he used to frequent when full time, cutting his teeth on New Year baby stories and centenarian citizens celebrating survival.

Kelly was clutching one of the items from the box he had discovered under the floor at home. It was a building society passbook from the 1980's, showing an opening balance of £30k put into an account in his name.

The date the account was opened was within days of another account opened at a local bank, again an opening balance of £30k and an opening statement showing the account in his own name.

Within the passbook there was space for the account holder's signature and at home, he had tried to discern the signature written in light sensitive ink, but being invisible to the naked eye he hadn't met with success. He'd also tried holding it up to the light to see if he could make out any sort of indentation on the page but also failing in this task, he went on to the internet and ordered himself a UV reader, the kind usually used for checking forged notes and waited for the post to arrive.

When it did, he eagerly switched it on and placed the signature page underneath it. At first he didn't understand what the scrawl meant but then he clearly saw the words 'general authority'.

Still puzzled, he'd gone back to the Internet and searched for the unfamiliar term and discovered that it was likely that another signatory signed on this account and Kelly's mind turned immediately to his father or Kathleen.

Of course he was most puzzled by where his father had obtained the amount of cash detailed in the accounts, he'd simply never had that amount of money. On closer inspection of all of the accounts evidenced in the box, all of them were opened within days of each other.

Kelly moved along in the newspaper offices to where the archives were kept.

He opened the pages for the editions spanning the week leading up to when the accounts were opened but found nothing of interest save for fading adverts and suburban scandal.

He stayed there for hours searching for something, some clue. He expected to find news of an inheritance or behest, a football pools win, an obituary of a famous family member previously unknown to be connected to the family.

Frustrated, he pushed his stool away from the inclined desk and threw his head back, letting his tense muscles relax before heading for the water cooler in the corner of the office.

The bottle gurgled as it emptied and Kelly refilled the quickly drained contents of the condensation-covered cup.

He returned to his stool and moved to the next volume. This time he decided to look at just the front cover headlines rather than look at each page in the newspaper.

He flicked his way past murder, corruption and terrorism as despondency crept in and reminded him that he was looking for a needle in a haystack in a possibly non-existent haystack at that.

Just as he lazily scanned a new headline, his eye was caught by a photograph on the back sports page of the previous edition he had turned over.

It was a picture of a racehorse in the winner's enclosure, happy owner and trainer holding aloft champagne and silverwear.

He didn't see anything particularly unusual in that, it could have been any big equine winner on any back page.

His eye was arrested however because he had seen this picture before in the previous volume he'd looked through.

Finally enlivened by the search, he pulled the previous volume back over to where he was sitting and started to flick hurriedly through the pages.

Several copies in, he found what he'd remembered underneath a headline of 'Who Dares Wins stolen – owners anguish'.

The photo had been reproduced in a larger format than previously and the people crowding around the winning horse were more discernable.

Behind the trainer on the left of the photo, a woman raised a glass to the camera. It was unmistakably Kathleen Bruce.

Down Royal racecourse was established in 1685 by Royal Charter in the reign of James II.

It settled in to its home in the Lagan valley near Lisburn soon afterwards following a move from Downpatrick.

Whether racing for the Silver Bell or The Royal Plate, generations of bloodstock have crossed the finish line after thundering around the clockwise track.

1958 and Saturday the 10th of May saw Queen Elizabeth the Queen Mother attending the racing at Down Royal. Her car dropped her off at the side of the track and the crowd was parted to allow the royal visitor to head for the stands.

Ladies in neat pastel two-piece suits and conservative hats applauded as Queen Elizabeth walked by. Men still making use of drab post war suits strained to see over the forest of millinery to catch a glimpse of the royal guest.

Tommy dug an elbow into the side of a generously built lady in a lime green hat to catch sight of the regal vessel as she cruised through the slowly parting waves of punters.

Tommy was there to do deals for gamblers who would otherwise be refused by the turf accountants on the rail – those who were too regularly successful, those most often in the know and keen to place large sums.

He had arrived at the course early and ensured that he got to hear about the condition of the track, the horses, the changing odds before picking his moment and his price.

His mind retained the results of countless horses running on the many tracks around the country. He could see the silks, the numbers of the horses, the conditions, the winning odds. All there to be recalled whenever he needed the information to form his diligent, daily review of the race results.

With his knowledge, he split large bets between different bookies and paid a small cut to the acquaintances that would do the same.

He just had time for a pint before the races began and he headed for the bar to quench his thirst before seeing if his predictions would be correct. Betting with mainly other people's money had brought him success although he had once tried to go it alone but something was missing.

He needed the pressure of retribution that came with using other's money, a certain clarity of judgement emanating from a level of nervous tension not present when he used his own money alone.

He finished his pint and pushed his way back out through the crowd to the rail to watch the first race.

He watched the horses coming down the track, felt the hooves thunder under his legs as they neared the tape and took delight in seeing the silks of his chosen jockey eagerly thrusting for first place.

The frantic cavalcade hurtled towards the winning post and Tommy smiled with satisfaction as his prediction took the race.

Placed horses were committed to memory and he claimed his winnings and joined the crowd as it moved back from the rail towards the stands and another opportunity for liquid refreshment.

The atmosphere at the course was full of excitement and heightened anticipation as the Queen Mother made her way to make a presentation to the winning owner of the next race – The Governor's Cup.

Scores of people crowded around to catch a glimpse of the Queen Empress who congratulated Major Hughes, the owner of 'Copper Cottage'.

Applause and a few cheers from lucky winners accompanied the Major's beaming smile of satisfaction.

Tommy moved off to find a friend in the bar as he had a deal to discuss with him that promised to net them a few hundred pounds apiece.

He stopped in his tracks for a moment as he saw a girl in the crowd who looked just how his Gloria used to look. Realising that she was just a ghost from his past though, he smiled to himself reflectively and hummed 'April Love' by Pat Boone, ". . . every star's a wishing star, . . . don't let her run away . . .".

He took in the odds on the bookie's boards as he passed by, visualising every chalk mark, committing them to memory for future recall and furtive deliberation.

Chapter Twenty Two

Michael peered into Maggie's eyes as she held aloft a glass of cold Sauvignon Blanc, condensation forming on the outside of it.

"Cheers," she said and downed a healthy gulp before relaxing back into her restaurant chair.

On the walls were copies of Parisienne café scenes and metal signs from the 'Belle Epoch'.

On the tables, candle wax sputtered as it flowed down the glass necks of the wine bottles they stood in, trickling to form rugged fascias on the smooth glass.

A potted palm cast spiky shadows over a terracotta wall whilst laid back jazz pervaded the room and helped to build an ambiance.

Michael had seldom eaten out before. He'd picked a safe starter and main course by choosing food that was familiar to him.

Maggie on the other hand was drawn to the luxury end of the menu – if lobster had been on it, she would have had it.

A waitress handed warmed bread rolls to the pair and Michael set about his roll eagerly, crisp shards of the outer crust raining down onto the tablecloth.

"Can't take you anywhere can I," smirked Maggie as Michael consumed a buttery mouthful, washing it down with a meaningful draft of his glass of beer.

"Nothing wrong with a healthy appetite, I'm bloody starving," he replied, looking around to see if the starters had made it out of the kitchen.

"You eating yours?" he asked, eyeing up Maggie's roll greedily.

"Good grief Michael, you'll be starting on the plates next," Maggie stated, pushing her plate towards him so he could take her bread.

The starters arrived then thankfully and Maggie had chosen a risotto with black truffle, Michael a dish of coconut king prawns with mint and dipping sauce.

The prawns had been consumed well before the risotto had been half finished. Hungry eyes had stared at Maggie's plate and forced her to offer the remains of it to her dinner partner.

"Oh, I'm not sure I want to give it a try – what are those black bits in it anyway?" Michael asked, his inexperienced palate concerns just winning the battle with his rampant appetite.

"You've never tried truffles before then?" Maggie replied, trying not to sound too patronising.

"Only the ones my Mam buys at Christmas to impress Mary O'Leary, you know, those chocolatey ones," he added, "not that I get to eat them, I think she polishes them off as soon as Mary has commented on the price of them as she always does, asking, 'how do you always manage to get these Moira when I'm stuck with the usual tin of Quality Street from the supermarket?"

Maggie laughed out loud and placed her glass down on the table.

"What's so funny?" Michael queried, looking slightly angered lest Maggie was making fun of him.

"Oh God no, it's just sometimes you're all 'the big man' and then other times you're just peering out from around your mother's apron strings," she said, gazing into his blue eyes.

Michael's features hardened for a moment before realising that the woman opposite to him had some feelings for him and his tight lips spread out into a grin, his eyes twinkling as he met her gaze.

"So how long are you staying around for?" he asked, taking hold of Maggie's hand on the table.

"Oh, I don't know, depends on what's happening here to keep me interested," she replied, placing her free hand on top of his.

"Oh, and how long you keep out of the way of Declan, Maggie?" he enquired, mischievously.

Maggie's demeanor changed instantly, her eyes dropped, she pulled away her hands and she picked up her glass again, taking a significant swig of the wine as she did so.

"That's it Michael, spoil the moment why don't you!" she spat out.

"Ah Maggie, c'mon, I'm only teasing," he said, trying to regain eye contact again.

Maggie's lips remained in the solid pout that took hold after her outburst. She broke her self-imposed silence by tapping her long red nails on the tabletop and glaring at them as if looking for a reflection of herself in their glossy depths.

She let her eyes focus back on Michael slowly, calmly stating, "You need to understand what we're dealing with in Declan, Michael," and she shuffled slightly in her seat before continuing, "Declan is just not for making jokes about. The things that he's done . . .," her voice then trailed off and she displayed a touch of inner vulnerability behind the burnished exterior shell.

"Hey, hey, I've come across his sort before, I'm a big boy now you know!" he said quickly, looking for re-assurance in her eyes.

"He's capable of more than you realise Michael, you've got to understand that. Oh God, here we are, out for a lovely meal and we end up talking about him again," she reflected.

"That's the nearest I want you to get to that man again Maggie and I'm serious," he said, cutting off her attempt at interjection, "from now on it's going to be you and me, together."

* * *

Kathleen tried to hear the voice emanating from her mobile 'phone above the roar of buses and taxis surging along Belfast's Donegall Place.

She was standing at the corner under the clock outside the Anderson and McAuley department store – or at least outside the building that used to house the store with its grand interiors, trading quality goods over its five solid upper floors to the discerning shopper for nearly a century before. Over expansion for 'Andy Macs' and the bombing campaign put paid to many a store's pre-eminence as a grid of road blocks and security checks choked the city centre of life and caused the early demise of many a once thriving business.

The store's name survived in the inlaid lettering set in to the solid stone bases supporting the ground floor windows, a ghostly imprint of another era before the City was forever transformed by the turmoil of 'the troubles'.

Kathleen shouted, "Hold on a second," into her 'phone before carrying along the street, waving in and out of slowly moving pedestrians until she stopped again on the corner that once housed another illustrious department store, Robinson and Cleaver, with its copper topped domes vying with its neighbours for architectural stature on Donegall Square.

The building's clock still kept commuters informed of the time as they waited for suburban buses to take them away from the square just as it had since the end of the nineteenth century all under the watching glare of the sphinxes atop the nearby Scottish Provident building.

"Go on Michael, I've only got a few minutes to talk," she shouted, still frustrated by the traffic noise and she headed across the road and through the gates of City Hall to gain a modicum of solitude amidst the lawned environs of the white palace that dominates the commercial landscape of the square around it.

"It's going well Kath, I'm getting there. I just wanted to give you an update," Michael explained.

"Are you sure it is going well – I mean really sure?" Kathleen shouted into the 'phone.

"Oh aye, you know me and the ladies Kath, she's in safe hands with me," he confirmed.

"I absolutely do know about you and the ladies Michael, that's why I'm checking in on you – you've not exactly got a great history in that department now have you," she stated, before sitting down on one of the benches facing City Hall.

The line became silent for a few moments before Michael responded with, "I'm just telling you that she's falling for me Kath, I know it and another few nights and I think I'll have her hooked."

"Well, you'd best be right because we've only got one chance at this and I've waited too long to have things messed up at this stage. Are you hearing me Michael?"

"You're not the only one to have waited a long time for this you know, after all, if you . . ."

Kathleen cut Michael off mid-sentence and retorted, "C'mon, c'mon, I know you're strong, just don't let anything get between what we all want here Michael. Now where's your brother been these last few days?"

Another silence occurred before Michael explained, "Oh, he's been keeping a low profile, he's had a bit of trouble but I think things are calming down. I guess you're going to need to use him before too long."

"Give me another update in a day or two then and I'll head down there, I've got some business to sort out here first though." Kathleen didn't wait for a response before she pressed the button to end the call and replaced the mobile in her handbag.

Something about the years passing by, referenced by Michael, caused a wave of nostalgia to creep over her. Her mind wandered to thoughts of Michael's father and times of optimistic opportunity.

She had thought about him little over the passing years and had never really seen him as the family man he was, with views, desires, plans and aspirations as with any other.

Instead, she had always viewed him as a remote figure after he had died, her mind encapsulating her memories in a leak proof box.

She stared vacantly across the lawns and statuary for a few moments before checking her watch and gathering up her bag.

She got up from her bench and made her way past the rear of the Titanic memorial to the south side of the square.

Still distracted by personal reflection, she paced onward and didn't notice a figure leaving a cashpoint and carefully trailing her as she left the square and walked up Adelaide Street, heading for Ormeau Avenue and a meeting at an hotel in 'The Gasworks'.

She walked past Franklin Street and on to Clarence Street, becoming more focused and aware of her surroundings as she caught sight of the Tudor-Gothic style St Malachy's church at the end of the street, its octagonal turrets thrusting skyward, a sweet confection of Victorian brickwork.

As the street scene grew more quiet, she felt the urge to look behind her and as she did so, she caught a glimpse of a figure disappearing in a momentary flash in the corner of her eye.

She turned around again, convincing herself that it was just a trick of the light but instinctively more cautious than before.

Behind her, skulking in the sun starved shadows, a figure did indeed exist, stalking its target.

Declan paused for a moment and then resumed his furtive pursuit.

Chapter Twenty Three

Kelly was back in the newspaper offices, trying to find a link between his father, Kathleen and the life he now led. A life transformed away from suburban solitude to one that seemingly revolved around fraud and crimes that involved firearms and arson.

Something about the juxtaposition of the most modern journalistic IT in the newspaper office and the vast volumes of old, hard copy back issues stacked in front of him on the sloping desk made him smile.

He remembered the world that his father used to inhabit with a sense of confortable nostalgia, one of negatives and blown up prints, shiny metal and sticky printers ink that he had observed on the occasional trips with his father to the printing presses.

Gone were the smells of hot metal type and the overalls of the printers, gone the smell of photographic chemicals and typewriter ribbons.

Something of that world clung to the pages he now gazed upon, to the index cards and the binders replaced by anorexic flat screens and ethereal email.

Supermarket special offers displaying defunct coinage and automotive dinosaurs passed his eyes and still he searched on.

Sporting news presented tantalising glimpses of 'Who Dares Wins', the stolen horse that Kathleen had been pictured with, but it is a photo of a man on a building site that caught his eye.

It was the hat that attracted his attention.

A hat sat atop a head too large for it so that it was perched there perhaps temporarily before departing elsewhere with the next gust of wind.

Kelly stared more closely as the same man in the hat had been in the photo with 'Who Dares Wins' and Kathleen.

The shot was captioned, 'Terry Flanagan and the new site'. The article that accompanied the picture revealed that Terry was a builder by trade and seemingly made his way through housing developments when land was cheaper and planning laws more accommodating of serried ranks of bland housing which took no account of geography in its form or setting.

Kelly looked back at 'Who Dares Wins' and the figure with Kathleen – it was certainly the same man, the same hat. He made a note of the newspaper date and took a copy of the yellowing pages.

The PC Kelly now sat at whirred into action as he searched the Internet for 'Terry Flanagan, builder'.

His first search threw up countless variations, individuals in the USA, in Canada, in every corner of the English speaking world it seemed. He clicked back on to the search field and selected pages from the UK. This search was more successful and in an online trade directory for a few years earlier, Kelly found an entry for, 'T Flanagan & Sons, Builders, Armagh'.

The entry was accompanied by a photo of Mr. T Flanagan & his sons in front of a company van.

Kelly smiled as he noticed Terry's penchant for diminutive headwear, this time an ill-fitting baseball cap in dire need of pulling down over his inflated head.

Kelly opened his email account in a new web browser and pasted a link to the photo on to Sophie's email address. He then followed this up with a text to let her know to check her email inbox.

He didn't have to wait long before his mobile rang and Sophie greeted him with, "Hi Kelly, you've been busy I see."

He replied, "Any ideas?" not expecting a positive response, but Sophie said, "Actually I have got an idea, you know I recognised the name because they are the guys I used to see around in Armagh."

"Well it's either a small world Sophie or I need to change career and set up as a private detective," he grinned, as he pushed back into his office chair.

"I'll keep on searching here and let you know if anything else turns up, but I think a trip to Armagh might be in order."

Clicking through several more pages online, he found a link to a local Armagh paper and an article headed, 'Search goes on for local builder'.

Kelly read the article carefully and followed another link to a related story.

Terry Flanagan had simply failed to turn up at home after a days work. His distressed wife had told how she had cooked a stew for his evening meal and how she had kept it warm for hours whilst she kept returning to the bungalow's front windows, searching for the familiar headlights that failed to illuminate the driveway that night.

Mrs. Flanagan had 'phoned her eldest son at 9 p.m. and again at 10. Terry had said earlier that morning that he had a new contract to quote for in Belfast and whilst it was unusual for him to take work in the City, it wasn't unknown if the price was right.

At 11.30 p.m. that evening she couldn't believe her son's suggestion that he'd have got involved with business cronies and was probably sat in a bar somewhere sobering up before driving home. Terry never failed to come home on time or when he did, she always had a 'phone call from him.

She 'phoned the Police.

They called in the next morning, expecting Terry to have made contact or to have returned home in the early hours but instead they had been greeted by his wife who had not slept at all the whole night and was clearly distraught.

From that day on until the article was written, a number of weeks after the disappearance, not a sign was seen or heard of Terry Flanagan. No bank withdrawals, no telephone calls, only deafening silence.

Kelly finished his research and stared once again at the picture of 'Who Dares Wins', of Kathleen and Terry. What linked the two of them? Was it just joint ownership of the racehorse?

Something nagged Kelly in his head, the sequence of recent events in his life and the relationship between Kathleen and his father, Terry Flanagan's disappearance – all if it must add up to something more he thought.

Then there was Sophie, the girl who literally ran into his life one evening and was becoming an increasing part of it.

Kelly pulled on his jacket and walked down the echoing staircase in the 1960's block. He said, "Night" to the security guard and stepped out on to a cold and windy street – 'Baltic cold' he thought as a gust of wind rushed past, enveloping him in its dry easterly embrace.

Leaves tumbled along the pavement along with the detritus of the day in the city, an orange cellophane chocolate bar wrapper, a cardboard coffee cup, a cola can bashing and clanging along in a tiny cacophony of sound.

Kelly pulled his collar up around his neck and forced his way into the gathering storm.

Tommy could see Maggie sitting awkwardly on the tired sofa, waiting for information about the puzzling list of numbers. In reality he couldn't actually see her though as she was not there, she was a figment of his imagination. Instead, Tommy was slumped on the floor of the kitchen of his flat, a deep gash oozing coagulating blood onto the sticky lino.

In his mind he could see her quite clearly, see the day's events that led up to the violence and his injury.

He relived the disappointment felt by Maggie about the numbers, his first failure with data in all his years and felt a sharp pain gnawing away at his insides.

A dark figure forced its way into the miasmic scene, noises were muffled but distinctly emanating from Declan and a terrified Maggie.

The blows were recalled, the ones that had rained down on Maggie before Tommy himself got in the way of Declan's anger.

The blow that sent Tommy to the floor wasn't audible to the old man as he played the scene back in his mind.

He just remembered falling in what seemed to be slow motion until the sound came back to him when he recalled his head hitting the worktop then nothing more. Nothing except old memories, faded thoughts, sentimental sequences played over and over again in his mind.

He wanted to see Gloria – his Gloria – in his mind, but the image wouldn't come. The harder he tried, the more confused the images that came into his head. Instead of Gloria, he recalled a woman with the same hairstyle but this one worked in the newsagents he bought his racing paper from. The next time, instead of Gloria, he got another woman he never knew singing outside a pub doorway.

"What was her name," thought Tommy, "was it Gloria? It doesn't sound right now."

"C'mon Tommy," Gloria said as she finally appeared in his mind – older than he would have liked perhaps, after the drink and the perceived shame that followed in the wake of their childless marriage.

"Ah, there's my Gloria, there she is – lovely Gloria," he mused before the fuzziness and the pain returned.

"Can't feel my legs Gloria, can't really feel anything much anymore," he murmured, his labored breaths getting slower and more shallow.

Tommy surveyed the scene before him. For the first time he

saw the grease and grime gathered in the corners of the floor along the desiccated skirting and tutted to himself.

He saw the plastic tumbler lying there on the floor, the tear in the lino, the dirty nets at the window, the cracked tiles, the damp stain on the wall near the window.

He saw the tired worktops with their chipped edges topping well-worn cupboard doors inside of which he knew there was the mismatched crockery and mixed up cutlery gathered over the previous decades.

He looked up to the cracked tiles on the wall and automatically started to count them, checking the total in his mind as he had done every day since he first moved in to the flat.

He looked down at the figure on the floor and saw tired clothes sheltering a shapeless body. He saw the pale complexion starkly set against the drying and darkening blood oozing from the head wound.

He realised he was looking down at himself from the corner of the ceiling, surveying the scene below as if viewed through a CCTV camera and his mouth formed into its characteristic 'o'.

He felt so light, floating there, hearing the drip of the tap at the sink and hearing the distant hum of nearby traffic.

He felt no fear watching himself. It was as if he had taken off an old and heavy coat and put it to one side, regarded for what it had done, but discarded for something new.

The scene beneath him began to fade as light filled his eyes and for a moment he heard no sound.

A speck before him grew larger into view and moved nearer towards him as he moved nearer to it.

Tommy MacGuire could now make out what the growing speck was. His mother was there standing before him, shining out from their old front doorway from his childhood home.

He could see her smooth, brown hair, her paisley blouse and the long skirt that she used to wear on Sundays. His brother Freddie was clutching on to her skirt and he was laughing merrily, giggling and waving to Tommy as he came nearer to them.

His mother started to smile and wave too and Tommy was filled with warmth and elation.

His mother's smile widened to a grin and she said, "C'mon Tommy, we're waiting for you, it's time for us to be together, it's time to come home."

The light was gone as quickly as a switch being flicked off and all that was left was the tired kitchen, the dripping tap and Tommy MacGuire lying dead on the greasy floor.

Chapter Twenty Four

Moira Flanagan was out visiting one of her neighbours that she liked to impress.

This time it was Siobhan O'Neill, a friend from her school days who appreciated the airs that Moira cultivated.

Siobhan's family was not the poorest in the area back then but poor enough to feel grateful for the attention of Moira's family who were the first to buy a television set in the street.

The fact that Moira's father swindled his customers out of a little money here, a lot of money there over the years to pay for such consumer comforts didn't really signify – they still had the first TV set and the O'Neills were suitably impressed.

Whilst Moira gulped down another glass of sherry with Siobhan and exchanged opinions about the rudeness of the supermarket checkout girls in the nearby town, her son Michael was in the front room of his mother's house, gulping down another glass of red wine with Maggie and exchanging saliva with her on the sofa.

"C'mon Maggie, she won't be back for hours, he coaxed, pulling Maggie back up into a seated position on the couch.

"What's got into you tonight?" Maggie slurred, "it's usually me encouraging you."

"Is that you complaining there Maggie or are you going to have your way with me again?" he smiled, peering through relaxed eyes at his quarry.

Maggie paused before lunging at Michael, her lips locked on to his and her hands reaching under his t-shirt to lift it off him.

He reciprocated, fumbling at her top before pulling her up and leading her through the sitting room door and towards the stairs.

Maggie grasped at Michael's buttons on the fly of his jeans with her manicured nails causing him to say, "Hey, c'mon, upstairs."

The couple carried on up the stairs and Michael closed the bedroom door behind them and pushed Maggie back onto the bed.

Watching outside for signs of life in the bedroom, Kathleen paused for a few moments before checking over her shoulders and making for the front door where she carefully lifted a key to the lock and turned it as quietly as possible.

The lock gave out a 'click' as the barrels retreated and Kath put downward pressure on the handle until she felt the levers allowing the door to move.

She put her shoulder to the door and grasped the handle firmly so that she was in solid contact with it and pushed it open an inch at a time until she made a large enough gap to fit herself through.

As she moved into the gap she knocked into the door slightly and the hinges let out a groan. She froze instantly and listened intently for any noise coming from the house. She heard nothing though for a few moments until she heard some re-assuring groans from upstairs that let her know she had not been heard.

Once inside, she closed the door again as quietly as she could, propping a 'phone book behind it to prevent her having to close it properly but also preventing the door from blowing inwards.

She stepped across the carpeted hall and into the sitting room where she headed for the sofa.

Looking around, she spotted the handbag she was looking for and knelt down on the carpet alongside before picking it up and emptying out the contents on to the floor.

Her hands now felt around the inside of the bag until she stopped and let out a quiet, "Yes" as her hands felt the paperwork she was expecting placed between the bag outer and the lining.

Kathleen carefully retrieved the papers, opening them to check that they were Maggie's copies of the bank sort code lists and placed them inside her own coat pocket, replacing the papers with some replacement sheets to ensure that a quick check of the lining would not betray that the papers had been switched.

She replaced the contents of the handbag, sneering slightly as she noticed the shades and brands of makeup.

She paused again to check for sounds in the house before slowly checking around the sitting room doorframe to ensure that her exit was clear before retracing her steps out of the house and back to her car parked along the lane.

"Too easy Maggie . . . too easy." Kath said as a grin broke across her face.

After the graving docks in 'The Titanic Quarter' had long since fallen out of use and long before the massive re-generation project that had created 'The Arc' and the Titanic Visitor Centre, a figure had stood by the side of the Lagan river, contemplating what he had just done.

The morning had been grey with gusty winds and rain that had come and gone with annoying regularity.

Terry Flanagan had driven along Queen's Road singing loudly to Radio 2 and pulled his van into the side of the road adjacent to Abercorn Basin.

A blast of rain hit the van's windscreen, causing Terry's previously clear view to turn awash and blur his surroundings.

As the water drained down the glass, Terry picked up his wallet and placed it into a pocket of his much worn jacket that he always put on when attending business meetings.

He stopped singing and instead cursed quite audibly as he opened the van door and stepped out into the heavy rain.

He locked the van and quickly shoved the keys in a pocket before pulling up his jacket collar to stop the worst of the rain travelling down his neck and on to his shirt collar.

He paused, suddenly remembering that he had a cap in the back of the van.

He moved quickly around to the rear doors of the vehicle and fumbled with his keys again to find the key to a padlock that now served as security for the back of the van.

As he stepped back from the doors, his left foot found a sizeable puddle which promptly began to seep in to his 'best' shoes.

Cursing again, he pulled open the doors and rummaged around to find the much-used cap that he quickly rammed on to his now wet hair.

His 'phone buzzed in his inside jacket pocket and he thrust a wet hand in to retrieve it.

"Where are you?" Terry asked, struggling to hear the response above the hammering rain.

"Aye, it's a little wet," he added, forcing half a laugh into his voice, "no, I'll be there in a minute. I'm just by you."

He replaced the 'phone and locked up the back of the van. From where he stood, he needed to push through a space in the chain link fence and step onto the gravel that demolition had left behind.

Here and there, scrubby plants pushed through the rough and uneven surface, a mixture of yellowing leaves and occasional floral reminders of the summer days that had now passed into autumn rains.

The stones felt sharp through the thin soles of his shoes and he moved gingerly over the rubble and clinker.

The last useless vestiges of an old red brick wall now blocked his path and he put his left hand down on it for stability before stepping over the low courses and onto the broken brick shards and dust on the other side.

The wind came again in another heavy gust which flattened the opportunistic plants sideways before it caused swirls that repeatedly lifted and teased them back towards vertical again.

Terry's cap wasn't moved by the wind, he had rammed it down firmly on to his head for a change and this provided him with a sense of protection from the elements.

He looked up when the wind dropped and saw the man he was there to meet standing with his back to him on the edge of the dock wall in front of him.

Hamilton dock brought coal into Belfast for many decades but by now its use had ceased and it acted as a receptacle for air blown dock waste that bobbed up here and there on top of the turgid water.

Across the basin, a freight ship was moored up along the dock that was still in use and it tugged at its moorings as if to test their strength and resilience to the storm.

Other than the skip and the torpid lapping of the wind blown waters, the two figures were alone at the edge.

"This place has changed Terry," said the figure he had come to meet, "not at all what it was when I was a lad."

"Some would say it's progress Declan, I say it's vandalism," pontificated Terry as he reached out to shake the hand of the man before him, "good to see you."

"And you Terry, now how's it going?" asked Declan as he turned to face Terry square on.

"Ah, could be better Dec, but I can't grumble and you'll have seen my pride and joy has won for me again no doubt?"

"Ha, yes, and I was wise enough to put a small wager on for myself Terry so I guess I've got you to thank for a nice payout."

"Nothing to do with me Dec, I just made a lucky investment in the horse and I can't say I've even had a moments regret for that." Terry's voice boomed out as the wind dropped again, leaving him feel a little self-conscious even out there amidst the empty post industrial desolation.

Declan's face hardened from jovial chat to business and he paused a little before asking, "Have you brought it Terry?"

Terry's face forced out a grin before he stammered, "Yes, yes, yes I've got it Dec. There's just something to discuss with you first though, call it a sort of business proposition, a kind of . . ." Declan cut him off.

"Not interested Terry, don't try and build up your part and I'll save you your respect by not engaging in that conversation. Now c'mon, hand over the details as we discussed and we'll both leave here happy."

Terry didn't know what to do, he hadn't expected Declan not to want to hear about an opportunity. He shifted nervously and broke eye contact with the man before him whose demeanor had hardened once again.

Terry decided to try again. "All I'm saying Dec is that if we finish here, we, well you, will miss out on what I think we can do next, you know, maybe double your money?"

I've said I am not interested Terry, hand over the details now please," Declan stated, "I'll not ask you nicely again."

Terry's bravado had been prodded and he was ready to retaliate, "Maybe not and just maybe you're not ready for the details Declan, do you want to think again?"

Declan's eyes now betrayed the determination beneath and Terry began to feel uneasy. "Look," he said, "Kathleen and me, we're . . ."

"Kathleen?" spat out Declan, "You're trying to tell me you're here messing me around because of Kathleen?" He walked a step closer to Terry, who instinctively moved a little backwards in response.

"Well, we think it's going to be best not to liquidate the assets just yet Dec, you know, leave it a while, let the story cool down a bit, what's the rush and all that?" Terry's hands were at his sides, palms open, trying to show his openness and desire to negotiate.

"You wouldn't even be in this without me Terry, much less that little girl who has caught your eye," Declan sneered, "what does the lovely Moira think of the competition?"

"You bastard!" retaliated Terry, "leave my wife out of this, if it wasn't for me and Kathleen you'd have never had the opportunity, never been able to get close to what we've achieved."

"Oh don't let this get nasty Terry, that would not be professional now would it," Declan shook his head from side to side as he said it, "give me the list NOW, I want those details, I want my share."

Terry could sense that the conversation was over, could see that Declan was immovable.

"Okay Declan, okay, we don't need this to end badly," Terry said soothingly, "I can give you the details, you can use them with the list you've already got and you can access the accounts. If you struggle, I guess I'll be hearing from you." Terry tried to lift the mood by laughing nervously once more.

His hand trembled a little as he reached into his inside jacket pocket for the crucial paperwork. He pulled out the sheets of type written numbers and started to hand them to Declan who grabbed at the sheets.

Terry, startled by this, fumbled at the papers and lost grip of some of the sheets. These were grasped quickly by the wind and flew up into the air leaving Declan with half of what he needed.

"You stupid bastard!" screamed Declan as he watched the sheets play in the wind before they escaped its clutches and drifted down onto the waters of Abercorn basin, the spume topped water quickly submerging the illusive information. He tried to keep his eyes on the spots where they had landed in a vain attempt to plan a rescue mission.

Quickly realising the hopelessness of the situation, he looked around to Terry only to see the man starting to make off across the rubble, back towards his van.

Declan immediately gave chase and pursued his quarry.

Terry's legs, used to building sites though they were, were clearly unaccustomed to this level of physical exertion and they screamed out for more oxygen to Terry's heart that was already racing to pump more adrenaline soaked blood around his flaccid physique.

Declan, much the younger man, was soon on top of Terry and flew at him to bring him down to the ground.

Terry collapsed onto the uneven ground and let out a loud cry as his face hit the stones and the corner of a random brick.

"What are you doing?" cried Declan, "you are going to take me now to get those details again! I need another copy today Terry, today!"

"No, no, I'll bring you another one Declan, I'm sorry, I just panicked." Terry lifted himself up from the ground again but Declan slammed him back down enough to generate another loud cry from Terry whose head once more was pummeled by the brick.

"No, we'll go and get the copy now," asserted Declan, dragging Terry up with him, whose legs then found it hard to find their balance.

Terry, although clearly at a disadvantage screamed back, "Fuck off, you'll have to wait for it Dec, you've lost your chance today."

He started to run as fast as he could towards the chain link fence and his van, hurriedly fumbling for the keys in his pocket as he grasped for breath, his ankles twisting on the stones and debris.

Declan's face turned dark purple with rage and he raced ahead to cut off his progress and block his route to the van.

Terry, his breaths getting shorter and shorter, turned about as fast as he could and started off in another direction, determined to reach the top of the dock where he knew an access road would lead him back to the road his van was parked in, vainly hoping to beat Declan to the van or at the very least escape elsewhere in the area until he had chance to return later.

Declan changed his direction and sprinted as fast as he could on the ground after Terry. However, as he raced on and focused on the man ahead, he missed his footing, his shoe getting caught in a twisted metal rod sticking out of the ground.

Declan now crashed earthwards and landed heavily on his hands, causing him to scream in agony as a fingernail was torn away as it had thrust downwards to find stability.

He sat down for a couple of seconds to take in the blood streaming from the uneven wound, groaning, before hearing Terry's pig-like grunting, his laboured breaths mixing with audible whines as Terry relived every fearful nightmare he'd ever dreamt of being pursued.

Declan's face grew calm. He knew what he needed to do to assuage his anger, to rid himself of the humiliation of defeat.

He picked himself up in time to see Terry reach the road at the top of the dock that led back towards the van.

Declan gave chase, not after Terry, but towards the gap in the chain link fence where the van sat.

Terry rounded the corner of the access road to see Declan standing by the van already. His whines and the panting grew again as he desperately looked about for another route.

Declan calmly started walking up the road towards Terry and as Terry decided on a new direction, Declan pulled out a revolver, aimed it at him and pulled the trigger.

Terry stopped in his tracks as he heard the shot fly by him and embed itself with a crack in the pavement nearby.

"I'll take you, I'll take you now," Terry whimpered, as he looked round to see Declan raise his bloodied hand again and balance his aim.

Declan calmly ignored the plea and squeezed the trigger. A second shot rang out and hit Terry in the head, a burst of blood flying out on impact.

His body spun around slightly before collapsing awkwardly to the ground.

Declan replaced the gun and raced up to where he lay, quickly grasping hold of Terry's jacket to find the van keys.

Terry's mobile 'phone clattered out onto the tarmac at the same time as the keys did and Declan paused to look at it before quickly realising he needed to get rid of it.

With his bloodied grip, he scraped at the back of the 'phone to remove the battery which he then threw over the chain link fence. The SIM card was snatched from the metal clip and put into his own pocket before the other part of the 'phone was thrown into the dockyard on the other side of the road.

Declan grabbed the keys and raced back towards the van, When he reached it, he got in and sped along the road to the body that was now getting soaked by the driving rain once more.

He pulled the van up just short of the body and quickly put it into reverse, spinning the wheel around so that he could back up to the motionless corpse. Finding the key for the padlock, he wrenched open the back doors and climbed in to clear a space amidst the half empty cement sacks and concrete spattered buckets.

Jumping back to the ground, he tried to lift the body into the van but couldn't succeed in making Terry's shoulders stay inside.

He propped the body to sit up against the bumper of the van and tried to haul it up inside the van by putting his arms under Terry's armpits and lifting, but he couldn't stand upright enough to get Terry's bulk into the back.

Conscious that he was in a deserted but still publicly accessible area, he jumped out again, put his shoulder into Terry's chest, grasping hold tightly of one arm and hauled him up onto his shoulder.

Declan gasped for air as he strained under the weight and set off for the top end of Hamilton Dock.

In his mind, he'd intended to make the other side, to tip the body into the channel itself, but exhausted, he let go of his burden at the first opportunity and the body headed down towards the grimy water but not before Terry's head made purchase with the dock wall on the way down.

Declan didn't wait to watch the body sink below the water but instead checked over both his shoulders to ensure that he wasn't being observed before racing back to the van and driving it off to the top of Queen's Island where he pushed his foot down hard on the accelerator to push it over the waste ground.

The van bumped up and down, bouncing violently this way and that as Declan struggled and fought with the steering wheel.

Just before the edge, before the open waters of Belfast Lough, he got out of the van and gingerly edged it forward with his hand on the steering wheel and his shoulder in the open doorway.

When it was far enough forward, he slammed the door, moved around to the back and pushed the van into the water with his remaining might.

This he did watch, observing the waters stream in through the passenger window he had left open, hoping that it would sink without trace to the bottom.

Declan flung the van keys into the water behind the vehicle and made an about turn, leaving behind the mortal remains of Terry Flanagan and his trusty van to the grime of Belfast's shipyard past.

A number of days later, Terry's body popped back up in Abercorn Basin, the heavy black waters topped with shimmering oil gently pushing him into the debris strewn side where no dock wall remained, just gravel and rubble and weeds to offer their silent tribute. Nobody saw it amongst the rubbish as nobody was there to see it and eventually the tides swept it out of sight again until the wake of a passing ship sent it once more below the surface.

Chapter Twenty Five

Brendan Flanagan was waiting in a bar for his brother Michael to show.

He had been trying to make a pint of stout last for the past twenty minutes, but the dregs were losing their appeal and after checking his watch, he decided to down the remainder and he got up from behind the table he was sat at and moved over to the bar.

It is an oft-quoted cliché but his feet really were sticking to the floor, the once piled carpet now an amalgam of an over-trodden surface littered with black grease spots and beery residues.

Brendan moved his feet about on the spot before the bar; sub-consciously peeling his feet away from the tacky surface time and again, trying to catch the eye of the barmaid.

Elaine was otherwise engaged, chatting to a couple of the bar's permanent fixtures that usually frequented the premises at lunchtimes.

She noticed Brendan from the corner of her eye and tried to extricate herself from the unceasing attention of the regulars whose only real absence occurred on market days.

"Ah but you're still only a young thing," said one of the pair, ignoring her attempt to escape.

"Oh, I bet there's life in you yet, John," she chortled away, adding, "I'm just going to serve this customer."

"Ah well, I might just find a bit of life for you Elaine, ha ha!" John replied, providing her with a display of his uneven and gappy teeth as he did so.

Elaine moved along the bar to where Brendan was still moving about on the tacky floor.

"Hello stranger, you've not been in here for a while," she stated, straightening up the bar towels as she addressed him.

"Oh, I've been busy Elaine, but hopefully things are going to get back to normal soon."

"Glad to hear it, we've been missing you," Elaine said, actually intending to say that she herself had been missing him but finding herself speaking on behalf of the pub instead of herself, keen not to sound too interested in him so soon after he'd returned to the bar after an absence she had most certainly noted.

"Get me another pint will you and take one for yourself whilst you are at it," he offered, reaching for his wallet from his back pocket.

"Thanks for that, I'll just have a tonic water if that's okay," she asked, reaching down behind her for a pint glass for his stout.

"Tonic water, I thought you liked a vodka or two, you're not going all tee-total on me are you now?" he asked, looking straight into her eyes.

"It's only lunchtime Brendan, if you're in later, I'll let you get me that vodka?"

Elaine started to pull the pint, smiling quietly and hoping that he would take her up on the offer.

"Ha ha," he laughed, "you might just be in luck on that one."

"I'll take one of those too," said a voice alongside Brendan – it was Michael who had come to the bar and made his way up to his brother.

"Oh, you will, will you," Brendan complained, "well, I think you'll be getting this round in as you've kept me waiting," and offered his brother a cheeky grin, mostly to amuse Elaine rather than to wind up his brother.

"I'm not that late," Michael replied, "stop your complaining, I'm here now. Are you hungry? I could eat a horse."

Brendan raised his eyebrows and looked at Elaine, "Younger brothers, who would have them, eh!"

"So what are you having Michael," she enquired, "a pint?"

"Yeah and what food do you have on?" Michael asked, picking up the A5 sized menu card from in-between a pot containing cutlery and a bottle of budget tomato ketchup.

"All day full fry or Shepherds Pie," Elaine replied as she started to pull the pint.

"You mean the same as usual then? Diane not tried anything new for a while I take it?" Michael said, a grin letting Elaine know that it wasn't a criticism, more an acknowledgement of the unchanging set up at the Cross Keys.

"We had Lasagne on last week I'll have you know," she retorted, "nobody wanted it, but we had it!"

"Oh, I'll go for the fry then, I've not had a proper breakfast today," said Michael before he grasped the now settled pint and lifted it to his lips.

"Take a seat, I'll bring it over when it's ready," Elaine confirmed before disappearing from the bar for a moment to rouse Diane from daytime TV in the kitchen.

Brendan and Michael sat down at their table, the walls around it full of old fashioned adverts on mirrored glass for long forgotten brands from breweries that nobody remembered, including 'Dunville's Royal Irish'.

Something about the pub that day reminded Brendan of the days his father used to take him in a pub at lunchtimes in the school holidays.

His father had been instructed by Moira to take their eldest son off her hands for the odd day here and there and Terry Flanagan thought that they might as well provide his son with the full extent of his daily pursuits which included a few drinks with pals at lunchtimes. Terry though, made it quite clear to Brendan that if he told his mother that was where he spent his lunchtimes he'd be in for a proper hiding.

Moira of course knew exactly where Terry spent his lunchtimes and happily turned her cheek if it meant her husband came home at a decent hour in the evening and didn't fritter away the time he should spend with her, sat in a bar like so many other husbands she knew of.

Michael could tell that his brother was lost in thought, his eyes lacking focus and staring in the vague direction of the frosted window.

"Not boring you am I?" asked Michael, giving his brothers nearest foot a kick under the table.

Brendan came back from the past with a jolt, "What, no, just remembering how Dad used to bring me in places like this, don't know why I'm thinking of this today in particular."

"Something to do with what we're here to talk about I suppose." said Michael looking around hungrily at the bar.

"Maybe Michael, maybe. What's clear to me is it is about time we finally got our inheritance, I'm tried of working for others and not claiming what's ours," Brendan stated, stabbing his index finger in the space in front of his brother's face for emphasis.

Michael felt uneasy about the vehemence which his brother placed on each word, unsettling utterances jarring with the 'usual' Brendon he was used to being with.

Brendan continued, "I've got the key Michael, THE key that Mam said didn't exist. I finally went to check out what Dad told me all of those years ago and wouldn't you know it was actually there where he said it would be."

"Wha . . . not the one he said was at Mount Stewart?" Michael queried, a half grin beginning to stretch across his mouth as he began to understand what this could mean.

"Oh yes, the very one and right where he said it would be," explained Brendan, "all we need now is the papers that you've got from Maggie and we're going to have what Dad worked so hard for."

"Well, we've got the papers," Michael confirmed, "I arranged for Kathleen to have access to Maggie's bag last night and she's replaced the papers so she won't notice – not for a while at any rate."

"Michael!", Brendan hissed, conscious of anyone else listening in at the bar, "Why the hell did you let HER have them so soon, I'll not have her getting her hands on what's ours.

Just then, Elaine appeared from behind the bar with Michael's fry up and Brendan kept his mouth shut for a while whilst she busied herself with knife, fork and sachets of tomato sauce.

Brendan paused for a moment and gave Elaine an unconvincing smile as she retreated back to the bar.

He continued, "Get those papers back from Kathleen, Michael and we're home and dry. Why did you let her get her hands on them first for God's sake?

"Hey, I thought we were working with her on this one – she does have some claim doesn't she?"

"No, she does not," Brendan stated, "she may have been involved with Dad through the whole set up but you can't tell me that any of that planning, the numbers, the locations, c'mon Michael – no way was that down to Kathleen."

Michael, unsure how to respond to this sudden change in views and allegiance displayed by his brother, turned his attention instead to his all day breakfast.

He sawed off a section of budget sausage and stabbed it firmly with his fork before dipping it into the golden yolk of the crispy brown fat frilled egg.

"I don't see how we're going to keep Kathleen out of this Brendan, Christ, she even knows I'm meeting you here for a pint today," Michael said, tackling the bacon from amidst the coagulated baked beans.

"I'm not letting her use us forever Michael, I'm your brother and we're going to do this for US. She thinks we have our uses for sure, but do you honestly believe she's going to look after us come the end of all this? I think we both know the true answer to that one." Brendan put down his pint and looked out towards the window, "We'll not antagonise her just yet but she'll soon find out that we're not the pushovers she seems to think we are, scurrying around doing her bidding." Brendan turned back towards his brother and asked nonchalantly, "Another pint?"

The freshness of the morning had come and gone, leaving behind the turgidity of early afternoon. Maggie had finally roused herself after the night she had had with Michael a few hours before.

The bedclothes were strewn around the foot of the bed, mostly trailing on the floor where Maggie had flung them when realising that Michael wasn't coming back between the sheets anytime soon.

She was thirsty, that dry thirst that follows too much red wine – a desiccating dehydration that leaves your mouth aching for water.

Maggie had already pulled her clothes on and sat on the edge of the bed applying makeup in her handbag mirror. A smell of baking drifted upwards from the kitchen below and Maggie felt safe, a long distant memory of stability coming back to the surface with the hunger inducing aromas.

She considered her options. 1) Ring Michael and get him to come and pick her up ASAP. 2) Descend into Moira's world below and bide some time before Michael returned.

Whilst she pondered this thought and rummaged in the handbag, she stopped suddenly and stared at the bag in her hands.

She distinctly remembered leaving the handbag downstairs the night before, before coming upstairs with Michael, but her handbag was there by the foot of the bed when she woke up. Her mind pieced together the previous night again and amidst the happy recollections she once again stared at the bag trying to work out how it came to be in the room.

She shuddered for a moment as she imagined Moira coming across the bag and how she might have decided to bring it upstairs and into her room in a quiet moment.

She also wondered if Michael might have brought it upstairs for her on seeing it downstairs on his way out that morning.

Deciding that Michael will have been the one to bring up the bag, she rummaged again for more makeup and instinctively did a visual check of the contents – purse, lipstick, tissues, perfume, papers . . .

She lifted out the papers and knew instantly that something was wrong. The ones she had been carrying had been stapled together but the bottom sheet had been changed, this being the same problem that Tommy had found. These sheets looked similar, exact almost for the fact that the top sheet had just one set of original staple marks in it whereas the original sheet had had multiple staple marks betraying the re-stapling that came from the switch of the bottom sheet some time ago, the one that Tommy had noticed had been changed when he had struggled with the last clues.

Maggie's heart started to quicken as she tried to imagine who had switched the papers and when.

She searched through them frantically, trying to see any other noticeable differences in the columns of numbers but all looked fine from her initial review.

She even doubted herself for a moment about the staple marks, thinking that maybe she'd been mistaken about those. A sickening realisation come over her though as her mind confirmed what she had first suspected – the papers had most definitely been switched.

Anger replaced the confusion in Maggie's mind as she realised how foolish she had been to trust Michael, to trust another man so soon after Declan.

Filled with a mounting rage, she hurriedly adjusted her clothes and stormed out of the bedroom and down the stairs. At the bottom, she looked in her bag again to pull out her mobile 'phone which she took out of standby and quickly scrolled through to find Michael's number.

The 'phone rang at the other end but only connected to Michael's voicemail, "Answer Michael you bastard!" cried Maggie and she ended the call before the beep allowed her to leave a message.

"Hey, hey, what's all this about?" asked Moira who had come out of the kitchen wearing an apron over her clothes, her hands slightly pale from the flour she had been using to dust one of the work surfaces in the kitchen where she was baking.

"Your son has stitched me up, that's what!" retorted Maggie with vehemence, "Where is he anyhow?"

"I don't like the tone of your voice . . ." started Moira before Maggie cut her off with, "Oh shut up – just tell me where your stupid son is or you're no use to me just now."

"How dare you take that tone with me and talk about Michael like that," spat Moira, "just get out of my house if you can't be civil and don't bother coming back!"

"Oh don't worry, I'll not stay in this place a moment longer that I need to but until I see Michael, I'm going nowhere!" said Maggie, checking her appearance again in the hall mirror.

"Nobody gets to speak to me like that, not in my own home," continued Moira, "just get out of my house now you common piece of . . ."

"Ha ha," Maggie cried, "you're welcome to your house and you're welcome to your son but one thing is for sure – I've got unfinished business with Michael and he and I are going to sort it out and if you know what's good for you, you'll keep your interfering nose well out of it. To think that I actually felt sorry for Michael living here with you but now I see your family are all the same," Maggie grabbed the front door handle and yanked the door open, "you tell Michael that I'll be in touch and he'd better make sure that he gives me back my property when I see him or let me tell you, you'll all be sorry you crossed me!"

Moira opened her mouth, about to remonstrate with the invader in her home but before she formed any words, Maggie shouted, "Oh save it Moira, just save your breath!"

Maggie stepped out into the afternoon and turned back to grab the handle again in order to slam the door behind her but Moira had got there first.

"No you don't Madam!" said Moira calmly, "You go on your way and just watch your own back because people who cross my family get burnt Maggie, BURNT!"

Chapter Twenty Six

Dark clouds of doubt and unanswered questions joined the billowing steam rising from a bathtub, scarcely visible but tangible enough to force the recumbent bather to screw up his eyes and rub his face, urging the airborne droplets to carry away a heavier burden on their ceiling-ward journey.

Why was he here, directionless between betrayals of past trust and uncertainty of future direction, indecision, angst, worthlessness? The vultures of self-doubt were gathering, attracted by the scent of self-diagnosed failure.

The mixer tap dripped icily into the foam topped lake beneath and Kelly lifted up a toe to let the cold water trickle down his foot and ankle.

He shifted slightly in the tub, causing a wave to bounce off the end of the bath and travel back to wash over him.

Water circled over his body, causing the hairs to waft in the current like strands of seaweed being submerged and then exposed again by an advancing tide.

Kelly stared down in a daze onto his torso and watched the water gently washing to and fro, swirling eddies forming when he shifted again to re-start another wave.

Peace descended, save for the therapeutic drip of the tap and Kelly felt some relief from the haze in his mind.

He started to drift off into slumber, his mind replaying images of photographs and half remembered conversations as he did so.

He fought against the tiredness but succumbed as his heavy eyelids clamped shut, plunging him into a detached darkness.

As he drifted off, Kelly saw Kathleen in his mind, getting out of her car on the driveway next to his when he was a teenager.

Kelly had shyly peered out from behind the curtains of his bedroom upstairs at the front of the house, keeping himself back from the glass as he stared at her progress towards the house and her own front door. As she went, he had wanted to get a better look and so he'd carefully leant forward a little more to see the last of her before she went in to the house.

Kathleen was of course fully aware that she had an admirer in the window and carried on her progress until she was just out of view when she quickly stepped back and waved playfully up to the bedroom window.

Peeping Tom started with shock once he saw the wave in his direction and he had dropped to the floor faster than his teenage frame had moved for some time and he'd stayed there, back hunched and on his knees below the windowsill, trying to convince himself that maybe she had been waving to someone else but knowing absolutely that it was him she was waving at.

He'd crouched there for a minute longer, hand clasped over his eyes in despair at his own embarrassed state before deciding to crawl on his hands and knees towards the bedroom door, lest he should be spotted again.

"Should have just waved right back," Kelly said to himself in his half slumber.

Drip, drip, drip, continued the tap and Kelly was watching Kathleen again as she'd dashed through the rain to get to her car on another day whilst he was perched in his first floor observatory. It was summer and her white top showed where the big raindrops had made the fabric translucent as she'd struggled to find her key from her bunch to open the car door.

Drip, drip and Kelly returned to the steamy tub just before the bath water seeped into his open mouth as he slid lower in the water.

The shock of the water level near his face made him search

quickly for the bottom of the bath with his submerged hands where they slipped momentarily before enabling him to hoist himself up in the water, gasping for air as he did so.

He reached for the chain with his toes and he pulled out the plug and stayed lying there for a minute or two, letting the retreating waters carry away some of his memories down the thirsty drain.

Moira's words still echoed in Maggie's ears as she strode away from the bungalow, cursing audibly as she hammered her heels into the turgid tarmac, hair swaying, jaw gnashing, eyes flashing.

She was a little way from the house before she realised that it was still a good walk to the village, to the hope of a taxi away from the stench of fresh air pervading her urban nostrils.

Her inner thoughts took over from her external utterances of rage and she pondered how best she could track down Michael, to confront him before Moira poisoned any possibility of him even picking up the telephone to her in reply.

Maggie stopped dead in her tracks and fumbled in her handbag for her mobile. Punching the screen, she dialed Michael again, intent on demanding an explanation.

Michael's voicemail connected again and Maggie screamed in frustration as she pressed the screen to end the call. As she did so, she spun around to turn away from the glare of the sun as she struggled with the clasp on her bag and noticed a car in the distance driving purposefully along the road from Moira's dormer bungalow.

Maggie saw the opportunity instantly and hurriedly straightened her skirt and brushed off some invisible lint from her jacket as she started to walk along with smaller, more gracious steps.

Swinging her handbag, she was aware of the car nearing her and turned to face it to try and wave it down for a lift, seeing it as her best opportunity on the narrow country lane.

The sun reflected brightly off the windscreen as she tried to ascertain the sex of the driver so she could alter her approach and she still couldn't quite tell who was at the wheel until the car slowed and pulled up alongside her.

As she bent down to talk through the opening window she couldn't help but let out a startled cry as her eyes adjusted to the occupant inside. Her eyes widened further with astonishment as the eyes staring back belonged to Declan.

Maggie moved quickly and turned swiftly away from the car, heading back down the road the way that she had come as quickly as her heels would let her.

Declan hurriedly put the car into reverse and pursued his quarry down the road, swerving this way and that as he tried to get used to steering down the lane using only his mirrors to afford their distorted view.

At a bend in the road he hit the high hedge topped bank and the car grated along for a moment before he hit the brakes. He acted quickly and flung open his door and hurtled after his prey who was now only a few feet ahead on the road.

"Maggie Haugh!" Declan screamed out, "Stop there or I swear I'll kill ya!"

Maggie let out another shriek and couldn't help peering back over her shoulder and she caught sight of Declan only feet behind her. She then turned back around too quickly for her footwear and one of her heels snapped sideways underneath her leaving no support for Maggie who crashed forward to the ground, sending her bag down the road, its contents scattering in all directions. Lipstick and blusher rolled quickly into the side of he road.

She let out a cry as she tried to get back up on her feet but that was only a precursor to the scream she let out as Declan reached her and grabbed hold of her jacket to pull her over.

"Get up!" he shouted. "C'mon, get up!"

Maggie didn't reply but tried to slip out of his grasp but he held her tight.

"Stupid bitch!" Declan cried again, loosening the grip of one hand so that he could slap Maggie hard on the face, the blow sending out a loud crack as it made contact. "Get up and get in the car!"

Maggie's bottom lip was cut badly and blood poured down her chin and onto her clothes. She sucked in air but instead got a mouthful of blood and she choked loudly, coughing repeatedly until her airway cleared.

Declan had started to physically drag her back towards the car and Maggie's shoes scraped and scracked on the tarmac as she tried to get a purchase on the rough surface in a vain attempt to resist her tormentor.

Declan gave her another forceful yank and Maggie was pulled upright momentarily before collapsing to her knees once more.

By this time they were back at the car and Declan shouted, "Get in!"

Maggie stayed on her knees for a moment sobbing black rivers of mascara that merged with the crimson tide from her ballooning lip before wincing at the next approach Declan made.

She now reached up for the open passenger door and dragged herself in and on to the seat. Declan slammed the door after her and hurriedly went around to the drivers side, restarted the engine and set off with a screech of burning rubber.

Further down the road, Michael was negotiating the lane on his motorbike and Maggie was still aware enough of what was going on around her to recognise him through the tears she was valiantly attempting to hold back.

As the motorbike came towards Declan's car, Maggie mustered her strength and waved her arms frantically into the windscreen.

Declan cursed her and landed another heavy blow with his left hand in response, the heavy signet ring scraping Maggie's face again and creating a fresh cut.

Michael quickly negotiated his way around the swerving car, thinking, 'Bloody stupid driver' but failing to notice the flaying arms of Maggie behind the windscreen, simply opened up the throttle again to make faster progress along the road towards home.

'The Baltic' was the largest ship in the world when she was built in 1904, closely following after were White Star's "Oceanic' and 'Celtic' and the 21,000 ton 'Cedric', all built in the harbour at Belfast with its spacious river quays and four graving docks spawning world famous leviathans.

Where else exists such a deep and picturesque arm of the sea, for fourteen miles the channel reaches between Antrim and Down and into the heart of Belfast. Ideal for shipbuilding, the only dangerous reef being called the 'Briggs' by the Irish and the "Clachan' by the Scots.

On the north side, all that is left of the shipbuilding era now are the empty docks, the echoing sheds that once employed many thousands and Samson and Goliath, the two yellow gantry cranes on Queen's island that help to anchor the city in the psyche of many even if they haven't visited the place.

The confidence to build Samson in 1974 even though the troubles were claiming lives and livelihoods all about, seems hard to appreciate today with the benefit of historical hindsight, yet the yellow siblings still stand over the world's largest dry dock and see occasional use for ship repair and metal construction.

Kathleen's father was one of the then 30,000 workers at Harland & Wolff before he met her mother and whisked her off her feet at the 'Fiesta' dancehall on a Saturday night.

Mary had eyed Jim as he entered the ballroom with his friends, black hair slicked into a quiff and she remarked to her friend Sheryl that she 'Wouldn't mind a dance with him'.

Sheryl commented that he wasn't her type and anyway he was clearly 'a bit of rough' but she knew that's what Mary went for.

Mary's father had been a captain who knew the coast better than his own back garden. He knew the approach to Belfast Lough, knew that when entering from the south you'd encounter tides that ran hard, knew where caution was required about the reefs formed of wormy Subellamia Spinulosa which could add another 60cm to the seabed.

Once Mary had danced with Jim and they were sat on an upholstered bench on the side of the dance floor, they chatted over a pint and a Brandy and Babycham respectively.

She grew still more interested when she learnt that he worked in the shipyards – something about the link to the sea stoked her interest and encouraged her to let Jim put his arm around her shoulder after another drink.

At the same time, Sheryl had been trying to like a bricklayer with wavy blond hair and an overbite, but her heart wasn't in it. She giggled politely and allowed her admirer to light her cigarette and refill her glass of Advocaat and lemonade but her gaze was mainly towards Mary and Jim. She wondered how she was going to accept that her friend would soon busy herself with her 'new fella' and leave Sheryl sat in at home with her mother and a flatulent poodle.

Mary always did that with men, always keen to go out with Sheryl when she was in-between blokes but you'd hardly hear from her when she was being courted.

Sheryl would always accept this however and comply with Mary's fickle friendship, but the thought of returning to 'nights in' instead of nights on the town made Sheryl look again at the bricklayer and respond a little more warmly to his calloused advances.

She looked over at her friend one last time before getting up to dance and saw Mary's immovable helmet of backcombed hair heading towards Jim's Brylcreamed barnet.

Black bouffant, jet black then and later dyed to cover the grey – the same grey that her daughter Kathleen now carefully hid with trips to expensive city salons.

Mary's family had money, not much money, but comfortably off enough to buy Mary and Jim a house in one of the better areas of Belfast. Mary's father had passed on a few years before and Mary's mother didn't hold the prejudices her husband had spouted and welcomed Jim into the fold warmly, knowing that her daughter's happiness should come before social position.

Mary's mother often wondered herself though if she would have held such forward thinking views if she hadn't had the security of a private income.

There were enough neighbours still keen to be seen at social functions at Mary's parents' home to render any worries about future son in laws to fade into insignificance. A curiosity only, one to push around one's mind whilst contemplating whether to have chicken or beef for the wedding breakfast. Not that she didn't want the best for Mary, far from it, but she had a healthy enough understanding about the changing society they found themselves living in and recognised the tide had turned in respect of offspring obedience.

Mary and Jim settled in to their new, paid for home and began to start a family. Jim kept on travelling to the shipyards but arrived in his own car, parking it along the side of the dock road, praying daily as he left it that it would remain pristine until his return at the end of his shift.

Perhaps it was the banality of this regular family life at home that pushed Kathleen to look for a second existence, one that stretched her resolve, excited her passions and led her negotiating a path along a knife edge, no space for the slightest slip or momentary lack of concentration.

Where others could undertake the graft, Kathleen would always let them continue, happy to view the results and benefit from the resulting proceeds. Some tasks though require the instigator to act alone, to see through their vision in person, to step closer to the fire that has been set.

Kathleen sat in her car outside her childhood home watching someone else's family, someone else's life, continue in the surroundings once so familiar to her.

She switched her gaze to the house next door – to Kelly's childhood home where he still lived amongst the remnants of the past – those left at least after the raging fire some months before.

Inside the house Kelly watched the final inches of water race towards the plughole and sleepily decided that he needed to get out of the tub.

Just as he was hauling himself out, the doorbell chimed.

Kelly cursed as he stepped on to the waiting bathmat and reached over towards the towel rail over the radiator.

The doorbell rang again twice in quick succession, followed by a knocking at the door and he rushed to yank the towel from its resting place and flung it around his waist.

He was still dripping water as he raced down the stairs, one hand steadying himself on the bannister, the other clutching the towel slipping down his hips.

Kathleen noticed movement coming down the stairs through the frosted pane of glass in the front door and shook her hair provocatively whilst waiting for the door to open.

"I'm coming," called Kelly as he descended the last few steps and reached the latch.

He opened the door a crack and could not stop himself from stepping back slightly in surprise as he stumbled over, "K . . . K . . . Kathleen!"

Kathleen raised her eyebrows as the door swung open and revealed the man in the towel standing before her before saying, "Interrupting you I see," and allowing her gaze to travel down the still wet torso facing her.

Kelly blushed. Not just a red face, but a dark, burning furnace of a face that could heat a small home. A teenage blush, one that also made him feel devoid of the towel still clinging about him.

"What . . . what are you doing here?" he stammered. In that one small sentence he wrapped up all of his feelings about Kathleen and she sensed it. His once teenage fixation, his adult temptations, his disgust and loathing as he'd discovered the photo of her in his father's bed and the unanswered questions about financial fraud.

"I've come over to see you of course," she purred, "and my, haven't you all grown up, the last time I saw you like this you'd just stepped out of a paddling pool in the garden."

Kelly felt a sense of anger and frustration building inside him, particularly with the over familiar teasing from her on his own doorstep.

"What do you want, I've got a lot of things I need to do Kathleen," he stated.

"We need to talk John," she continued, "c'mon, we've known each other too long for this."

Kelly paused for a moment and then decided to grasp the opportunity to find out more information, to try and make some connections so he can satisfy his ardent curiosity and regain a semblance of normality.

Fractured pieces of childhood presented themselves in Kelly's mind, clouding his judgement, leaving himself more open than he'd like to psychological manipulation at the hands of his first teenage lust interest.

"Alright," he said, stepping backwards into the hall, "come in, I'm just going to put something on."

"Mmm, wouldn't want you catching your death would we," Kathleen added playfully, brushing past Kelly just enough to make him even more uncomfortable.

"Go through to the kitchen Kathleen, I'll be back down in a minute and put the kettle on."

Kelly then sprinted back up the stairs still clutching the towel until he reached the top and turned into his bedroom. As soon as he flung the towel down his florid face turned ashen instantly and his mouth dropped open.

He was frozen in an instant as he realised that in the kitchen cupboard next to the kettle and the coffee jar, were the pass-books and bank details that he'd found in the box under the floor of the front room.

He was momentarily unable to decide what to do, swaying slightly until he allowed himself to take a breath and regain his composure.

He rushed to the wardrobe and grabbed a pair of jeans and hurriedly pulled them on and made for the top of the stairs, still doing up the buttons as he went. He raced down the stairs and quickly pushed open the kitchen door.

Kathleen turned around quickly, positioning herself carefully in front of part of the worktop. She tried to act normally but Kelly instantly knew what she had already seen.

Kathleen tried to catch him off guard saying with a smile, "No clean shirts up there?" but her manner was too forced to be natural. Kelly did not return her false smile.

"What have you got on the worktop there Kathleen, something interesting?"

She laughed awkwardly before replying, "You're just not happy to leave things alone are you, always looking into things you just don't understand. Your father wouldn't want this you know."

Kelly was the next to laugh. "Ha, ha, don't you dare bring my father into this, how dare you question my actions when you've clearly used my father and somehow decided to use me too between you. He paused, looking for a reaction before continuing, "I need answers Kathleen and I want them now."

She stared at him, judging his resolve, assessing his implacability before speaking, "Stay out of this Kelly, you're nothing but an innocent in all of this and that's the way it needs to stay, the way your father would want it."

Kelly cut her off instantly, a fire within making his eyes sparkle with intent. "My father, ha, where's he been to offer parental guidance and support then Kathleen, eh? He's been much too busy playing around with you it seems to fulfill that role in my life, so don't try to put me back in my box, it's not going to work."

She smiled to herself, not a smile of glee or happiness but one of steely resolve and calculation.

"No, I don't suppose it is John. You might not want me to mention your father but you're more like him than you might care to think. He knew what he wanted too." She stepped away from the worktop and towards Kelly until she stopped right in front of him.

"Keep out of this John Kelly, keep the hell out of it or I'm not going to be able to protect you from this anymore."

She placed a hand on his shirtless chest and ran it through his chest hair before he could pull back from it. "Please believe me John," she added softly, lifting up her dark eyes to his, "I'm doing what's best for you. Put your trust in me and all this is going to turn out the way it should."

Kelly lifted up an arm and grasped Kathleen's hand, pulling it off his chest. He tightened his grip steadily until Kathleen winced in pain.

"Just you get the hell out of here Kathleen and I suggest you don't come here again unless you're going to come clean on all of this," he added, as he threw her arm away from him.

She backed away towards the worktop again, flinging her hair out of her eyes as she did so.

Kelly was aware of a faint rustling of paper as Kathleen's right hand crept back to grasp the paperwork she had already taken out of the cupboard whilst Kelly was upstairs.

"Get the hell out off that Kathleen and get the hell out of here!" cried Kelly, racing over to retrieve the papers back.

She grabbed at the remainder of the passbooks and statements and turned her back on Kelly in an attempt to stuff what she could into her waiting handbag.

"Get off that, it's not even your property, it's all in my name. Put it down NOW!" he demanded, grabbing at the strap of her handbag as he did.

Kathleen continued to fight him off by turning her back on him and forcing him away by scraping her manicured nails of her free hand into his upper arm.

"Your property, ha ha, oh John, as if any of this was ever your property!" she said mockingly but Kelly jumped forward again and grasped at the bag once more, this time succeeding and sending the contents scattering across the floor.

Amidst the contents a revolver spun along the floor before coming to a rest by the kickboard of the kitchen units.

Kelly was frozen in surprise and took a moment to take a breath, giving Kathleen the time she needed to drop to the floor and to pick it up. She stood up and pointed the gun directly at him.

"You're making too many mistakes John and I'm sorry but I can't answer for what might happen to you if you keep on with this insane interference," she stated calmly before adding, "I'm taking these papers and books John, primarily because they belong to me, not to you. I suggest that you let me leave with them and just forget you've even seen them."

She stooped down again whilst keeping the gun pointed at Kelly and calmly picked up the contents of the bag that had been spilled and replaced them one by one into its receiving depths.

Kelly was impotent in his physical reactions but internally, his mind was reeling from the realisation that the woman standing before him was so different to the one that he'd had for all these years in his mind.

He'd even begun to soften and maybe even to forgive her for the furtive relationship that she'd had with his father, trying to believe that maybe she had been the party being led astray, the one so besotted that she was incapable of rational thought. He now saw her though for what she was and any last vestiges of warmth towards her had turned into nausea.

He turned his back on her in disgust and looked out of the kitchen window, startling himself suddenly as he remembered that she had a gun in her hand and that it was still most likely pointed directly at him. He knew though that she would not use it, or at least that she wouldn't if he let her take what she wanted to and let her go on her way.

Kathleen had finished her collecting activities and closed the bag. She walked the couple of steps towards Kelly and thrust the muzzle of the gun into the small of his back, just enough for him to noticeably wince, primarily from the cold metal against his bare skin.

"Don't think about contacting me or contacting anyone about me John because if you do, you'll not be around to experience the satisfaction for very long. Thanks for the bits and pieces too, good of you to take care of them for me."

With that, Kathleen exited the room and slammed the front door behind her as she left the house.

Kelly stood there numb, emotions frozen amidst the soaring levels of adrenalin coursing through his veins. He felt humiliated, used, belittled and at that moment made the decision to fight back, whatever the potential hazards and consequences might be.

His first step to regaining his pride was to return upstairs to his bedroom where he opened a wardrobe door and parted a number of jumpers and woollen scarves stored at the bottom.

He pulled out a large book and lifted off the cover so that he could access what he had left beneath. From inside, he took out the pages of photocopies, duplicates of passbooks and bank statements that provided him with the same information that Kathleen had taken from downstairs.

He sat down with them on his bed and started to try and decipher their significance, determined to beat Kathleen, to put the jigsaw pieces together to see the picture emerge from scattered confusion.

Chapter Twenty Seven

Seagulls cried overhead as they whirled about on the breeze that was flattening great swathes of dark water in the Belfast docks, sending building ripples out from where it first touched the surface, movements that seemed to suggest the water rushing away from the wind.

Grasses clung to their rooty anchors amongst age worn cracks and the remaining rubble surrounding the unfinished side of the Abercorn basin as the wind pulled them this way and that, lifting, swirling and buffeting the slender leaves sprouting from desiccated crevices.

Juxtaposed alongside were the three main blocks of The Arc apartment development, waiting for company in the creeping regeneration beginning to change the area that would soon render the scene unrecognisable to the dockyard ghosts.

From above, the dock walls and basins were still discernable and the Lough waters still lapped upon the same shores but atop the concreted harbor walls rose new incumbents in the scene bringing people to live here in the new apartments with their gleaming kitchens and leather sofas that faced wall mounted flat screen TVs.

How long before these tenants would move on and leave an area to change again – fifty years? A hundred? Who knows what will have priority in the centuries yet to come – sea view serenity or overcrowded survival sucking life from every square foot it tries to consume to house and feed and heat a burgeoning population clinging on to the vestiges of consumerisation?

The prow like walls of the Titanic Visitor Centre thrust out from the centre of the building, a rippling surface of solidified waves clothing the pointed bows, reflecting the colours of the nearby harbour waters.

Maggie had her back to this vigourous modernity and faced instead the rear of the Harland and Wolff drawing office, its red brick and terracotta facades shouting to no one about what lay inside. She was more comfortable with the scale and materials of this building as she battled with the wind and chose to stay on the same spot.

An angry bruise, still swollen and yet to fully colour, surrounded her left eye. She had carefully covered it all that she could but even Maggie's makeup wasn't deep enough to cover these wounds.

A tear welled up in the tight and reduced corner of her eye and began to run down her face – a combination of the biting wind and the irritation caused by the liberal application of warpaint.

Declan had inflicted similar 'gifts' upon Maggie before and as the blow fell that caused it, she'd just let out a dull cry as she also knew that a more robust reaction to the pain would only metre out further retribution from her callous tormentor.

Emptiness filled her mind. She heard the wind, saw the movement in front of her of windbourne detritus, but barely blinked as she phased out into a world of nothingness.

Her hands turned numb with the cold wind and this finally caused her to flinch, more an involuntary response that made her move her hands slowly into warmer coat pockets.

Declan was nearby looking for something along the chain link fence. As they'd both arrived at the spot, the wind had caught hold of the piece of paper he'd been clutching as he'd got out of the car and carried it off to be sucked onto it.

Although he had told her not to move, Maggie had wandered off whilst he ran along the fence line, chasing after his document which insisted on becoming airbourne again each time it was within his grasp.

The paper came to rest in a muddy puddle amidst the weed-strewn gravel and was caught fast as the water began to seep into the paper's fibres.

Declan let out an expletive and caught hold of the corner that was least at risk of full immersion. He hauled the paper out of its watery resting place and held it at arms length as the filthy water drained from it to the thirsty ground below in meandering trickles.

Kathleen meanwhile, was standing at the top of the Titanic dry dock, peering down into the cold harbour waters forcing themselves against the dry dock's outer metal gates. The only noise she could hear apart from the buffeting breeze bouncing an empty drinks can along the dock wall was the sound of a spattering spout of water that had forced its way through the dock gates and was cascading down into the vast stone void below of the dry dock.

Cut out figures were arranged in the bottom of the dry dock providing a retrospective tableaux of activity that would have taken place when there was real life in that place.

The figures were life size but were miniaturised by the immense scale of the dry dock's depths, frozen spectres of industrial decline.

Kathleen was thinking about Terry Flanagan, remembering the passion that she had had for him and his lust for her.

She often visited this spot when in Belfast as she felt close to him here. It was always a place they'd be assured of some privacy when prying eyes seemed to surround them elsewhere.

His absence still caused the raw wound inside her heart to flare up and draw her back to the dockside.

Little did she know that her beloved's body was resting in the dark waters beneath her, shifted slightly by time and tide.

It was so close to her that she could have seen its decomposed and worm riddled form if the water had not been so full of silt and waste and assorted effluents from the Lagan's journey seaward to obscure her languid gaze.

Those empty eyes reflected the empty space left in her heart as she recollected times past. The breeze picked up her hair and sent it streaming away from her face and this soothed her, making her feel at one with the elements and in tune with her introspection.

Kathleen had felt loneliness gnaw away at her since Terry's disappearance and she soothed the psychological sores inside of her with an unceasing hunger for work and the acquisition of wealth from whatever source she could.

Sometimes though, not even her capitalistic fervour could quench the gnawing hunger and that's when she came to stare at the sea and the scenes of yesteryear before her.

Maggie meanwhile had continued her aimless wandering and was within sight of the dry dock. Declan, having finished picking up his documents, looked about him and started to shout, "Maggie!" on top of the breeze.

His voice though, was carried away on the wind and she did not hear it. Instead, she continued on towards the old engine house along the dock edge.

"Maggie!" he cried out again as he quickened his pace in the direction she must have headed in.

Maggie was now aware of his cries but decided to head on towards the figure standing near the water's edge to make the most of her remaining moments of freedom.

Closer now, Declan shouted out again, "Maggie!" and quickened his pace. She heard him and kept her head down but his cry was loud enough to pull Kathleen back from her introspection.

She turned around and was taken aback to see Maggie, hands thrust in her pockets, standing a short way off in front of her.

"Maggie, Maggie, what are you doing here?" Kathleen stumbled out.

She recognised Kathleen's voice and looked up from the ground. Kathleen could see the swelling about Maggie's eye and immediately knew who was responsible, particularly when both women heard, "Maggie!" shouted out again from Declan.

Despite past mistrust and deceit between them, the two women knew instantly that they had a kind of connection, a bond of sorts.

Maggie virtually fell the last few feet towards Kathleen as she mouthed, "Declan, Dec . . ." before Kath grabbed her arm and pulled her towards the building. They managed to reach the Titanic dock and Kathleen realised that they could keep on the opposite side of the building from him if they hurried and she pulled Maggie's hand forcibly to get them both out of sight.

They stumbled amidst the gravel that covered the ground between the engine house and the water. When they reached the end of the building, they paused to peer around the side to see if they could see Declan.

"Maggie!" came the frustrated cry again from Declan and Maggie managed to whisper, "Are you parked nearby?"

"In front of White Star House," Kathleen replied, "we can get there if we go now, c'mon." With that she once again grasped Maggie's hand tightly and they dashed towards the office building and their escape.

Kath continued to pull Maggie on behind her, not taking any account of the fact that Maggie was still quite dazed and as they went, Maggie's feet couldn't keep up and she went over on a heel and let out a shriek as she landed on her side on the uneven ground.

Declan didn't shout out again but instead turned his attention to the direction the sound came from and quickened his pace so that he too rounded the end of the way Kath and Maggie had already gone.

Kathleen had already dragged Maggie back on to her feet and was once again running with her. Declan, heart pounding, saw the pair ahead of him and shrieked, "Kathleen, Kathleen!", before having to catch his breath for a moment as he clutched on to the red brick wall of the building.

His mouth was dry but he managed to blurt out, "Stop now or you'll both regret it!" before forcing his heavy legs in front of each other again in pursuit of his prey.

The women neared Kath's car and Kath thrust her hands into her coat pocket to grasp for her car keys. Fumbling with them, she slowed her pace a little to enable her to single out the key fob and 'zap' the central locking.

The door locks obligingly unlocked and the car lights flashed in welcome as they neared it. Declan, also seeing this activity, was spurred on even more to reach them.

"Get in, c'mon, get in!" Kath urged to Maggie and hurried to put the key into the ignition. As they both slammed the doors shut, Kathleen was too intent on starting the engine to think about locking the doors and just as she started the car, Declan reached it and grasped out at the handle on Maggie's side having approached from the rear.

"Kathleen!" cried out Maggie as she fumbled again to find out how to lock the doors in the car that was new to her.

Kathleen had by now started the engine and slammed the car into first gear and stamped her foot down on the accelerator as Declan pulled Maggie's door open.

Maggie's screams were carried away as the forward motion wrenched the car from Declan's hands and she was nearly thrown from her seat before the car door caught again and stayed shut with their forward progress.

Declan cried out in pain as the car wrenched at his wrist and shouted after the escaping pair, "Come back you bloody bitches!"

Sophie was strolling through the Victoria Square shopping development, perusing the contents of the shop windows with disdain as she went by.

Most items were 'too expensive', a few 'too cheap looking'. Other items of clothing simply looked ridiculous to her, pulled over and around pouting mannequins or suspended by industrial guy ropes, slowly being fried under the intense glare of the penetrating spotlights.

Blasts of warm air escaped through open doorways and dissipated in the cool air of the mall as air was funnelled through the space from Upper Church Lane and out towards Cornmarket.

Sophie slowed her progress and looked at her reflection in another shop window, taking in the thin dress, the unlined jacket, bare legs sticking out of abused brown boots.

Her eyes flicked back to see through the reflection and into the department store's inviting interior. She paused, pondering for a moment whether to go in, but instead decided to walk on as she remembered her purse devoid of ready cash or obliging credit cards.

Once she reached the end of the covered space, she turned around on her heels and walked back through the mall with determination towards Castle Lane and Arthur Street, heading towards Café Vaudeville and a meeting later on with Kelly.

Sophie had suggested the venue as a place to meet when Kelly had contacted her two days before. She'd never been in the Vaudeville but had walked past the imposing doors and was curious as to what lay inside.

She entered and walked with purpose to a table in sight of the entrance so she could see Kelly come in.

A number of shoppers and business people were taking coffee and devouring flaky bakery fare around her where later in the day, Champagne and cocktails would replace the morning repast.

A waitress headed her way with a smile and asked, "What can I get for you?"

"Oh no, nothing just now thanks, I'm waiting for someone."

Sophie then kept her head down and re-read the menu on the small table in front of her.

She didn't spot the door open and Kelly coming in until he was nearly at the table.

"Hello stranger," he said warmly, "okay if I sit here?" breaking the ice as he grinned down at her.

"Oh, ha ha, yes, please do." Sophie replied, her face coming alive and a smile was returned.

"Have you ordered?" Kelly asked, picking up another menu.

"No, I thought I would wait for you first. How have you been anyway?"

"Oh good, good thanks and you?" he enquired in response, placing the drinks card back on the tabletop.

"Oh grand thanks, grand," she replied politely, not sharing her ongoing worries over money that were only made worse by the prices for coffee and cake in the hastily suggested venue.

Sophie had spent the last couple of years in and out of dead end jobs that paid the minimum wage and also didn't tax her brain – a conscious decision as repetitive packing duties enabled her mind to move into a calm state where she wasn't troubled by conflicting issues or unresolvable conundrums of how to achieve aspirational gain.

She actually looked forward to the fuzziness that came with repetition, her mind on autopilot, her hands conditioned to set robotic movement.

Workers chatted between shifts, conversations about partners, children, television. About football, nights out, shopping and crass celebrity.

Sophie smiled and said little, comfortable with her protective introspection.

She took away her meagre wage and waited for events to unfold around her to change her world.

"What do you usually have here?" asked Kelly, browsing the card again, "do you get in here a lot?"

Sophie was brought back to the present and paused for a moment, wanting to say that yes, she did come here a lot with friends, with family, with a host of fictitious fancies. She wanted to tell of the episodes of enjoyment, of wild nights out, but instead her integrity simply suggested the response, "No ... first time, I've never been in."

'Ah, I thought that you must have been here before – well it's a nice spot for sure. Anyway, I've not been here before either, looks like we've both missed it so far."

Sophie smiled slightly and then a warm grin of relief spread across her face as Kelly stated, "My treat anyway."

"That's really kind, thank you Kelly. I'll have a latte I think. So how have you been since I last saw you? It was a bit of a surprise to hear from you after last time. I didn't know if you were mad with me or . . ."

"Oh no, God no, you were just being upfront with me I suppose, but listen . . ." he broke off to give the order to a passing waitress, "listen, I know you'll think me mad but I have to know more, so much of my life seems to be caught up in this, maybe has always been caught up in all this and it will drive me out of my mind if I don't at least try to work things out."

Sophie stared at Kelly across the table, pitying slightly his naïve enthusiasm, his desire to cut through deceit and obfuscation. She let him continue.

"You know I told you about Kathleen, well she's been over to the house."

Kelly proceeded to bring Sophie up to speed on recent events and couldn't help feeling safer, more confident of success by inveigling his young confidant over coffee and cake.

"So what do you think? Are you going to come along with me to the north coast?" asked Kelly, "I'll pay for the trip, nothing for you to contribute at all."

Sophie's better judgement was saying, 'no' to the trip in her mind, to stay packing boxes and instead re-enter the dull world of numbing stability that she had built for herself. She picked up her coffee, looked around at her surroundings and a buzz of excitement entered her stomach. She felt the time was right to move on and replied, "Yes, alright, I'll come but I can't promise what'll happen Kelly. You know there's all kinds of people mixed up in this somehow."

"I know Sophie and thanks for looking out for me," he said, but noting a betrayal of surprise on her face added, "well at least thanks for giving me some guidance. If I don't do something with this now it is just going to eat away at me. I've been living in a world of ignorance for too long now and whatever happens, I suppose I also want it to be known that I can't be pushed around any more."

She smiled a pitying smile again saying, "If that's the only reason for looking for answers Kelly, then you're better off not knowing the answers. You on your own is no match for who might be involved in all of this."

Kelly paused and then said, "I know. It's more than likely just bravado taking over. You see, you're a steadying influence on me – all the more reason for you to come along for the ride."

Sophie smiled again but happily this time. "Sure I'll come, as long as you understand there's places I might not want to re-visit, where I might be leaving you on your own."

"Of course. I know that you've had a tough time of it in the past. I'm not looking to make any of this difficult for you and if it becomes difficult, you just need to tell me."

She sat there for a moment, took a gulp of coffee and explained, "You most likely saved my life that night in Ballycastle you know and whilst I'm happy to be out of the situation I was in there, I'm going to do the right thing and as least try to help to steer you to where answers might be. Don't expect me though to be there long term, you know I'm prone to moving on."

"Well, let's hope that we can both move on then after this?" Kelly finished his overly small espresso, wishing now that he had ordered an Americano instead. “So where’s best to meet up and how would next Thursday be?”

“Okay, Thursday it is,” she lied, knowing that she’d have to feign illness from her packing job or construct some other fabrication of reality for her fervent boss.

“How about Donegall Square, I’ll get off the bus there and if I’m not there when you are, you can circle back around and pick me up?”

Kelly considered this for a moment, thinking what a terrible location it would be to try and pick up someone with luggage in the heart of the city centre but simply said, “Yes, fine, shall we say 10 o’clock and we can be up along the coast for lunch?”

The following Thursday, Kelly was up early, packing a bag with everything he thought he might need for the trip ahead. Having forced a number of items into the remaining space of his bag, he turned around to see t-shirts and a jumper still on top of the bed and cursed as he surveyed the already over full bag and wondered how he was going to fit what he needed in to its mean environs.

Mindful of potential uninvited visitors to the house, he had already changed the locks and had recently installed a burglar alarm, all easy problems to solve for a committed would be entrant to his home, but at least they enabled him to have a little piece of mind knowing that he had done all that he could before leaving the house.

The box of papers, passbooks and documents though were travelling with him, spread out beneath the boot cover that topped the spare wheel in his car. He considered this the safest place and one that he wouldn’t have to touch unless really necessary as he had since photocopied each document again, leaving one copy in his travel bag and another set positioned between the slip case of a Folio Society volume of ‘The Fables of Aesop’ in his book shelf at home.

He took a last look at himself in the bedroom mirror to tug down some of his dark hair that insisted on creeping up at his temple and took his unzipped and overflowing bag down into the hall.

He went through to the kitchen to pick up a bag of rubbish he had cleared out from the fridge, chucked in the last of a loaf of bread he'd been using the last couple of days and headed out of the front door, zapping his car unlocked as he did so.

Once the burgeoning bag was propped up in the boot, he indicated and pulled out into the road in the direction of the city centre.

Behind him, just far enough away to be unnoticed, but near enough to keep a track of the direction he was taking, a silver Audi once again trailed its prey.

Chapter Twenty Eight

Kathleen pulled up her car in front of Tommy's flat. Maggie was still staying with Kathleen but hadn't accompanied her on this trip due to the possibility of her coming across Declan. Kath though had taken the precaution of keeping him busy elsewhere in the city with a small 'difficulty' with one of his business concerns that she had thoughtfully engineered with one of the Flanagan brothers, but wanted to make this visit alone.

The day was one of flat light caused by a pervading gloom. The streets and pavements were still damp from earlier rain, grey lampposts acting as a conduit to bring down the grey sky to the gloomy voids between depressing urban decay and desolate weed strewn cracks in the pavements.

Cars of all shades joined with white vans in contrasting with the varying coloured hues of doors and window frames along the street.

In sunlight, the variety might add a level of warmth to the buildings but in this negative light, they added to the sense of jumble in the street, a pulled down metal shutter here, wire meshed windows there. Peeling paint on derelict front doors masking a sense of how the street once looked in its heyday when there were neat blinds and swagged curtains at the windows and polished boastful brassware on the doors.

One resident thought it pleasing in later years to paint the brickwork of the property adjoining Tommy's a shade of pink and this was now peeling away in patches, leaving exposed brick or substandard undercoat showing through underneath – an architectural vitiligo.

Kathleen dropped her 'phone into her handbag, checked her face in the visor mirror overhead and opened the car door. As she did so, she carefully checked the road, trying to check if anyone else was around to observe her furtive progress towards the flat.

She took a deep breath as she moved towards the steps leading up to the front door, mindful of how Maggie had described the last time she had seen Tommy with Declan.

Maggie had been very open with Kathleen, too numb to display her usual hutzpah, too weary now to worry about trying to keep her own hands on the codes and information that she had.

For the first time in Maggie's adult life, she had decided to let some of her inner self show through, to be vulnerable and she left the façade behind in her borrowed make up bag.

Kathleen pushed the buzzer for the flat and stepped back but at the same time, noticed that the door was slightly open.

She stood there for a moment, wondering whether to go back to the car, to 'phone Brendan perhaps, but instead decided to shout through the gap.

"Hello Tommy, are you there?" she enquired, waiting motionless to listen for a response.

"Hello," she said again, this time knocking on the door with her hand.

Hearing no noise from within, she cautiously pushed on the door which gave slightly to her touch, the hinges groaning slightly as years of city detritus was ground between the metal plates.

The small vestibule area was dank, the kind of gloom that only gave into light on the few truly bright summer days when the sun was at its highest point. Then, the light showed up every flaw in the paper covered walls, showing the cobwebs clinging voraciously to peeling corners, showing the ill fitting mat running up in a threadbare progress to the inner door.

Kathleen once again shouted out, "Hello," as she got accustomed to the gloom. Hearing no reply, she pushed at the next door and went in to the small flat.

Once inside, her nostrils recoiled at the smell of the un-emptied bin in the kitchen, forcing her to wretch for a moment.

In front of her, her view of the kitchen was obscured by the high back of the old fashioned sofa, its replacement loose covers in red elasticated velour gaping about seat pads whose battle to maintain a semblance of form and substance was long since over.

She paused for a moment, wanting to leave the flat and to return to the warm environs of her car outside with its heated seats and surround speakers, but she was too tempted by her desire to understand where Tommy had got up to in his quest to understand the numbers.

She spotted a door ajar leading from the kitchen area and into the bedroom and started to move towards it.

As she did so, the full area of the kitchen came into view and at first, out of the corner of her eye but then absorbing every part of her vision, she saw Tommy lying there at the base of the kitchen units.

His body was lying in an uncomfortable position, one arm trapped under his body, the other lying limp by his side although the fingers of his hand still seemed to be clenched together.

His face, waxy grey, his cheeks sunken and smeared with coagulated blood from the wound on his head which had left a pool of blood on the linoleum floor. His eyes were dead, lifeless in a lifeless cracked skull.

Four or five bluebottles lazily droned about the body and crawled amidst the cranial gash.

Kathleen took in the trail of blood smeared down the unit

doors and onto the floor and realised that she was stood amidst the drying pool that had seeped from Tommy's skull.

Her stomach turned over inside her and she gasped to take in air, to breathe again after being frozen there as she had taken in the scene.

The full strength of the smell in the room filled her throat and lungs as she recoiled in horror, her mouth wide open in shock and she felt the saliva in her mouth readying itself for vomit racing up her throat.

She forced a hand over her mouth, choking back the first of the rising acid and then managed to free herself from the spot as her flight mechanism kicked in and she raced to the nearest space away from the body.

She slammed into the bedroom door as her feet propelled her forward haphazardly. She was stopped by the bed as she entered the room and her vomit was thrown out of her mouth and onto the nylon cover of the old fashioned bedspread.

She stood there, gasping and propped up on her knees against the bed as the acidic cocktail poured onto the cover which in itself made her continually wretch until she tore herself away and slumped onto the floor near the head of the bed and the wardrobe.

Sitting there for a moment, she calmed down and reached into her bag for some tissues to wipe her face with.

Having done that, her mind began to race with the enormity of what she had just seen, of what Declan had done, of the danger she herself was now in.

There was no doubt in her mind as to the fate of Tommy in the next door room, no need to check for signs of life, but her mind did switch to what Declan had wanted from Tommy and why he'd been forced to use violence, leading to accidental death or otherwise.

Kathleen knocked the curtain as she got up and she noticed Tommy's red tin placed there between the wardrobe and the adjacent wall.

She paused for a moment and then listened intently for a short while to satisfy herself that no one else had been around to hear her dash away from the kitchen and into the bedroom. She then stared at the soiled bedspread and back to the tin and decided on a course of action.

She picked up the tin without pausing to try and open it and placed it with her handbag on the floor whilst she gathered up the vomit covered bedding into a heap. She paused again to steady herself, suddenly feeling nauseous and the memory of the scene awaiting her again in the kitchen caused her to shudder involuntarily.

She made her way quickly out of the room, unable to avoid taking in the body in the kitchen again, clutching on to the bedding and the tin before her, imagining it to be protective armour against the dead body.

Then she froze on the spot, panicked by the thought that she might have left traces of her presence, fingerprints etc. on the doors and surfaces and she put everything down again whilst she considered what to do, her back to the cadaver.

She then took the scarf from around her neck and made for the sink and gingerly turned the tap with the scarf, letting the slow trickle of water spill over the bottom of it.

Turning the tap off again in the same way, she hurried past the body and back to the bedroom door which she scrubbed at where she thought she might have touched it, conscious that she may just have smeared the traces of her presence rather than erase it, hopeful that she might have completely obscured it.

She picked up her bag, the tin and the bedding again and stopped at the front door to start scrubbing that, trying to remember where she might have touched it on entering.

The air outside the flat was exhilarating after the sickly sweet smell of death, decay and rotting rubbish inside and she hurriedly looked about the street again before satisfying herself that there were neither pedestrians nor any visible security cameras in the immediate vicinity.

She made her way back to the car slowly, having to force her legs to work as they had started to shake beneath her and when there, she opened the boot and placed the bedding and the red tin inside.

Later, Kathleen was at home with the tin and a melancholy that wouldn't leave her as she began to try and make conversation with a bath-robed Maggie who she came across making her way across the hall and into the sitting room.

"Hi Maggie, I've had a tiring day, I'll be back down later on," was all she said in the end before climbing the stairs to reach her room.

Maggie wondered what Kathleen was carrying in front of her as she spied the garish bedding and what looked like a box but decided not to ask her, happy to turn on the TV for company.

Once Kathleen reached her own room, she wished she had left the bedding downstairs, instead she placed it on the bathroom floor whilst she took a shower, its presence horrifying her every time she caught sight of it.

Once dressed again, she returned to the bathroom with a black bin liner and turned it inside out so she could grasp the stinking pile of bedding without touching it and sent it to the bottom of the re-inverted bag.

She wretched as she struggled to knot the loose plastic of the bag, to seal in the horror of the visit to Tommy's flat.

With the bag firmly closed up and held at arm's length, she went back downstairs and was about to place the bag in the wheelie bin but then she worried that someone might find it and possibly link her with the flat. Instead, she zapped the locks on her car and placed the bag into the boot, ready to hurl it out again in some quiet spot on her next journey out.

Maggie offered her a cup of coffee when she returned inside after having asked Kathleen, "Tell me about it over there Kath, what did you find?"

The other woman couldn't keep her emotions in check any longer and broke down for a few moments, choking back tears but eventually able to say, "Oh God Maggie, it was truly bad, it was all so bad. Declan left Tommy for dead in that disgusting flat."

"What . . . did you find him there still, was he . . . is he alright?" asked Maggie, confused by what Kath had actually seen.

"God no Maggie, no. He's lying there still on the kitchen floor . . . blood, blood all over the place. The flies . . . oh . . ." she breathed deeply and continued, "I can still smell that flat, I can't get rid of that smell. I threw up all over the bed back there in the flat. It was just like hell."

"Oh Christ Kath, shit, what if someone has seen you there?" asked Maggie before turning ashen and saying, "Oh God, Declan. He's really done it this time, I tell you it's going to be me lying there someday, the absolute bastard!"

Maggie shivered as she took in the news and Kathleen grasped hold of Maggie's hand, taking another deep breath before saying, "We're going to stick together you and I, we're going to be alright."

Maggie shook her head. "How can we be alright Kath. He's going to find out what he's done to Tommy, he's going to come after me. God, if he finds out you've been in there too . . ."

"Right, stop that now Maggie. We cannot let ourselves think like that. What we are going to do is to work out this mess once and for all and then we're going to leave here for a while whilst everything settles back down. With any luck Declan is going to get sent down for a long time for what he's done."

Maggie laughed a little. "So even if he does, how long does 'accidental death' or 'manslaughter' get these days, he'll be back out in no time Kathleen, back after me. He's not going to leave either of us alone until at least one of us is dead."

Kathleen let the moment of Maggie's angst pass a little before saying, "He'll go down, he'll go down. His DNA has got to be in that flat Maggie and I could just imagine an anonymous call to the Police suggesting that they might want to centre their enquiries in Declan's direction."

"But what about you, what about me? We've both been in that flat."

"Yes . . . we have, but we've got each other to cover each other's back. We can say that we were both there but left Tommy on his own with Declan in the flat."

Maggie cut across her, "But the taxi driver, he knew there was something wrong . . ."

"Even if they find him Maggie, you can say that you were frightened by Declan, that you knew he could be violent and I'll say the same, c'mon, we've got to stay focused, got to ensure that our stories match," Kathleen pointed out, trying to convince herself as much as Maggie.

"Oh and whilst I was there I found something that I think is going to be useful Maggie, but you've got to work with me, to tell me what you know."

Even a few days ago Maggie would not have trusted Kathleen, but now, after the scene at the docks, after the reality of the situation had been brought into sharp focus by the discovery of Tommy's body, she was willing to let her guard down. She could see that she had nothing to lose at this stage other than her own safety and possibly she might gain a measure of security from her collaboration with Kathleen, both physical and financial.

Over coffee, the pair of them pieced together the fragments that they both held, of the number sequences, the disappearance of the horse 'Who Dares Wins', the key from Mount Stewart obtained by Brendan and the numerous pass books and accounts in Kelly's name.

They then set about Tommy's red tin.

* * *

Tommy's red tin had been with him as long as he could remember. He'd lived with it in his mother's house for all the years he was there and took it with him when his mother died and the house was eventually vacated.

At the bottom, amidst the oldest memories, Tommy had kept a set of cigarette cards, their painted likenesses of the football heroes of another era fixing his childhood at a particular moment.

When his younger cousin had shown an interest in the cards in his younger years and seemed intent on their destruction, Tommy had locked them away from sight.

Tommy had hounded friends, relations, neighbours, just about anyone who would talk to him until he'd finally managed to complete the set, sometimes receiving one or two from odd jobs or errands. He'd hoped to be able to send away for the album that could safely contain his collection but there never seemed to be the time nor the stationery in the house to enable him to do so.

Instead, the cards were kept in a brown envelope inside the tin and maintained in strict numerical order with the spares sorted, again in order, at the back of the main pile.

In another used envelope he'd kept a few stamps from overseas that had been sent to people in the streets nearby from relatives who had fled to find a better life. Small coloured squares, evidence of colonial dominance and efforts to further self-government through Dominion. Paper pieces of overseas, gummed upon mother country bound familial correspondence.

His mother's small bible had joined the other treasures forming the base layer in the tin, its leather cover still smooth and neat and flexible, softened from many years of devotional duty.

Next to the bible, a small collection of early photographs, his mother pictured amidst a painted backdrop depicting a fanciful landscape. Colour had been added to her lips and cheeks post development to lift the solemnity of the sepia.

An uncle sat on a fringed leather banquette, his frame heavily clad in weighty fabrics and solid leather footwear to counter balance the lugubrious mutton chops crawling across and out of his proudly angled jaw.

Another relative, who'd been accidentally drowned in a wash-tub whilst his mother had hung out the washing, was pictured in happier times, wrapped up in blankets in the bottom drawer of a kitchen dresser.

Aunts, cotton dresses clothing tiny frames atop buttoned up brown boots, puppies at their feet and clustered in their outstretched arms.

Such articles comprised the total family history that Tommy had left, the rest lost in the hurried residential departures in wartime and later neglectful rot.

This layer, near worthless in monetary value but priceless in sentimental value for Tommy, formed the base of the tin above which sat assorted documents and papers of value to him that he chose to keep safe in this red tin, the same tin that was now occupying the attention of Maggie and Kathleen who were beginning to make connections and solving mysteries through their collective knowledge of recent events and past recollections.

Chapter Twenty Nine

Transport House came into view before Declan. One of Belfast's most recently listed buildings, it only thrust itself up into the city skyline in 1959, the work of JJ Brennan and echoing an earlier ground breaking style seen at the bus terminus in Dublin.

The trade union building is clad in sea green tiles and sports a tiled mural depicting industry – mainly soviet in tone with twelve workers marching out one behind the other away from the cube like factory and into the street.

A liner is berthed alongside and surrounded by heavy cranes in a prosperous dockyard. Overhead a futuristic delta winged jet glides overhead, its 'quiet spike' piercing the ceramic skies in which it flies, presiding over successful industry and collective harmony.

Declan stared up into the windows surrounded in black composite, his view mainly obscured by vertical blinds, some hanging in serried ranks, others drawn back in places, no longer echoing the rank of factory workers all alike, marching together across the exterior wall.

He was trying to find Janet Nicholson, trying to collect money that was owed to him that was now overdue.

Janet represented a family with links to Declan but one that invariably seemed destined to need the support of him in difficult times and needed to pay back with interest when they could usually least afford it. She had originally worked for one of the banks who had their headquarters in Belfast until redundancy was offered and at the time was welcome to enable debts to be settled and space to be gained between the parties.

However, Janet's husband's business had been going badly and they'd been forced to seek assistance again in order to maintain the family home.

Janet had worked at the union for the last five years and enjoyed the certainty of her position there even though she had taken a pay cut after leaving the bank.

She was sitting at her desk overlooking the Albert clock, waiting for the hand to show her that she could leave for lunch and for a meeting with Declan.

She took out a mirror from her handbag and checked her dark hair, making a small adjustment before reaching down into the deep bottom drawer of her desk to lift out a large brown envelope filled with cash from a job her husband Roy had completed on the side, very much out of hours and barely legal.

All day she had fretted about keeping the packet in her desk at work, knowing on one hand that no one would dream of rummaging through her desk for anything whilst she was sat there but she still had turned the lock to keep the drawers safely shut. A nagging doubt though kept worrying her, a sense of the unknown, of what 'could' happen to put them in an even worse position with Declan.

She pushed back her wheeled office chair and tried to sound as matter of fact as she could as she said to a colleague opposite to her, "Right, I'm off to lunch, see you later on."

Sandra Gibson had sat at the desk opposite to Janet's for the whole time that she had worked at the union, chatting continually to Janet about late night television, family holidays, stories in the gossip columns. "Oh wait Janet, I'll come out with you," said Sandra, beginning to log off from her computer terminal and roughly tidying her desk.

Janet paused for a moment, unsure how to stop her friend from coming with her saying awkwardly, "No, no, don't bother, I'm only going out to do some errands."

"Don't be silly honey, I'm keeping you company, you don't know who is lurking about out there on a Tuesday lunchtime," she laughed, "and anyway I'm bored sitting here so you can cheer me up on the way," Sandra stated, pushing back her own chair.

Janet was frozen for a moment, trying to think quickly of a way to be forceful without hurting her friend's feelings.

As she was thinking, Sandra provided an escape route as she said, "Just give me a couple of minutes, I need to go to the little girl's room, wait for me downstairs?"

Sandra moved off towards the loos on the stairwell and Janet loitered outside for a moment before she started to hurry down the stairs as the door of the loos closed behind her friend.

Janet reached the bottom of the stairwell and paused again to catch her breath, then took out her 'phone and made a brief call.

Opening the double doors of the building, she stepped out on to the pavement under the austere concrete portico. She allowed her eyes to peer across the High Street for a moment until she caught sight of Declan waiting patiently for her opposite the entrance in front of St George's church.

Janet's heart raced as she began to step out to meet Declan, ever mindful of his unpredictability. As she did so, she reached down into her shoulder bag and brought out the money filled envelope that was stored inside a supermarket carrier bag.

She moved closer to Declan, trying not to make her route too obvious and as she passed the bag over to him, he grasped her hand, making her cry out a little in surprise.

"All there is it darling?" Declan asked.

Janet felt sick with fear and hatred for the man holding her wrist but managed to say out loud, "Every bloody penny."

She trembled a little as he let go of her hand.

In the background, an idling motorcycle waited, its engine a steady throb.

Roy Nicholson had received a cue from Janet by 'phone a short time before and had found his most forgettable leathers to wear and had taped over the identifying branding on the bike.

Sandra came out of the double doors of the building and into the street just in time to see Declan let go of Janet's hand and take the carrier bag from her.

Panicked, Sandra let out a cry and hurtled into the road in the direction of her friend but her cry was drowned out by the roar of the accelerating engine of Roy's bike.

Roy approached Declan and Janet at high speed, the engine building higher and higher and as he neared the pair, he swerved towards Declan and grabbed at the carrier bag, tearing it out of Declan's grasp.

As he did so, he opened up the throttle again and tore off, the bike swerving side to side as he tried to control its forward volition, intending to head back towards Victoria Street.

Roy didn't see Sandra in the road until he had run into her, sending her backwards with huge force and at speed and spinning her around onto the ground, her broken limbs tangled underneath her soon to be lifeless body.

The carrier bag of money burst on impact, showering the scene of carnage with assorted bank notes and Roy joined them on the floor as he was thrown from the bike, which spun onto its side and came to rest at the kerbside leaving behind a trail where it had made contact with the road.

One wheel of the bike was still spinning as Declan recovered himself and quickly picked up the remnants of the carrier bag's contents before running off into the nearby streets leaving Janet screaming from the depths of her body for her husband and also her best friend lying broken in the road being gently showered by Ulster Bank confetti.

Maggie's talons tapped Michael's number into her mobile, maroon marvels stabbing the keys as she tried in vain again to reach Moira's boy.

She didn't want to speak to him, didn't want the inevitable awkwardness that follows a badly ended relationship. She did though want answers and to truly discover if his deception with the papers in her handbag was solely down to him or if it was instigated by another.

Both her heart and her head told her that Michael had not acted alone, but who was he working with? Brendan perhaps or Moira? Was it Declan again, or even Kathleen? Her recent generously provided sanctuary, gained from Kath over the last few days had blunted the usually sharp wits of Maggie Haugh. She had to resort instead to tortuous attempts to reach the man who she knew she could wield some influence over – Michael.

The line rang and once again, his voicemail clicked in. Maggie seethed inwardly but thought quickly. This time, rather than her usual abusive tirade, she changed tack and instead said, "Michael my darling, it's Maggie. Look, I've said a lot of things I probably shouldn't have, please, please will you call me back, I just want to talk. Bye my darling, bye."

The end of a talon ended the call. Maggie's eyes sparkled a little for the first time in many days. She liked the feeling; it was as if her old self was coming back, returning for the start of the next act in her life.

Michael's 'phone rang. He saw the name flashing up on the screen and he placed it down on the table next to him, as if by putting it there, he was transferring responsibility for it.

He watched the name flashing, wanting attention. He had no intention of answering it but felt a note of guilt when it stopped and the screen displayed 'one missed call'.

He picked up the 'phone again, re-claiming ownership and noted that there was a new voicemail waiting for him.

Dialing the access number quickly, he wanted to hear the message, wanted to hear Maggie's voice. He knew that he should listen to his own inner voice and to ignore it, to press the key to delete it, to keep the distance between them but he couldn't.

Lust lures the unwary just as a trap ensnares its prey, for temptation is a drug that torments its victims and toys with their emotions, sapping usual sensibilities.

Michael was motionless at the end of the line, listening to the message, appreciating the softer tones in her voice.

His heart beat faster and he pressed the key to end the call as his stomach quivered with excitement, followed by rapid reality and a sense of despair as he wrestled with the decision about what to do next, which card in the pack to play.

Kelly and Sophie were pulled up outside their guest house on Quay Road, Ballycastle, the neat terraces with small gardens in front looking welcoming, helped by the watery sunshine just struggling through the low clouds.

The pair were shown up to their respective rooms on the second floor by their hostess, Mrs. Donnelly who made a point of reminding them that no take away food was to be eaten in the rooms although they do have a welcome tray with tea, coffee and hot chocolate alongside a packet of shortbread that they were advised would be replenished on their third night, should they choose to eat it.

They met up again in the small lounge by the front door that was given over to residents. Sophie was already there when Kelly came down the last flight of stairs to the ground floor.

She was leafing through a selection of tourist leaflets and local interest books left out by Mrs. Donnelly to inspire her guests to spend as much time as possible out of her establishment. She wasn't wholly anti-social as a hostess but certainly saw the property as her own home and carefully vetted her intended guests as they booked and as they entered the premises, allocating rooms based on her own peculiar analysis of social status.

Cautious acceptance got the second floor, those with grander sounding names or addresses the rooms on the first floor. Those who did not meet with her visual inspection criteria were relegated to the third floor rooms in the eaves.

Mrs. Donnelly herself was quartered in the basement which was actually more appealing than it might first sound as the property being Victorian, the basement storey was actually only half below ground level and her kitchen window at the bottom of the front bay afforded a good vantage point to clock in and out her guests.

So as Kelly and Sophie set off down the stairs at the front of the property, Mrs. Donnelly twitched into life as a spider does when sensing movement on its web and dashed to the window in time to watch the leaving pair make their way along the front path and out onto the street between the small gate piers.

Mrs. Donnelly delighted in telling fellow 'hospitality' colleagues that the constant footfall of guests coming and going over her front steps and effectively over her own subterranean abode made her feel as if she was a modern day Julia McQuillan, a nun in the 17th century of Bonamargy Friary near Ballycastle who was buried at the entrance to the chapel so that she might be trodden over by all and sundry on their way in and out.

Mrs. Donnelly's husband had arrived on the scene like a modern day Sorley Boy MacDonnell and whisked her off her feet, depositing her at his mother's house on Quay St in Ballycastle after marriage as he went off for weeks at a time on business trips in the south.

Unlike Sorley Boy though, Mr. Donnelly did not achieve much in his working lifetime but the couple did stand to inherit his mother's house and eventually the couple could call it their own.

Years of poor business deals and little income resulted in no pension provision so on his death, Mrs. Donnelly swallowed her pride and opened the doors of her home as a business. Kinbane and Dunluce might be in ruins, but Mrs. Donnelly's castle was still extant.

Kelly and Sophie had decided to go for a walk on their first afternoon, deciding that answers to all their questions could begin to be sought the next day.

They'd taken the car out along the coast and were walking along the Gray Man's path at Fairhead, the path sometimes being known by its name of Fhir Leith.

The entrance at the top was very narrow and the path wound its way around the rugged coastline. The pair looked close as they helped each other along the way and over obstacles as the path grew more difficult.

The dolerite cliffs towered above the sea, up to 643 feet in height and the continual pounding by time and tide had scattered assorted slabs of rock down at their base.

The day was beautifully clear and the pair paused to take in the views to Rathlin Island and on to Scotland and the empty headlands to the west of Feorlan across the narrows at this point.

Kelly had been here before and loved the view and the feeling of connectivity to the isles and to the headland across the channel. The nearness and also the 'can't quite touch' distance all added to the mystique.

Kelly's father brought him out one summer to walk up Knocklayde, to take in the mountain air and extensive vistas from Carn na Truagh.

Kelly was fascinated at the time by the possibility of having a Neolithic passage tomb beneath his feet and had asked his father to take him back again. Like many promises made by his father, this one too would go unfulfilled as the man let his lustful urges rule his actions and he instead left Kelly to remain with his mother and their shared memories of family life.

They met a couple of climbers as they walked along the path, jangling carabiners and dusty with chalk, their fingers wrapped with metolius tape to avoid 'Fairhead rash'.

Salt water fizzed on the shore in-between the rocks and pebbles, the warm sun sending up clouds of invisible ozone for the walkers to breath in.

"Ah ozone, take in that sea air Sophie!" said Kelly as he filled his lungs.

Sophie smirked and replied, "It's not actually ozone, the smell's a sulphide – we did it in school."

Kelly laughed, "Ha, whatever, whether it's a sulphide or ozone, it's good to get a lungful of it."

"Ah, well there's another thing, how can breathing in a sulphide actually be good for you, sort of a contradiction don't you think?"

"I hadn't realised that we had a scientist in out midst Sophie, I'll think twice before I open my mouth next time!" said Kelly with mock indignation.

"Oh sorry, science was the one thing at school that actually interested me, I'm sounding boring now though aren't I," relied Sophie, pulling her face into a wince.

"Not at all, it's good to hear about your interests, didn't you want to do something with that?" he asked, looking into her eyes for an answer.

Sophie let her eyes drop involuntarily and added, "Didn't really get the chance I suppose, too many other things going on."

Kelly nearly replied, nearly made a comment about going for what is important to you and having goals, but something told him to leave it there.

"Time to go back?" Kelly asked instead and started to head back along the path to the car park.

Sophie smiled a tired smile and confirmed, "Yes, time to go back."

When they reached the car, Kelly paused for a moment, inspecting a thorn that was sticking prominently out of his offside rear tyre.

"Where's that come from?" he asked rhetorically before bending down to remove the offending detritus.

Sophie had wandered nearer to the main road, dawdling along and appreciating the warming sun on her face.

Several cars passed by along the road unnoticed by Sophie until a silver Audi came along at some speed. The occupant was listening to the radio, but his eyes were drawn to the figure staring out absent-mindedly from the kerbside whilst she waited for Kelly to finish dabbling with the car.

The Audi suddenly stopped in the road with a screech of brakes and a slight skid of tyres on the carriageway.

A car that was travelling behind it had to swerve violently to avoid it and moments later blasted the Audi with its horn in shock and anger.

The sound of the emergency stop and the car horn woke up Sophie and both she and Kelly turned their attention to the road.

The Audi's passenger window opened and the occupant in the driver's seat was stretching across to get a good view before he called out, "Sophie!"

She turned pale and immediately started to move back towards Kelly's car. Kelly was startled by the noise and the voice shouting out Sophie's name and stared towards the road.

Sophie started to run towards Kelly, blurting out, "We've got to go now!" grabbing at the passenger door handle when she reached it.

"Do you know that man?" asked Kelly, fumbling to get the car key in to the ignition.

"Brendan – he's bad news Kelly, please can we just go." Sophie implored, hurriedly looking back to see if she had been followed.

"I swear that's the silver Audi that's been following me Sophie, who the hell is this Brendan?" he demanded, reversing into the middle of the car park.

"Just drive Kelly, please, I'll explain later," stated Sophie, her left hand raised up to cover her face from view from across the road.

Kelly moved the car forward and out towards the road.

The silver Audi had meanwhile pulled in to the side of the road. The driver allowed Kelly & Sophie to drive out onto the main road whilst Sophie sunk as low as possible into the foot well of the passenger seat, hoping that she had not been seen.

Brendan was on the 'phone by now and connected through to the person on speed dial.

"Kath," Brendan said, "it's me, I've just found them."

Chapter Thirty

Eamon Gibson sat at his desk in police headquarters listening to the desk 'phone ring beside him.

His colleague and fellow DI Garth Spencer looked across to Eamon, about to ask if he was going to answer the call but was beaten to it by Eamon breaking out of his trance and lifting up the receiver.

"Eamon Gibson," he said quietly, his eyes still staring into empty space.

"Okay, yes. No, I appreciate that, thank you."

These minimal words left his mouth before he replaced the handset and looked down at his desk.

Garth paused, unsure whether to talk to his friend, searching for an opportunity to connect across the desk.

Eamon let out a deep sigh, prompting Garth to say, "Hey, are you alright?"

Eamon paused for a while before taking a deep breath, saying, "That was the funeral directors – just finalising things for tomorrow."

Garth's stomach turned in knots as he felt his friend's grief.

Only a short number of days ago, Eamon's wife had been killed in an accident outside Transport House. He'd heard something going on in the office, presuming that it was just one of many events that could take place in an average week in the Police force. He'd also noticed the eyes of his colleagues though, looking over at him and then quickly looking away when he tried to make eye contact.

His DCI had broken the news to him that his wife Sandra had been scooped up from the road where she had been mown down by the motorbike.

They'd tried to stop him from coming in to the office, to ensure that he grieved properly, but steely resolve and self control drove Eamon back into the office the next day to enable him to observe the attempts to piece together what had happened to Sandra as she'd just popped out on her lunch break.

He'd been asked respectfully to stay away, to come back after the funeral but he just kept coming in to the station at the crack of dawn and going home when the lights went out.

He was instructed though to keep away from the investigation itself and the team looking into it were situated on another floor but Eamon's DCI had not counted on an old school friend keeping him informed of every aspect of the case as it was being worked on, fuelling his anger and burying his sorrow.

"C'mon now," Garth said quietly, "time for you to go home, time for you to get ready for tomorrow."

Eamon's eyes flashed up angrily at his colleague, about to remonstrate, to bite back just as he'd verbally attacking anyone who had come near to him in the last few days. As he met his eyes though, he could not mistake the compassion within.

Eamon's eyes welled up and he choked back his emotion, taking a deep breath to try and steady his outward persona.

"Shall I drive you home?" Garth asked.

"No, no, I'll be fine, I . . . I'll see you, see you tomorrow, right?" replied Eamon, reaching into his top desk drawer for his car keys.

"Aye," Garth affirmed, "I'll see you tomorrow."

Dawn. Bright skies and chattering birdsong sat awkwardly with Eamon as he turned over in his empty bed to reach for his wristwatch.

The light streamed in through the gaps in the curtains partially lighting the room, showing Sandra's bedspread, her bedside lamps, her choice of furniture, her taste.

It was still too soon for him to get up, to face the day. Instead, he turned over again, shutting his eyes, but he was too awake to allow sleep to return and he let out a sigh before throwing back the duvet and swinging his feet to the floor.

He stayed in the shower longer than was usual for him, letting the water run steadily over him and on down the plughole, the noise of the torrent of water helping him to blot out what was to come.

Later, he sat on the sofa in the seat he always favoured, trying not to notice the pictures of Sandra on the mantelpiece, her magazines on the coffee table, her box of chocolates by the armchair.

After what seemed like an eternity of silence he was startled by the ringing of the doorbell.

He looked up at the clock above the fireplace and his stomach churned again as he realised the time had come to travel to Sandra's funeral, to say a final goodbye.

Garth had arranged to come to the house to meet the funeral car and travel with Eamon to the church, he shook his friend's hand and took a seat in the back of the car with him.

The car pulled slowly away from the kerb and Eamon watched everyday life continue out of the car window.

Children walking as normal to school, guys in lurid Lycra cycling to work, pensioners waiting at bus stops for discounted travel.

Nonchalant normality abutted abject grief and Eamon vowed violent vengeance.

Black tarmac freshly laid pervaded the air as it steamed into submission, letting go of its acrid vapours as it shone and glistened into dull solidity.

Kelly choked on the fumes as he exited his car, looking nervously at Sophie and her sudden introspection.

The council lorry shed more tacky stone onto the coned off highway along the road, making good the subsided repair work of an 'out for a quick buck' utility company.

Mrs. Donnelly was ready for them as they made their way along the front path to her front door, waving up from the basement window and receiving a brief acknowledgment from Kelly.

As soon as the pair had shut the front door, Mrs. Donnelly moved over to her telephone and dialled a number.

"Hello, it's me," she whispered into the handset, "they're back in."

The voice on the other end said, "You think they'll be there for a while?"

"Oh, I think so, given the time, but I'd come over before the end of the day in case they decide to move on," she added, keeping her voice unnecessarily low given the number of floors between her and the guests in question.

"You'll be sure to let me know if they do make a move, in fact try and keep them there Auntie won't you?" asked Brendan, before ending the call.

Kathleen stood next to Brendan and smiled confidently, before saying, "All coming together nicely Brendan, all coming together nicely."

Upstairs in the guesthouse, Kelly and Sophie were talking about the day and about the man that she had seen on the roadside at the top of the cliff i.e. Brendan.

"He was always with her, always around at the house, as if he owned the place, I couldn't stand him but my Mother wouldn't hear anything said against him from me, she just used to say, "He's good to your Aunt and he's good to us Sophie."

I don't know how and don't know why we had to put up with it."

Kelly had been listening to Sophie for a few minutes now, politely nodding and adding encouraging noises where he thought that he should.

He was though, bewildered how Brendan was linked to Sophie. After listening for another couple of minutes he simply asked, "So how do you know him, know Brendan I mean?"

Sophie stopped mid sentence and looked at Kelly as if he hadn't been listening at all, her eyes wide with incredulity. "Well, he was with my aunt, I've said that already."

Kelly clearly looked blank again so Sophie added, "With my Aunt Kathleen – your father's Kathleen, who else Kelly! It has always been about her, you know that by now."

Kelly's jaw dropped as his mind raced to piece together the links, mental images flashed through his mind and in every one, she was there. Central to every scene, the flame about which many a hapless moth burnt its papery wings.

The image of dust like scales erupting from a light bulb filled Kelly's head as he sat there open mouthed, his eyes glazed over with introspection.

Sophie shook her head in disbelief at Kelly's naivety, part pitying, part wanting to nurture someone who has clearly been affected by Kathleen and her entourage in a way that she could relate to herself.

Kelly's mind meanwhile snapped back to the present and he blurted out an additional question, "So Brendan was seeing your Aunt Kathleen then?"

"God knows what their relationship was or is Kelly, all I know is that he was always around like a dog obsessed with its mistress, following her everywhere, doing exactly what she asked without ever questioning why, or who would be hurt by any of his actions."

"And your mother, did she ever see a problem with this relationship like you did? Good God, I'm still getting over the fact that you are her niece. All the years that I've known her and I never knew she even had a sister," stated Kelly, "where was your mother when Kathleen lived next door to me with her parents then?"

"Oh, my mother was a good twelve years older than Kathleen," explained Sophie, "and Mam left home early herself, fell in love with a waster who she met on a ferry to Dun Laoghaire and I'm the result!"

Kelly's mind was filled with images of the past, all mixing together one on top of another, a combination of the sea air from the walk along the cliffs and the mental exertion of it all leaving him feel quite drained.

Sophie observed the tiredness in his eyes and was about to suggest that they have some time back in their rooms before dinner but Kelly's mind was still fizzing with attempted tries to form meaningful connections out of it all.

"So why didn't you acknowledge this Brendan earlier on, I mean I get that he wasn't your favourite, but had things got so bad?" he asked, mindful of how Sophie had seem full of panic earlier on.

"Oh right," smiled Sophie, "I suppose it was the shock of seeing him like that, out of the blue. I mean I didn't imagine I'd fade into the background around here but after that night at Whitepark I've sort of cut myself off from all that."

"Not that night I nearly ran you over?" probed Kelly, "at Kathleen's place?"

"Ha ha," laughed Sophie, "to think I'd gone there to try and reach out to Kathleen," she paused in thought before continuing, "you see, I'd lost Mam and gone away to London, I wanted to get as far away from here as possible, but something drew me back. Maybe I wanted to talk about her to Kathleen. I don't know – anyway, we were there in the house a few doors away from Kathleen's that my Mam and I had rented. Kath had kept it on and I'd stupidly imagined it was because of nostalgia, but by the look of it she'd installed Brendan there, ready for her to take him out for a walk whenever she fancied. Giving him a bone every now and again for being a good dog."

Sophie's face betrayed signs of disgust at the recollections she was sharing with Kelly. He waited for her to carry on, but after a pause that seemed liked minutes, she took in an audible gulp of air and continued.

"I'd let myself in at the back door, the key was always under a flower pot at the back. I thought I'd surprise Kathleen by making her a cup of tea ready for when she told me she'd get back. I put my bag upstairs in the bedroom I'd always used but I couldn't help looking in at Mam's room on the way.

Her things were still there – well, her furniture, you know, all the same really except that Brendan's clothes were strewn on the carpet and the bed was unmade. He'd been smoking in there too, an over flowing ashtray was spilling across the bed side table." Sophie looked down, letting the image subside a little before continuing, "So it all sort of washed over me, the grief I mean. Anyway, I felt like I was going to throw up or something so I went into the bathroom, sat on the loo for a while just listening to the silence.

After maybe ten minutes though, I heard the front door open. Kathleen had come back in with him, talking in raised voices, you know, when someone clearly doesn't know that you are there. If you don't say, 'Hello' right away, you leave it for a minute or two and then you think, 'I can't say I'm here now, they'll think I've been listening.' So I just sat there a bit longer and thought I'd make some obvious noises like flushing the loo, using the sink and so on but Kathleen was getting more and more agitated and Brendan was starting to slam things down in the kitchen, so I listened and waited for my moment to make my presence known.

Anyway, one thing I did hear very clearly was that they were talking about Brendan's brother Michael and discussing whether he should get his share of 'the money'. Kathleen clearly didn't think he should as she was saying that she could just leave with Brendan, go abroad for a while and leave Michael behind.

Brendan initially thought that all this was a bad idea, it was his baby brother after all that they were discussing but Kathleen just kept saying, 'You know it makes sense, you know it does'.

He then said what if Michael found out what they had done and she just replied, 'I'd need you to do what you've done to the others who have got in our way.' Anyway, with this Brendan really got angry and started shouting at her and objects starting flying around the kitchen from the sound of it.

When this happened I thought I'd had enough and made my move, creeping out of the bathroom and I started to slowly creep back downstairs a step at a time, trying to stay as silent as I could.

As I reached the bottom step, Kathleen was screaming back at Brendan, most of it too jumbled for me to make out properly above the sounds of smashing crockery but I did hear her say, 'You good as killed my sister with all of your taunts and your innuendo and your lies'.

Well, at that I just made my way along the hall in the dark, not bothering so much if I made a sound but I went and tripped up over a bag that had been left by the front door and the contents scattered here and there and amongst the stuff was a handgun, just lying there on the hard flooring.

Well the two of them in the kitchen now heard me alright, me picking myself back up and trying to gather the contents back together. Anyway, Brendan swore and started to come into the hall. I just panicked, I grabbed the gun – for protection I suppose – and flung open the front door, thank God it wasn't locked.

You know the rest, I just sprinted down the drive and along the road and that's when you nearly knocked me over. I left you that gun when I left the next day, thought you looked like you'd benefit from it I suppose."

Kelly waited patiently for Sophie to finish her account of the night in question, cursing inwardly again about how deceitful his one time friend Kathleen actually was.

"She's got a lot to answer for," he stated with conviction, "and she can't keep on hurting people."

Kelly though didn't have a clue how to stop her and Sophie hadn't got the confidence or the support she felt she needed. As she read the expression on Kelly's face though she began to have a little hope, a chink of positivity pervading her inward gloom, a glimmer of expectation stirred her determination and buoyed her spirit.

Elsewhere, Kathleen and Brendan were talking intently, racing over the facts and actions and finalising plans to finally access the money they've been following for years. They moved on to talking about Kelly and Sophie but the discussion was a short one.

"You need to ensure that they don't get in the way Brendan, you need to ensure that they keep quiet," she said, placing particular emphasis on the last word.

"How quiet?" he queried in return, looking into Kathleen's eyes.

Kathleen sat there motionless, her mouth fixed in a hard smile before replying, "Quiet as in silent Brendan, certainly John Kelly, he needs to be quiet for good."

Chapter Thirty One

Michael had finally 'phoned Maggie back, intrigued by her change of tone, excited by the chance of speaking to her, to feel a quiver of excitement inside himself again.

Maggie's soothing tones caught him off guard and he found himself arranging to meet her, the other trigger being Brendan's recent absence to trail after Kathleen again.

Michael was feeling resentment towards his older brother, tired of being treated as nothing more than a workhorse, being sent on errands and collection jobs that Brendan felt beneath himself to do.

Family ties were one thing but Michael struggled with his part in deceiving Maggie, his usual disinterest in relationships being turned upside down by the thrill of illicit encounters and the teenage like chemistry that seemed to exist between them.

Michael was standing on the East Strand in Portrush, next to Holger Lonze's 'To the People of the Sea' sculpture, its gold sail tops shining brightly in the afternoon sun, a visual echo of the days when the Drontheim fished along this coast.

Michael reached out to touch the bronze sails and was surprised at how much heat they had stored from the day, a reminder of the way that heat forged their forms in the workshop, latent energy. His hands copied the movements of the sculptor smoothing his line.

Michael had been walking next to the White Rocks, stretching from Curran Strand to Dunluce Castle, a myriad of caves and arches harbour sea life and they have weathered to form Elephant Rock amongst others, a limestone leviathan holding back the cliffs whilst drinking up the azure sea.

He was enjoying the late afternoon warmth and the sound of the waves as they lapped limpidly at the shore. The onshore breeze had died down now, soon to be replaced by a seaward flow as the land cooled at a faster rate than the surface sea temperature.

He checked his watch, something he'd been trying to avoid since the last time that he'd looked, nervously excited about the meeting ahead, nervously worried that Maggie might not show up.

Just as these thoughts swirled around his head he saw the unmistakable form of Maggie walking down the Strand, weighed down by bags bearing the name of Henry Hamilton's White House department store on the main street.

Michael laughed a little, the delay was so typically Maggie as was the delay caused by shopping, probably buying bags and shoes she didn't need and beauty products that were seemingly priced to reflect the thickness of the cardboard of their cellophaned presentation boxes, the heavier the card, the more expensive the contents.

"Hello," said Michael, grinning to show his well formed, just white enough teeth.

Maggie always thought how like a schoolboy Michael looked. Sure, one with all the required adult attributes, but a youthful grin and a slight ruddiness to his cheeks along with his simply cut shiny black hair lent him the look of one younger than his years.

This amused her, not in a mocking sense, more in a way that was endearing and talked to feelings that she hadn't experienced much in her life to date.

"Hi," replied Maggie, letting her bags rest on the dry turf whilst she reached out to touch his hand, staring intently into his eyes.

He let her grasp his hand and instantly felt excited to be back in her presence. They looked at each other for a few moments before they leant in and kissed passionately, delighting in the sensations coursing through them.

They peered into one another's eyes for a moment before they both let out a laugh, "Missed me?" Maggie asked, tightening her grasp around Michael's waist.

"You bet," he replied, rubbing his hands along her back.

"So why here, do you have a holiday hide-away you haven't told me about before," she asked, staring out along the coastline.

He laughed again, his cheeks dimpling, "Ha ha, no, just doing some work nearby."

"Ah," she said in a lower tone, "you mean that you're here with Brendan then?"

"Let's not talk about all of that now," he stated, making her look into his eyes, "I just want to be with you, not anyone else."

Maggie was about to remonstrate with him for being so evasive, for virtually admitting to herself that she was there in Portrush to suit Brendan and Michael's latest work location but she managed to stop herself, not wanting to break the moment as she ached for his touch.

They linked hands and Michael led her away from the East Strand and into the town where he had booked a restaurant with a view and a hotel room to stagger back to after a bottle of bubbly. They would indulge themselves in reliving their past lust for one another until the early hours.

Maggie was lying in the bed that she had shared with Michael, her head propped up on her elbow, staring at his face as he breathed in and out softly beside her.

She giggled and laughed as quietly as she could but her shaking frame and barely contained joy woke her partner up.

"What's the joke?" he asked sleepily.

"Nothing, nothing, I'm just, well, I'm happy," she explained, a wide grin spreading across her face.

Michael just looked at Maggie's face, taking in the spirit she had regained but also noticing the distinct naturalness she now had. Gone the hard exterior, gone the defences, this was Maggie as she started out, trusting, passionate, genuinely human.

"Are you serious about being happy . . . with me I mean?" he asked, mirroring her pose by propping himself up onto his own elbow.

Maggie didn't reply for a while, staring into his eyes before answering, "I really am. I love being with you and I don't want this feeling that I've got to end Michael, just promise me we won't distrust each other again?"

Michael smiled readily and replied, "I was so, so worried that I'd lost you after – well, you know, after that night at my Mam's."

Maggie broke eye contact and turned away before saying, "I know what you did Michael and I know why you did what you did but I can never accept you putting your brother before me like that again. Is that clear?"

Michael reached out and rubbed his hand along her arm, "The clouds are parting in front of me I can tell you that Maggie, I can see now that I've just been another pawn in Brendan's game but he is my brother and I won't forget that."

"I don't want you to forget it Michael, I want you to remember it, to remember every time that he got you to do things you didn't want to do, things you know now were the wrong things."

"If we're together, I can be strong Maggie, we can be strong together and face whatever it is that Brendan's wrapped up in with Kathleen. It's not going to be easy – far from it."

Maggie lifted herself up to sit on the edge of the bed, "Oh I don't doubt for a minute that Kath's got a lot to answer for but hasn't Brendan got a pair of eyes in his head? Can't he see what she's like?"

"I thought you and her got on, especially after Declan? Why the change of heart?"

Maggie explained, "That night, when you took the papers, copied the papers – whatever, I knew in my heart that wasn't you behind it. I knew it was something Brendan will have tasked you to do but I didn't realise until very recently just how much your brother was involved with her. Now I do know and I also know that she'll stop at nothing to get the money she think is hers to take."

Michael shuffled along the bed to sit beside her. "I know all this revolves around some hidden away money but I don't get why you are so involved in it too Maggie? Is it just through Declan?"

Maggie snorted, "Ha ha, I've got to pay my own way in life someday Michael. This isn't about sponging off Declan."

She looked away into the distance for a while and turned back to him saying, "That money is my money, Michael. Not Kathleen's, not Declan's, certainly not your brother's, just mine."

Michael looked at Maggie quizzically, wondering how to frame his next question. The sounds of a hotel trolley being wheeled down the corridor seeped into the room and were followed by a sharp rap at the door and a cry of, "Good Morning, room service."

Maggie quickly got up from the bed and padded across into the bathroom saying, "You answer it, I'm not dressed."

Michael stood up and looked around to find something to put on.

"Oh Christ," he said as he rummaged around in the trail of last night's clothes that the pair had torn off each other in their haste on their way to bed.

"Won't be a minute," he shouted towards the door whilst he continued his hunt.

Lifting up Maggie's dress from the carpet he found his boxer shorts and hurriedly pulled them on before dashing to the door and opening it to the youth waiting outside. The kid was dressed in an over large waistcoat sporting a name badge that let everyone know his name was 'Keith'.

Keith lifted up the a large tray from the trolley whilst the door was being fully opened and moved into the room with it asking, "Where would you like me to put this Sir?"

Michael looked around for a clear surface and had to move several of Maggie's possessions on to the floor to make space for the tray on a desk next to the TV.

"Can you sign this for me please?" asked Keith, handing Michael a pen and the bill for room service in a small leatherette wallet.

Michael was wholly unused to the concept of room service and suddenly felt very exposed in both his state of undress and in his uncertainty as to how much he should tip at the bottom of the bill.

"Do I pay you now?" he asked, his already ruddy cheeks colouring strongly whilst he looked around for his wallet.

Keith couldn't stop himself from visibly starting a little, raising his eyebrows at a question that he'd never been asked before.

"Err, no Sir, you'll pay at reception when you check out."

Michael was embarrassed but relieved and simply handed back the bill unsigned to Keith who took it momentarily before explaining, "You do just need to sign the bill please Sir, it's then added to your bill at reception."

Michael felt yet more self aware and his cheeks burned brightly as he scribbled his name on the bill and added a £5 tip, thinking that £1 was too little and any more than £5 certainly too much.

Keith tried to sound genuinely pleased, which he was, but said, "Ooh, thank you Sir," but this came out with more than a little tone of sarcasm and his own cheeks coloured too and the two men headed back to the door, one desperate to leave, the other desperate to close the door, flop back on to the bed and to let his florid complexion return to a calmer shade.

Maggie came back out of the bathroom and smiled, "Coast clear?" she asked, walking to where the breakfast tray was positioned.

She was wrapped in one of those over thick hotel robes emblazoned with the name of the establishment on the lapel.

Michael sank back on to the bed, sighing, "Aye, coast clear!"

From this position he heard Maggie crunching on a piece of toast she had unearthed from a crisp white napkin.

"You know you said just now that the money was yours Maggie, well how exactly do you mean?" queried Michael, sitting up again, his cheeks now recovered.

Maggie stopped consuming the toast and turned to look at him, stating once again, "Because it is mine."

Michael frowned and felt awkward, unsure whether to leave the conversation there for now or to press on. He decided on the later.

"Well, I mean Brendan seemed to think that Kathleen has at least a share of the money, I mean I don't know all of the details but he says she has been trying to get her hands on it for years."

Maggie laughed wistfully and replied, "Oh, I'm quite sure she has Michael, I'm sure she has."

She walked over and sat down on the bed beside him.

"If I tell you something now, I have to know that you're on my side, that you're not going to go running to Brendan or Kathleen," she said, spitting out the last name with some vengeance.

"If you can't promise me that, there can be no us Michael."

He looked at her with intense eyes and responded quickly, "You can trust me Maggie, I swear you can. I know that I can't make Brendan see what Kathleen is like any more – it's gone too far for that."

Maggie butted in quickly, "So you're telling me that if Brendan came to you today after our conversation, swearing that he'd finished with Kathleen, that you wouldn't trust him, wouldn't believe him? That you could turn your back on him, is that what you are saying?"

Michael's eyebrows lifted up in surprise at the vehemence of her question but he also understood that her intensity denoted the need for reciprocal trust from him and his unswerving loyalty to her cause. He dropped his eyes towards the floor before stating, "I love my brother Maggie, he's the only one I've got, but I'm absolutely swearing to you now that your secret, whatever it is, is safe with me. Brendan doesn't trust me any more it seems with the simplest of tasks and information so I'll not feel guilty about putting my own happiness before his this time."

With this statement, Michael turned to face Maggie and said, "I want to be with you, I want to look after you, maybe even grow old with you and if Brendan doesn't like that he can go to hell."

Maggie returned his gaze and her outlook softened.

"Okay, I can hear that you mean it and I want that too," she confirmed, taking a deep breath and shifting on the bed to give herself more space.

"That money is truly mine Michael because it was, well, it should have been my father's."

Michael looked confused but sensed that she would go on to explain more. He simply said, "Go on."

"My father was a good man Michael, a hard working man. He did his best to look after his family with not a great deal of money to work with. We lived in a staff flat when I was growing up, just the three of us, Mam, Daddy, me. I know it's a cliché, but we were happy although we were comparatively poor.

Daddy worked for this old Colonel in a big house on the Stormont Road and we lived above the stables there because my father had a gift – he could train racehorses and train them well.

The Colonel was just about keeping everything together, financially I mean – the house, the grounds, the horses. My Daddy knew that things were tight so he worked extra hours when he shouldn't have for no pay and he had to beg and borrow tack and feed so many times.

I loved it there though. Imagine, every little girl's dream, a cosy flat above a stables always busy with activity and the chance to be around horses every morning and when I got home from school."

Michael looked intently at Maggie, struggling to take in the fact that the tough woman before him was once a gentle little girl, spending her time with horses. He loved her more for it though as he visualised the stable yard and the blonde girl playing amongst the stalls and tack.

"So that was our set up. My mother just about making ends meet, my father doing a job he loved and me amongst the horses, happy as can be and never wanting to be anywhere else.

There was a particular horse, 'Who Dares Wins', that my Daddy had been training and he did a fantastic job. The old fella in the big house was ecstatic, he had a horse that was being placed and then began to win races. It was all like a dream until one day it all went wrong.

Someone broke in to the stables one night after a big race and took the horse away in a horsebox. Not only that though, they took my Daddy away in that lorry too that night when he tried to stop them taking the horse. He'd been there with 'Who Dares Wins' again out of hours, doing more than he needed to with the tack and the feed and these thieves in masks had come face to face with him. He tried to beat them off himself but that just made them more violent and they tied him up, taped up his mouth and threw him in the front.

My Mam heard the noise having been woken up and she ran down to the yard in time to see the horsebox being loaded. The guys taking the horse tied her up too but just left her in the yard.

The Police found him by the roadside a few miles away. They said he'd probably been pushed out of the cab when it was travelling at speed. He'd hit the road and that was it, he was gone."

Maggie paused for breath, her eyes fixed and unblinking.

"I'd been hiding under the bed when I'd heard all the noise and Mam screaming after the lorry as it left the yard. It took my Mam to crawl back upstairs still half tied up before I came out to help her."

Michael started to say something but Maggie cut him short, "Things weren't the same after that, never could be the same. No money, no job, no home. The Colonel died soon after – he lost all interest in life and died alone in that big house surrounded by newspapers stacked up to keep out the draughts racing in to the one room he ended up living in.

My Mam took to drink, then she took to taking out her frustrations with life on me when she was drunk. I was that kid in school with the smelly clothes, the one with no friends, the one hiding the bruises I'd got just for being there."

Maggie looked down now with tears dripping from her eyelashes which worked their way down her face. Michael held her but she didn't return his embrace, numb to the consoling affection in her state of recollection.

Her voice broke up a little when she continued, "So you wanted to know why that money is mine didn't you. Well it's mine because those thieving bastards got rich selling that horse on to an illegal stud somewhere. It's mine because they also killed, no, they murdered my Daddy, they caused my Mam to become an alcoholic and they caused me to become what I am today – a mixed up joke of a woman living to wreak revenge on the ones who destroyed our lives."

Just for a moment Michael saw through the anger, the bitterness, the anguished despair and saw the vulnerability underneath her hard exoskeleton. It was but there only fleetingly, a casual visitor, an infrequent outward migrant soon driven away by life's harsh and turbulent tribulations.

Chapter Thirty Two

Declan had been following Maggie for the past two weeks, trailing her from a distance but close enough to fix onto her scent – hunter and the hunted.

For years he'd bankrolled Maggie's existence, for years he had lied and robbed and cheated to keep them both in alcohol and designer clothes, in cigarettes and ambitious automobiles. For years he had loved her.

Sure, he'd beaten her but he assumed that Maggie accepted that he had a weakness, after all, she always forgave him, she knew that it was 'her fault' when he lost his temper – at least that was how he comforted himself when he saw the result of his dreadful actions.

Maggie was his possession, a trophy to parade in front of his dubious associates, an accessory to furnish his world with a touch of underworld glamour.

Like many possessions though, this one had lost its appeal for Declan but his over developed ego would not let him allow her to be with anyone else.

He couldn't donate this one or sell it on, but he could destroy it and he intended to do so.

He was back on home turf as he'd grown up in Port Stewart, not far from Portrush. His life today bore no resemblance at all to the careful upbringing that he'd had. In his early years he'd been schooled at Dominican College in the building that used to be the Montagu family's O'Hara's Castle, built on the cliff top overlooking the town and the Atlantic Ocean. On a site a hundred feet above the sea, Declan had been educated in Christian ideals, a spirit of trust and of independence, but this had all come to nothing, the result of involvement in the drugs scene of the 80's and a subsequent dependence on illicit activity to fund an ever more addictive habit.

Maggie had helped him to reduce this dependence, to move to a more recreational rather than a habitual intake but this had recently changed. The loss of Maggie's need for him weighed heavily and his weaknesses for the drug, for the desired abstraction from a solitary existence focusing on past recollections of their partnership, ate away at him and forced him to seek more regular solace.

A new day had dawned in Port Stewart and Declan had been awake for some time, allowing his building frustration, anger and jealousy creep into all the remaining benign spaces in his consciousness.

He turned his back on his hometown to head to Portrush and his prey.

Arriving there after a reckless journey along the A2, he settled down in the car he'd parked a safe distance from the doors of Michael and Maggie's hotel. He didn't have long to wait.

The couple came out of the building hand in hand and headed for Michael's car in the small car park. Declan turned on his ignition and watched carefully so that he could pull out after them as they left.

Maggie was in the passenger seat of the car and the memories of the hundreds if not thousands of times that she had accompanied him, ate away at Declan still a little more.

The couple joined Main Street and then headed east along the Bushmills road. At the junction with Ballybogy Road, Declan nearly lost them as a car pulled out in front of his own car and proceeded to drive at a sedate pace until shocked into submission by Declan's acceleration towards their rear bumper, forcing it to pull over.

They travelled past Dunluce Castle and on through Bushmills, past Causeway Road and on to Whitepark Road and Ballintoy.

After driving down Harbour Road, they parked up outside the café in the car park overlooking the rocky bay, white waves sliding over the top of black and green basalt boulders.

Declan was careful to park up to the left of their spot so that he was far enough away not to be seen but close enough to see them to his right as they made their way into the sea front building.

He stared out across Boheeshane Bay towards Larrybane Head but he didn't see the scene in front of him, instead he allowed his anger to increase further as he imagined Michael and Maggie sharing coffee and cake across a cosy table in the café.

His glazed over eyes nearly missed the couple's exit from the door forty minutes later until he was woken from his stupor by their car doors being slammed shut.

Once again he left a safe distance between the cars and trailed them as they made their way back up Harbour Road and on to the B15 again, driving past rugged gorse and heather topped peaks and the occasional grazing sheep until it pulled off at the sign for Carrick – a – Rede and they wound their way down the side of the hill to the car park.

Here, Declan was once again cautious and was aided by the cover of a number of other cars already parked up so that he didn't have to worry about being spotted. He watched the couple as they gathered what they wanted from their car before making their way along to the cliff top path.

They stopped to buy tickets and afterwards paused on the top of the path to take in the scene before them, weak sunlight forcing its way through the slow to lift cloud cover. This then shimmered on the top of countless wavelets surrounding Carrickarede Island and warmed the guillemots and razorbills crowding the rocky ledges, animating them amidst sounds of the guttural crowing calls of 'goarr, goarr'.

Declan kept his distance as he watched them begin to descend the ladder steps once they'd passed through the gate built atop the bare rock.

Maggie meanwhile felt sick as she looked down into the waiting chasm to her right, only a small wooden post and rail fence keeping her fixed on her descent down the wooden steps.

"Oh God Michael, I don't think I can do it," cried Maggie, clutching on to his arm as she looked across the rope bridge reaching out in front of them that connected over the sea to the small island ahead.

Stretching for 65 feet in front of them and at a height of 80 feet above the water below, the swaying suspension bridge was first put in place as many as 350 years ago to enable salmon fishermen to reach the spot their catch would travel through to spawn in the rivers Bann and Bush.

"C'mon, of course you can!" Michael coached, stepping on to the first of the wooden planks himself and holding on to the rope handrail supporting the flimsy net of knotted ropes forming the sides of the bridge.

The last of the land was left behind as Michael pulled a nervous Maggie onto the swaying bridge, white spume topping the swirling waters as they crashed about the black rocks beneath.

Maggie let out another shriek much to the amusement of a Dutch couple waiting to cross behind them.

"It's high," said the husband, "my wife does not like heights either."

His wife stood behind him shaking her head in mock horror.

With this, Maggie found her composure and allowed Michael to lead her over the bridge until they reached the three steps up at the end of the walkway when they reached the island.

The island itself is small and inhabited by seabirds clinging to its rocky cliff sides. Another post and rail fence shepherds tourists away from the steep drop to the right and the path winds its way across to the highest point of the island and down to the flatter end against the sea.

Declan had hung back, leaning against the fence through the entrance gateway to the descending ladder steps, watching Michael and Maggie with abject disgust as they had made a show of themselves getting across the bridge.

He seethed as he watched them walking hand in hand towards the middle of the island, laughing at an unheard joke between themselves. He paced up and down, tempted to follow them but decided instead to stay where he was and to wait for their return.

Meanwhile, Maggie was telling Michael what a fantastic day she was having, so pleased that they had made the trip out, so pleased to be together. Michael sensed Maggie's warmth before she spoke and was ready with words of agreement and a reciprocal squeeze of hands.

The brighter skies were now filled with fast moving clouds as time progressed. The air-cooled and couples peered out into strengthening seas caused by the growing wind.

The light level dropped and the once playful waves now surged higher and higher over the rocky shore and began to send drops of spray flying into the air. Most people had seen enough and decided to make their way back over the bridge, but Michael and Maggie stayed a while, gazing out across the now grey surf into nothingness.

Declan, now even more impatient, was cursing audibly as people came back across the bridge, his temper becoming harder to control. His eyes looked through each person, unable to focus on anything except the couple still to make their way back to the mainland.

Whether it was the building cold or whether it was rage or a combination of the two, Declan was visibly shaking. He didn't sense this himself, he was numb to his surroundings and fixed only on the middle distance and the wire and rope suspension bridge.

After another ten minutes had passed, Declan stopped shaking as he spied the couple finally returning across the thrift-fringed path and back towards him.

Just as Declan was numb to his own cursing and shaking, he was equally unconscious of his forward volition, moving with speed towards his deep-set target.

He reached the bridge and grasped each wire handrail firmly, blocking the exit.

Maggie and Michael strolled towards the first wooden slats and it was Maggie who spotted Declan first, seeing him in her peripheral vision like a ghost solidifying from her past.

She gasped as she realised who it was, a quick combination of fear, anger and terror washed over her and she pulled Michael forcibly to a stop.

"What?" he said as she tugged at his arm again at the elbow.

"There, bloody there!" she cried, thrusting her arm out towards Declan.

Michael now stopped himself and they stood together staring over towards the demon placed on the other side.

Maggie spoke first, "What the hell are you doing here?" she shouted across the gap.

Declan, either because he could not hear her above the building seas below or because he chose not to, did not acknowledge the question and instead simply stood there, clutching on to the sides, swaying a little in the strengthening wind.

"C'mon," Michael said, I'm not going to be put off by that bastard," and pulled at Maggie's hand to follow him.

She shook his hand away in annoyance and turned to face him.

"I'm NEVER going to be free of him, I might as well just go over there and leave you here," she said in anguish, "he won't be happy until he has finished me off for good."

"I won't let him!" stated Michael firmly, "You're with me now and he is going to have to get used to it at some stage."

"Oh, you've really no idea, just no idea." she sobbed, "He's nearly killed me before and he's never going to be any different!"

Declan noticed their raised voices now and shouted across, "Lovers tiff is it? You sicken me walking around like you've not got a care in the world!" He waited for a response before adding, "I want you back with me Maggie, we've got unfinished business."

"NO!" she shouted back, "No, we have NOT got any unfinished business, I'll never let you lay a finger on me again, NEVER!" Her voice trailed away on the wind but Declan heard enough.

"Aw, c'mon Maggie, there's no need to be like that, we were meant to be together, you know that!"

Maggie's blood boiled and she cried out, "Fuck off, just fuck off you pathetic, sad man!"

Declan's face dropped and he started to shake again.

"You've got something I need Maggie Haugh, you've got the papers I need, you know where that money is and I'm going to have it and you are going to give it to me so help me God."

Declan took another step forward onto the next plank on the bridge and Maggie, seeing this, pushed Michael ahead of her so that he was further forward.

"What are you doing?" he asked, "Let's leave him be for now and go back over afterwards, he's got to get bored at some stage."

Maggie was about to remonstrate with Michael but Declan beat her to it.

"What do you see in that one Maggie, eh? He's a pathetic excuse for a man and always has been."

"You shut your face!" Michael shouted back. "You are a sick bastard, you need help!"

With this, he pulled Maggie with him on to the bridge and said to her, "C'mon, we're going across, he's not stopping us."

Declan, seeing them move forward, did so himself so that he matched their pace across the planks, like a pawn mirroring a move on a chessboard.

"Get out of the way Declan!" Maggie shouted and he replied, "No way, not until you give me what is mine!"

"I owe you nothing!" she shouted again, "I never did."

"You ungrateful bitch!" he replied, moving fast now into the middle of the bridge, causing it to jump up and down and start to sway.

The pair on the other side were forced to grab on to the ropes to steady themselves again but Maggie lost her footing and stumbled forward, her left foot heading through a gap in the boards, causing her to shriek out in pain as her ankle was twisted around.

Michael helped the distressed Maggie back onto her feet, blood oozing out of a gash caused by the fall.

He choked back rage as he held on to her and then cried out, "Get out of our way!"

Declan stepped closer again and planted his feet firmly on the planks and tried to get the bridge to sway again. This time it was Michael who fell, the movement sending him backwards and he let out a grunt as his body grazed against the cables.

Maggie watched Michael fall with incredulity whilst seeing the protagonist pulling at the sides again to make more movement.

Something inside Maggie snapped and she barely had time to think about what she was doing as she raced towards Declan and when she reached him, her hands flailed madly into his chest and his face.

Declan let a few blows land before grabbing her by the neck and throwing her around so that her back landed against the wire hand support.

The force of this sent her feet off the planks and she felt herself falling backwards uncontrollably. Declan reached out quickly in her direction but instead of flesh, he grabbed a handful of hair and Maggie's head seared with pain which translated into a loud shriek again as tears raced down her face as once again, Declan inflicted terror and harm upon her.

Michael pulled himself up quickly and rushed at Declan, landing a blow full in his stomach. Declan let out a cry as he was winded and had to audibly gasp for air as he was doubled over.

Michael now tried to help Maggie, pulling quickly at her arm again, She tried to get back on to her feet but her vision was now distracted by the plunge down to the heaving sea below and she just shut her eyes and sobbed.

Declan had now managed to catch his breath and he forced himself to focus on the couple and ignore the growing feeling of dizziness that was sweeping over him.

He lunged forward at Michael, pinning him against the side but Michael fought back, managing to throw a punch that landed square on Declan's jaw and his head was thrown back.

Declan fell backwards, stumbling as he went and he did not notice Maggie behind him on the bridge, still doubled over and crying. His head made contact with her halfway through a backwards step and this sent him off balance and the man tumbled back and over the side of the bridge, his arms circling madly as he tried to make contact with something.

The solidity of Maggie behind him had thrown him off his feet and he lurched sideways, his head heading over the rail first. One of his legs caught in the ropes and spun him around. He grasped out madly again in what seemed like slow motion and managed to stop himself from the downward plunge by grasping hold of one of the wires.

There he dangled, waves crashing beneath him, nausea and fear reducing him to high pitched and anguished cries for help. He tried to reach up with his free hand for another place to hold on to but he couldn't conjure up the will to ignore the pain in his right hand that had been badly grazed by the friction caused by his downward contact with the rope.

"God, help me, help me!" Declan pleaded, vaguely aware of a figure on the bridge above him.

The figure was Maggie and she looked down at him and smiled.

"Maggie, please, just help me," he whimpered and for a moment she considered doing that but Declan's anger returned and his whimper turned into a demand of, "C'mon! Bloody do something!"

Maggie held on to the swaying handrail and started to kick Declan's hand. He cried out with pain but didn't let go, so Maggie started to grind the heel of her boot down onto his fingers and hand with all of her might.

Declan tried again to reach up with his free hand, but the fingers in contact with the bridge were split open with the force of Maggie's pounding boot as she forced them harder and harder against the wire and rope, blood poured out from his shattered nails and mashed metatarsals.

He let out blood curdling cries and couldn't take the pain any more and he loosened his grip.

His free arm made one last feeble attempt to find a purchase as Declan let out a high pitched squeal. His bloodied hand let go of the rope and his other failed to make contact and he plunged downward, his limbs flailing this way and that.

The waves surged up to welcome him but the timing of their suck and pull left a drying rock exposed below and this is what Declan reached first.

His head and neck smashed into the rock as he fell and the rest of his body reached the water with an audible splash that was immediately replaced with another surging wave that lifted him off the rock and into the now deep water.

Blood coloured the surf as it forced his body through the narrow gap between the land and the island and out towards the open water.

Another wave surged in and flung Declan's body on to rocks nearer the shore, tearing at his clothes.

He floundered there feebly for a few moments before sinking beneath the water.

A gull cried out overhead, the sea sighed in response and above them all, Maggie Haugh laughed and cried like she'd never done before.

Chapter Thirty Three

Eamon Gibson had returned to the station, returned after grieving for Sandra, returned to some kind of stability to fill the deep cracks in his fractured emotions.

A call from his superior kicked him into action.

It seemed that there were reports of a struggle up on the North Coast. The couple from the Netherlands had done their duty and reported what they had observed. He did not know that those involved all had connections to the criminal community in the Belfast area and more importantly, had links to the unlawful killing of his wife.

He couldn't work on the case, he was too close but that didn't stop him from calling in favours, from seeking more knowledge from afar.

His closest colleagues, ones who knew Sandra well, were breaking the rules and helping him to quietly piece together the hidden connections coming to light in the case.

The net was perhaps beginning to close, the contents being squeezed together, less room to manoeuvre, less chances to escape as the gaps were being closed.

'Who Dares Wins' had been stolen and Kathleen and Terry Flanagan, all aided by hangers on – all of them had played their part in helping the process move quickly and efficiently, to create distractions, to engage stable lads, lorry drivers, a hard up vet.

All had one thing in common, they were all flat broke or in debt and were only too willing to profit from something they saw as a victimless crime. But then they assumed that the horse would have been well insured, assumed that no individual would lose out as a result of the theft – a comfortable crime perhaps.

What they didn't see or didn't care to see was Maggie's father dying by a roadside, her mother falling apart emotionally and physically and Maggie herself, ever more hardened and carrying the emotional baggage from her traumatic childhood.

Kathleen and Terry knew that they wouldn't profit immediately other than a few quid to pay for a few luxuries, but they had not planned on being without the proceeds for this long.

Terry Flanagan had known a contact that wanted to use the horse for stud work and was prepared to pay a fortune for it to be delivered to a quiet rural backwater in Co Wexford.

They'd always known that they'd have to launder the cash; to keep it moving to prevent any connections being made back to them so what they created was a smoke screen to work behind.

Kathleen found the person for the job and took him into her bed. She inveigled him into her world of corruption and delivered obfuscation in place of truth.

Kelly's father had been ideal. He'd amazed Kathleen with tales of the criminal underworld he'd come across through his work with the newspaper. He'd set up pools syndicates that had amazing, albeit conservative sums circulated through them and dabbled in stocks and shares and financial instruments before most of his generation had even considered doing so.

Once John had been sucked in to Kathleen's world of mire and corruption, once he couldn't live without being in her bed, she began to drip feed information about the horse theft and the cash payment.

Sure, she didn't tell the truth, she allowed him to believe that she was the wronged party, the one who he should fight for and fight for her he did.

John began to work out a complex financial web to hide the illicit funds. He set about splitting the cash into a myriad of bank and building society accounts in Kelly's name, this being in the days when many branches still had distinct local records and only early central computer data bases to link them together.

He hid the statements and passbooks from sight in various locations but did keep a coded reference as to their whereabouts.

He created the list of numbers, seemingly randomised, but actually containing the address and sort code and account numbers of each of the accounts.

He allocated numbers to the street names using a code that he devised and it was this list that Tommy had been working to decipher. The list that Declan had obtained by force from Terry Flanagan, that Maggie had then stolen on discovering that Declan and Terry had freely discussed the whereabouts of the cash proceeds from the theft.

The same list that Terry and Kathleen had forced away from Kelly's father John as they similarly forced him to write the letter he left on the kitchen table for his wife, Kelly's mother, explaining that he was leaving her and their boy.

The same list that once in Terry's hands had enabled Kathleen to asphyxiate her lover one night after they had made love, hauling away the body together.

Terry had taken the body to one of his building sites and buried it in concrete foundations.

This same list, Terry had kept from Kathleen, seeking to keep the profit for himself. The same list that once obtained from him by Declan and stolen by Maggie, had been worked on by Tommy, desperate to right the wrongs after discovering the part he'd played in causing Maggie's despair.

This same list had caused the death of four adults including the one who created it and also the one whose body still lay undiscovered in a Belfast bedsit.

* * *

Kathleen was on the 'phone to Kelly at the guesthouse. He'd taken the call as Mrs. Donnelly had told him that it was a neighbour from Belfast on the line who needed to speak to him about his house.

Kathleen had taken a risk that Kelly would buy the story, that he'd fall into another of her traps and she knew him well enough.

Kelly, ever conscious about the house after what had happened in the past, had indeed asked a kindly neighbour to keep an eye on the property and to let him know if there was any issue. The neighbour hadn't called of course, but Kathleen once again took a chance and came out of the winning side.

"I've got nothing to say to you Kathleen," he shouted into the receiver.

Kathleen was ready for this response. "It's your Dad, Kelly, he's been in touch!" She paused for a reaction but it did not come. "I couldn't believe it Kelly, he's got in contact and he wants to meet up with you."

Kelly's brain warned him not to accept this but his heart skipped a beat at the thought of being able to meet his father again. Sure, he wanted to berate him, to paint the scene of despair that had been caused to his depressive wife, but most of all he wanted to see him, to see how he had changed, to understand where he had been, to try and comprehend why he left in the way he had done and why he had been in an illicit affair with Kathleen.

Kelly had considered that this moment might happen ever since his father had left. He had determined across the years to assume that his father was never coming back, that he'd never have the opportunity to speak to him again and even if he had, that he would give his father the cold shoulder and let him know that he no longer cared why he had done what he had done.

He viewed the situation in a way that convinced him that his father had lost the right to any consideration.

Now though, now that he had got in touch with Kathleen, now that there was a chance – just a chance to see him, his emotions took precedence over sense and he even thanked Kathleen for getting in touch.

"I knew you wouldn't speak to me if she told you it was me on the 'phone John," she gushed, knowing she had trapped her prey.

"I want nothing to do with you Kathleen, nothing at all but you're the only link to my father that I've got," Kelly stated coldly, "why hasn't he tried to reach me himself?"

"Oh wow John, imagine what it must have been like for him, I suppose he wanted to test the water?" she replied, convincingly.

Sophie meanwhile was waiting upstairs, wondering why Kelly was taking so long to return.

These last few days had caused a lot of unpleasant memories to surface and she longed for a diversion to take her into an unconnected world but genuinely wanted to help Kelly, to stop him being one of Kathleen's hapless victims.

Kelly returned upstairs in a state of some shock but also undisguised excitement.

Sophie looked up as he entered the room and saw the different look on his face.

"The house?" she asked, starting to wonder why he was disguising a grin.

"No, not the house, actually it was my father, I mean he's been in touch!" He explained, wondering if he would need to tell the whole detail of the call.

"Your father!" exclaimed Sophie, how did he know that you are here?"

"Well, he's got in touch all the same," but Sophie interjected before he could finish.

"You've actually spoken to him?"

Kelly paused, trying to form a sentence that would still explain things without disclosing to her who was actually on the 'phone.

His mind wanted to believe that his father wanted to meet with him, but there was still a small element of doubt in the back of his mind that he sub-consciously didn't want to allow to grow.

"He wants to meet, I just can't believe it," he responded, "I can't believe I'm going to see him after all these years!"

Sophie studied his face carefully and asked again, "So you've actually spoken to him?"

Kelly thought quickly about his answer but too slowly to stop Sophie adding, "So who actually was that on the 'phone Kelly?"

He looked towards the window and then back towards Sophie before confessing, "Well, he has actually been in touch with someone we both know, someone he feels safe with."

"Who?" she demanded, "Who does he feel comfortable with?"

He responded, "I know what you're going to say, but I have to meet with him Sophie."

"C'mon, who the hell was it?"

"Okay, Kathleen, it was Kathleen," he replied and was then genuinely startled by the ferocity of her reply.

"Are you just stupidity itself? Can't you see what she is trying to do here?" Sophie then laughed to herself and added, "You just can't help some people, you really can't."

With this, she turned away before adding, "If you can't see through Kathleen's games Kelly, I can't help you. For God's sake, get a grip and listen to yourself and learn that the woman is just poison!"

Kelly felt his hackles rise and he wanted to shout back at her as he felt her words piercing his excitement. He managed to restrain his reply to, "So you'd have me just ignore him, to walk away without meeting him? You'd want me to miss the only opportunity I might get?"

He looked across at her, trying to make eye contact.

"Oh God Kelly, don't be so bloody naive, this is one of Kath's games, one of the ways she wraps you around her finger every single time!" she stated and moved to get up from the bed.

"What if it is him though – how can you want to deprive me of that. I've got to see him Sophie, sorry but I just have to try."

Sophie shook her head and explained, "I'm not trying to deprive you of anything Kelly because he won't have been in touch. This is just one of her games and you're going along with it all yet again!"

"Oh and you're such a good judge of character aren't you Sophie, so skilled in dealing with all of the situations that you've been in?" he added sarcastically.

Sophie shook her head and stood up. "I'm leaving you to it Kelly before I say something that I'm going to regret, you think long and hard and I'll come back later and I hope to God you've come to your senses by then."

Kelly didn't stop her or attempt to remonstrate because his mind was fixed. He wanted to see his father, wanted to help him to extricate himself from Kathleen if he was still involved with her, wanted to save the man who had betrayed him as a dog will go to the aid of the owner that abuses him.

He was mindful of the next blow but determined to protect his own.

Maggie and Michael had fled the scene at Carrick-a-Rede, Maggie still irrational and celebrating her escape from her nemesis. The couple had reached the car park and collapsed into the car, Michael exhausted by the struggle on the bridge and by the force he had to exert to drag Maggie away from the scene.

Maggie continued to laugh, but the waves of laughter grew shorter and they turned into a sobbing cry of despair. Michael was startled by Maggie's mirth and now scared by the wracking sobs now emanating from her core but he decided that the most sensible course of action was to get them away from the scene.

His fumbling hands managed to insert the key into the ignition of the car and he started the engine and rammed it into reverse to flee the parking space.

The car raced out of the car park and up the track towards the main road, before hurtling westward towards Ballycastle and Port Stewart.

Chapter Thirty Four

"Brendan, Brendan, where are you? I need to see you now, no, today!" Michael cried into the receiver of the telephone in Maggie's hotel room.

He paused, waiting motionless for his brother to reply before throwing his hand into the air with emotion as he said, "No, don't give me that crap about being busy Brendan, this is important."

He was forced to cut his sentence short as Brendan explained his plans that day with Kathleen to his younger brother.

Michael was struggling to keep it together, highly frustrated by his brother's easy rejection.

"Brendan, BRENDAN!" he shouted and the volume of his voice increased as he said, "I need to see you now because I think Maggie's killed Declan!" the last words were shaky and Michael felt his body quivering as the shock of the events began to sink in.

The line, once busy with a brother's excuses, grew silent.

"I'm serious, this is not a joke Brendan, I think that Maggie has just killed Declan. I was there. No, I was there myself with her, oh God, I don't know what to do," Michael sank into the armchair next to the telephone.

"Police?" No nobody else was there or at least I didn't see anybody."

He coloured immediately as his brother's voice rose in disbelief on the other end of the line and demanded to know all of the details.

"I'm not sure, no. I don't know," Michael continued in reply to a further barrage of questions.

"Where are you now Brendan? NO, I'm coming over and bringing Maggie with me . . . What . . .? No, of course I can't leave her here . . . Well, that's what's happening . . . she is coming with me. Right, right, okay. Yes, were on the way now."

Kelly meanwhile looked around the guesthouse bedroom, battling with himself and his conflicting thoughts about what to do next.

He knew that he must go and meet with his father, to have the opportunity to see him again.

Suddenly he recollected an image of his father from some twenty years ago.

He was struck by the thought of a more elderly father, one with grey hair, one with different glasses, different clothes, just different.

The image in his mind wasn't static, not a photograph. Instead it was a moving image from a New Year's party many years ago. His father was sporting a bright yellow paper hat and was blowing one of those rolled up paper 'ticklers' with a feather on the end. He could hear the ear-piercing screech emanating from the plastic reed at the mouth end, joining in unison with the other party guests.

Kelly shook his head, wondering why he had remembered this particular image. Perhaps it was because he wanted to remember a happy thought of his father, one where he was having fun and not one where he was arguing again with Kelly's mother. These arguments usually started in the kitchen when his father would come in late from work from whichever city centre pub he insisted that he'd had to go into to make the contacts he needed for his next work for the newspaper. He wanted to be in there with the action, find out where to be to catch a scoop for the following day's paper.

The evening was drawing in and in the growing gloom, Kelly stared at the same spot on the skirting board he'd been looking at with glazed eyes for the last five minutes whilst reminiscing about the past.

The gold nylon carpet in the room still retained its original bright hue next to the skirting board away from the wear and tear and flattening footsteps of a budget carpet's inevitable fate.

Kelly continued to stare in thought until darkness made him avert his fanciful gaze.

Morning dawned and Kelly hauled himself out of bed after checking the time on his mobile 'phone.

He padded across into the en-suite to use the loo and was startled at the image of his hair standing on end in the ancient vanity unit mirror, the result of a night of restless sleep.

He was about to step into the shower when he heard a knock at his bedroom door. He grabbed a towel from the rail and wrapped it around himself before answering the door.

Sophie stood in the doorway, dressed ready to go out and she simply pushed past Kelly and into the room.

"I see you are up bright and early," she said sarcastically whilst moving towards the window and pulling the curtains back sharply so that the room was filled with a cloud of dancing dust caught in the bleaching brightness as daylight raced in.

"Yes, well, I'm getting ready now," he replied, unsure as to what was going to come next after their angry conversation of the night before.

"Good," she replied, adding, "what time are we meeting this father of yours?"

Kelly's face betrayed involuntary surprise before he managed to answer, "Well, I said that I'd be there for ten thirty. So you're coming with me?"

"Ha ha," she laughed, "I wouldn't miss this one for the world."

Kelly grinned nervously and headed back to the shower, his mind full of anticipation, some excitement and the impending thrill of seeing his father that very morning.

After his uneasy sleep though, all this was mixed in with an amount of concern. He was keen that Sophie would not be proved right but he was genuinely desperate to see that his father was real, that he would see him in the flesh and change his last memory of his father, instead of the note left for Kelly and his mother as he'd moved out of their lives.

Kelly and Sophie drove their car up a remote lane off a main road and headed towards a farmhouse near Ballycastle at the end of a rutted farm track, which had become a base of sorts for Brendan and Kathleen.

The house was situated in a fold of land surrounded by dark trees on one side and fronted by a lush sward of green grass that provided interest for a number of russet and grey-flecked chickens.

The roof of the farmhouse was once thatched but was now covered with slate, making the building's profile much more angular that it would have been originally, its mossy golden sward replaced by grey slivers of stone that absorbed the light.

The harled walls were still lime washed and the front door retained its dark red paint, similar in colour to the deep red combs of the chickens pecking about at the green skirts drawn up tightly against the walls.

The car drew up on the rubbly hard standing with a crunch as randomly shaped pebbles scraped and shifted under the weight of the vehicle.

Sophie had offered on the journey over to stay in the car once they had arrived, but Kelly had insisted that they should do this together. Sophie expressed her willingness to help Kelly but also expressed her concerns about coming face to face with Kathleen and particularly with Brendan.

Kelly had been so wrapped up in his own world that morning that he hadn't stopped to consider the reunion of Sophie and her aunt.

He'd offered to drop her off in town or to try and organise a meeting elsewhere, but she'd replied that they had to meet again sometime and it might as well be now, particularly as there would be the distraction of Kelly's father at the meeting.

Sophie had also thought that if the meeting was indeed a scam, at least she'd be on hand to offer some level of support to Kelly and that it would open his eyes. She was keen today though, not to burst his bubble before he'd even finished inflating it.

The pair walked up to the front door and Kelly gave the knocker a load rap. Inside the house, raised voices were being badly disguised as the awkwardly audible argument was dulled once the occupants heard the sharp knock. Kelly looked at Sophie and raised his eyebrows in silent surprise as they waited for the door to be answered.

They heard footsteps heading across a tiled floor and Kathleen's voice saying, "Ring him back now please Brendan!"

She pulled back a bolt and unlocked the door and on opening it, she greeted Kelly and Sophie with a sickly artificial smile and a greeting of, "Ah, great, come in the both of you, come in."

Kathleen suddenly looked again at the pair and exclaimed, "Sophie! I hadn't seen you there for a moment, well I never, I didn't know that two of you knew each other?"

Sophie was filled with nausea at the artificial sentimentality in her aunt's voice and she merely raised her eyebrows in response and exclaimed, "Oh Auntie, you'll be telling me next that you didn't know I've been in town the last few days."

Kathleen's voice betrayed badly masked annoyance but her words were at odds with her tone, "Oh Sophie, what do you mean. Oh I know – you thought that Brendan must have seen you. Well he did say something to me but I told him he must have been mistaken as I thought you were in Belfast?"

Sophie shook her head and smiled in disbelief, "Oh I see, so there we are then, everything is a surprise this morning."

Kathleen felt her temper ready to blow after her argument with Brendan about Michael and Maggie's imminent arrival but she held it together enough to state sarcastically, "You must tell me how you and Kelly know one another sometime, it's all such a shock seeing you here together."

Kelly decided to interject at this point and said, "Well, you two have obviously a lot to catch up on but have we called at a bad time for you Kathleen?"

"Oh, don't mind Brendan," Kath replied, "he's just told me that our plans today need to change and the last thing that I wanted to do was to start changing arrangements at this late stage."

"Can we cut out the niceties please Kath for God's sake," added Sophie, "is Kelly's father here please – can he see him?"

Kathleen's eyes betrayed the venom she felt towards Sophie momentarily but again, she reined in her emotions enough to reply, "Oh yes, he's here, just not at the house as yet this morning."

Sophie turned to Kelly and opened her mouth but Kathleen quickly cut her off.

"He's not here but we can go and see him now," she stated, her eyes looking for contact with Kelly. They met their target and Kelly stuttered out, "W . . . well, err, err, if you think that's best."

This time Sophie cut in, "Oh come on, I told you she was going to do something like this didn't I. Why can't she produce this father of yours then when she told you to come now?"

Kelly met her gaze and he let her know through his glare that he was far from happy with what she has just said.

The last few days had provided Kelly with time to think and a lot of those thoughts had been about Sophie. He had been trying to work out what his feelings towards her were and whether their shared experience had forced them to get closer to one another as friends or whether they were bound together more deeply than by common factors and mutual antagonists.

He missed her when she was not around but he'd seen some of the fire inside of her and whilst he admired her spirit, he worried that she had too much emotional baggage, too much loss and sadness inside, creating a gap that he'd never be able to fill.

"So can I speak to Dad on the 'phone now then Kathleen if he's not here, sort of break the ice?" he asked, keen to show Sophie that he was calling Kath's bluff but also wanting to assume that he was still out there waiting and wanting to see his son.

Kathleen's face didn't betray the anger she felt at being confronted on her own doorstep but her words were tinged with an outward desire to mediate as she replied, "Of course, of course, why not speak to him first."

She paused for a moment in the doorway and then said, "Come in to the house, why don't you ring him from the back room, you can have some privacy there."

Kelly flashed a look at Sophie who shrugged her shoulders in reply and followed him through the front door that Kathleen held to one side.

Once they were in the hallway proper, she asked them to follow her and they made their way down the gloomy, flag stoned corridor as it dog legged to the left and then to the right, less and less light finding its way into the dark labyrinth.

"No money for the electricity meter?" asked Sophie as they stumbled along the wood chipped walls, much over painted with thickly applied gloss over previous decades.

"Right, just go through here," said Kathleen as she opened an old door and led them through into a musty room within. "I'm just going to sort the lights out," she added and left them in the room but as quickly as she'd left the room, she closed the door quickly behind her, leaving them in the dark.

Sophie let out a giggle and was about to say something but Kelly stopped her with, "Shhh!" he hissed, "listen!"

They both focused their attention in time to hear a lock being turned slowly in the door that they had both come through.

"Is that the door?" Sophie barked out, looking about the gloom of the room.

Kelly reached into a pocket and pulled out his mobile 'phone and pressed a button to gain some light.

He walked over to the door and pulled at the latch – no movement. The door was firmly closed and secured from the outside.

"I knew that we shouldn't have come here Kelly, what did I tell you!" she cried, "Try it again, it might just be stuck."

Kelly duly tried the door again, pulling at the handle and the latch at the same time. The door didn't move.

"Right, there's got to be a window," he said, activating his 'phone again.

All that the light revealed was a dark, dusty room filled with closed boxes and tea chests and an old table covered in a dated tablecloth and other household detritus.

The pair continued to circle the room with the aid of the 'phone light but could only see the locked door as their means of exit.

Kelly hammered loudly on the door, shouting out, "Kathleen, Kathleen, let us out of here now or I will 'phone the Police."

No footsteps were heard near the door but Kelly could hear the sound of a car crunching onto the gravel outside the house and an engine being turned off.

"HELLO!" shouted Kelly, "Is anyone out there?"

"Just ring the Police!" hissed Sophie. "This is just ridiculous. Ring them now Kelly or I will," and Sophie fumbled with her own pockets to reach her 'phone.

They were both trying to make calls on their mobiles but both soon realised that the signal here was non-existent. Sophie moved slowly around the room between the packing cases and boxes, trying to improve the signal but could not find a spot where it was any better.

"Shit!" she spat out, "what the hell are we going to do?"

The car door that had slammed outside belonged to Michael. He had just arrived with Maggie to explain the events at Carrick-a-Rede to Brendan. Maggie still looked strangely – preternaturally serene but her puffy eyes betrayed the tears she had shed over her lost love, a soul-mate, one who had caused her immense pain, distress and had tormented her both physically and psychologically.

The loss of him was incomprehensible to her and yet immensely welcome at the same time, relief mixed with abject despair.

Brendan ushered the pair in quickly, leading them through to the large farmhouse kitchen where Kathleen stood, looking out of the window, her hands resting on the edge of the Belfast sink in contemplation.

She didn't turn around to face the new arrivals until they had all settled down at the table in the middle of the room.

"What the fuck has been going on?" she stabbed out into the air, burrowing her gaze towards Maggie, expecting an impassioned response. None came however, Maggie simply turning to Michael for support and taking hold of his hand, her face showing the same waxen demeanor.

"Have you any idea just how much you've messed up everything?" Kath continued, "Any idea what we might have lost with your stupidity?"

Kathleen spat the last word out of her mouth and had to wipe away moisture from her lips with her hand.

Brendan responded first, his voice coming out in a loud hiss, "For God's sake Kath, we've got people in the house!"

"They can't hear us where they are now," Kathleen interjected.

"Who else is here – whose is the car?" Michael demanded, looking towards the door and moving his chair slightly so it scraped on the flagged floor.

"Not important Michael, not important," stated Kathleen, "just tell me what the hell has happened."

"I'm not going to be spoken to like that!" Michael continued and Maggie gave his hand another squeeze.

Brendan interrupted with, "Just tell her Michael, just do what you're told for once."

Michael's hackles rose with this patronising remark and he got up out of his chair and started to encourage Maggie to her feet but Kathleen commented, "Michael, please, we're all just stressed out, just let's all calm down and discuss this please."

Michael shook his head but chose to sit back down again, making no eye contact with either his brother or his lover.

He started to recount the events at the coast, answering Kathleen's repeated questions. Throughout the dialogue, Maggie showed no emotion, no connection to the words being delivered on her behalf.

Kathleen raised her eyebrows each time she listened to each new detail in disbelief and shook her head. Once Michael had finished answering her questions, she asked one extra one.

"Michael, I need to know the final piece of information and I think that Maggie knows it," she turned towards Maggie.

"Where did Declan keep his paperwork, his valuables, the information on the lists – we have to get hold of it NOW."

Maggie's static gaze broke and with a cracked voice she replied, "Is that all you are bothered about?"

"Oh Maggie, believe me I'm bothered about a whole lot more than that but I need to know where the information is if I'm going to help everyone here."

"HELP everyone? Are you serious?" said Maggie, her voice trailing away dryly at the end, "When have you done anything to help anyone but yourself?"

Brendan shook his head in anger, words of reproach ready on the end of his tongue. Kathleen got there first.

"You need my help now Maggie, so you need to help me in finding that last piece of information I need or believe me, I can do a whole lot worse that trading insults with ungrateful sluts!"

Michael's chair crashed to the floor as he raced out of it and flew towards Kathleen who did not flinch at his progress.

Brendan's intervention brought Michael to a full stop, his massive arms stopped his smaller brother in his tracks and threw him to the floor.

"STOP it!" cried Maggie, "Just stop it, I just want this whole nightmare to be over."

Both Michael and Brendan were surprised by Maggie's impassioned plea and they stopped their tussle.

"I'll not tell you anything Kathleen, not a bloody thing until you start to show some respect to me and to Michael. You think that we need you, well – you've just shown that you need us too so let's start all this again shall we?"

Kathleen's hands gripped the solid sink sides again until her fingernails felt numb whilst she considered her reply.

She sighed as she started to think about how to retain her position, her pride and her nostrils flared with annoyance but she knew she needed to buy some time.

"Alright, okay, we don't need to do this right now," she said, "let's all calm down and do this after we've all had time to think. Michael, Brendan will show you and Maggie to a room you can stay in whilst you're here – get some rest and we can do this later on."

Maggie?" started Michael before she responded with, "Okay, we'll do this later Kathleen but once we have sorted this out, that's it. I want out of here for good Michael."

Chapter Thirty Five

In Belfast, three teenagers were walking down Tommy's street, one kicking a waste bin as he went by, another kicking along an empty can of cola, the street ringing with the sound of aluminium scraping along the tarmac as the crushed can was dribbled along the pavement and in and out of the gutter.

At one property, they saw a light on in a front room window and dashed up to it, faces leering through the glass, before returning to their drink can soccer.

One of the lads put too much force into his next kick and the can soared into the air, sending it into a wall before it rattled down a stairwell into a void, inaccessible behind the old railings.

"Ahh you tosser, that was shite!" said one.

"Shut up!" said another, shoving the shoulder of the kid next to him, forcing him to fall off the pavement and stumbling into the road.

"Right!" the boy replied, and flew back onto the pavement, both hands making contact with his assailant. His shove in reply took the other off guard and he lost his balance, his backside landing on to the steps outside a property and his head bashed into the front door as he landed.

The front door though, instead of defending the interior within in its usual fashion, swung open and the boy landed half inside and half outside of the property.

Stunned for a moment and surprised by his location, he took a moment to get back on his feet. As he did so, he became aware of the eyewatering stench emanating from inside and he retched.

The youth who had sent him flying into the doorway was concerned for a moment that he had overdone it, seeing his friend dealing with peristalsis in the doorway and dashed up the stairs to help him up.

As he reached the top, several bluebottles raced into his face, escaping from the dark flat within. "Urggh!" he said and then the stench hit his eyes and he too felt nauseous at the sweet smell of decay.

"What is it?" cried the third, ready to join the others until the second boy hurtled down the stairs saying, "There's something dead in there!"

"Don't be daft," the third said, 'c'mon, stop messing around."

The first boy regained his breath and hurriedly joined the others. "God, what is that smell?" he spat out, "It's just RANK!"

The third boy, full of bravado, jutted in, "You're two girls aren't you? Scared by a front door, ha ha!"

"Something smells really bad in there," said the second, "maybe there's a body in there or something?"

"No way," said the third, "you watch too much television."

"God no, I think he's right, there's something dead in there," said the first.

"Oh what, like a pet rabbit or something – or a cat?" said the third laughing, "My Mam's probably given me worse for tea!"

"Hey, maybe it's a dog – all maggoty," said the second, "like that Chinese takeaway that had an Alsatian in the freezer."

"Oh, that's never true," said the first, "my dad says he heard a story like that when he was growing up too."

"Well, there's something in there and it stinks," said the second, "hey, what if it was a body or something, we might get a reward for finding it?"

"A reward? For finding a body?" Do they do that?" said the third, "Be kind of cool it there was, we'd be famous!"

"Well, I not going in there to find out," said the second, "what if there's someone else in there?"

"What do you mean, someone other than the dead body ha ha!" laughed the third.

"What about the Police?" asked the first.

"Oh, you mean ring them up and say, 'come and look at this flat, there's a stink inside' – it could be anything. They'd just laugh at us," replied the third.

"C'mon," he said, let's just go in there for a bit and if there's nothing there, we're not going to look stupid."

"I'm not going in there again," stated the first, "c'mon, let's just go, this is getting boring."

"Chicken!" stated the third, "What do you want, your mam to take you in there ha ha!"

"No," said the first, "but you go in if you want to, I'm not stopping you."

"Right, I will then," replied the third, "c'mon," and walked gingerly up the steps to the front door.

The second boy followed almost immediately but the first held back for a moment but conscious of being left behind on his own, rejoined the others. They pushed open the door and covered their noses with their hoodies to aid their progress into the gloom.

"What do you think you're doing keeping them in there?" hissed Brendan, gesturing towards the door behind which Sophie and Kelly were trying to gain a 'phone signal and intermittently banging the door.

"We need them out of the way," she replied firmly. "Once we've got what we need from them we can get out of here and finally finish with all this."

Brendan's face betrayed some irritation and concern and he replied, "And what if Maggie won't tell us what we need to know? What are we going to do then?"

"Oh, she'll speak alright, she'll speak," she added, "and if she doesn't want to initially, then she's going to have to be encouraged to, like we discussed."

"No Kath, don't bring Michael into this again."

"Bring Michael into this again? He's already well and truly in this Brendan, he's been mixed up in this ever since he set up with that brassy blonde upstairs!" she stated, her voice rising above a whisper now.

"But Kath, if . . ." he replied, but was cut off by her reply.

"Never mind 'if', we haven't got time for 'if'. She'll talk and then we can get what we need later on and then we can get out of here."

Brendan realised that he didn't have much of a choice and was always going to acquiesce to his lover's demands in any case, particularly if he wanted to stay with her and to benefit from some of the missing funds.

He actually feared for his relationship with his brother but like Kathleen, he believed that Michael's relationship with Maggie was based upon nothing but infatuation and lust. He believed that Michael had let him down as a brother, particularly as Kathleen and Brendan had only planned for Michael to be involved with Maggie just for long enough for him to gain her confidence and to gain the final piece of the jigsaw to lead to the location of the illicit money.

Michael had been a willing pawn, keen to please his older brother, keen to profit from their plans but Michael came to realise that a pawn was all that he was. As his feelings for Maggie grew and were reciprocated, he realised that he was being used with no guarantee of eventual reward. From that day, he determined to look after his own interests and those of Maggie too, ever more so following the revelations about the physical and psychological abuse she'd suffered both as a child and later on with Declan.

Kathleen continued, "In the morning, first thing, before they are properly awake, we are going to persuade her to talk Brendan, so get the car set up in the barn now but make sure that you're out of sight of your brother and then we can clear out of here."

* * *

Tommy had always been good with numbers. He could always work out the patterns, read the clues, see the things that others could not see.

Tommy had fed tidbits to Kathleen, tidbits to Maggie, to feed their desire for the final answer. All along though he had explained to both of them that he couldn't complete the work on the numbers, couldn't find the full answer that he needed, couldn't form his mouth into a characteristically small enough 'o' to solve the punishing puzzle left in the lists of numbers by the death of Terry Flanagan.

He'd needed, 'more clues', setting Kath off to interrogate and to interfere and Declan and Maggie off to a form of self-destruction.

All along though, after the numbers had come back to light, after Kathleen et al had waited patiently for the trail to run cold and the heat to die down about Terry's death, he'd carried on with his daily routine, his regular visits to the Chinese fish and chip shop, his deep study of the patterns in equine form in The Racing Post, his tots of whiskey taken from the blue plastic tumbler in the grease caked kitchenette.

All this regularity of habit though paled in comparison to his regular and deep study of his own bedroom wall, one patch in particular holding a fascination. One patch in particular holding his avid, avid attention.

Three boys entered Tommy's flat. Three boys, each determined to show a braver face than the next.

Three boys, part of a scene created many days before and left to be discovered in the future.

Three boys finding the scene today, about to tarnish their youthful innocence.

They entered the dark main room and let their eyes grow accustomed to the little light that there was, seeping in to the room from the kitchenette doorway.

"Hello?" called out one but his voice was softer than he had planned and he tried again, "HELLO?"

The second boy shoved the first from behind who was forced into the side of the decrepit sofa, its tired frame a result of settling and sagging over the previous forty years, one seat in particular showing the most signs of wear.

"Get off me," he hissed, as he regained his balance.

"I'm not staying here," said the third but the second boy grabbed his arm and stated, "We stick together."

"Maybe we shouldn't stay," said the first, "oh, the stink is even worse here!"

The second pushed them on with "It'll be something gone off in the kitchen, that's all, it smells flippin' rank." He continued, "C'mon, let's find out," and with that the trio moved on slowly, silently towards the open kitchenette doorway.

They peered in at the same time and were greeted by death itself.

The first boy physically recoiled and fell backwards into the lounge. The third let out a whining scream and raced for the front door.

The second boy was caught by sickening nausea and terror, frozen to the spot and he took in the scene of suppurating decay in front of him.

Tommy was in the same position he had been left in but his frame had sunk, his flesh was beginning to rot and maggots writhed visibly on the exposed skin.

The second boy's eyes were flooded with tears and his voice struggled to form any sound, tense vocal chords silently screaming.

"Sophie, Sophie!" called Kathleen through the closed door separating her and Kelly from the rest of the house.

"For God's sake let us out of here now!" cried Sophie in response, "What the hell are you playing at?" and she raced over to the door itself from her seated position on one of the old table tops.

"Oh, the door has jammed shut Sophie, I'm trying to work out how to open it with Brendan – don't worry."

"Well, get a bloody move on!" screamed Sophie, "We've been stuck in here for hours!"

They had indeed been stuck in there for a couple of hours – long enough for Brendan to visit the guest house and to rifle through their belongings looking for any clues that either of the pair might happen to have.

The willing landlady, happy to help her nephew, Brendan, had been only too willing to allow the furtive foray, unlocking the bedroom doors with a flourish to allow her visitor unimpeded access.

Brendan had seized the photocopies of the documents that Kelly had discovered under the floorboards of his house, the passbooks, the statements, anything he thought would be useful.

Kathleen, in her ever increasing desperation, had grown paranoid and had convinced herself that Kelly, Sophie or both, had found the link she needed and set about luring them to the remote farmhouse. This way, she could really keep them close.

Brendan for his part had ceased trying to offer alternative strategies to his other half and now merely carried out her will, partly out of devotion, partly out of a morbid fascination in seeing his partner work her machinations through to conclusion.

"Don't worry love, I've got a carpenter on the way, he's due very soon now."

"Oh, I suppose he's got delayed doing a job for Kelly's father has he?" replied Sophie sarcastically.

Kathleen pretended not to hear the challenge and carried on, "Oh, I don't know what the delay is but he's on his way now, I know that he is."

With this, she nodded to Brendan who had returned and the pair retreated down the long corridor back into the main part of the house and started to climb the stairs.

The pair reached the top and took a right, moving quietly along the upper corridor until they reached the bedroom at the end. Here they paused before Kathleen raised her voice and said, "Maggie, Maggie, are you awake love?"

From within the room, small sounds of movement could be heard.

"I just want a word with you Maggie, it is important," she continued.

With this, soft footsteps could be heard coming to the door, which was then opened after it had been unlocked from the inside.

The handle turned and Maggie stood there, blonde hairpiece betraying some snatched sleep through the way it was clearly flat on one side. She wore a lurid pink faux silk dressing gown, which clung to her shape and emphasised her ample assets.

"What is it?" she asked sleepily but the pair outside did not wait for a reply and instead Brendan leapt at the door with his shoulder, forcing it to catapult inward with a load 'bang'.

Maggie was thrown to the floor, letting out an agonised cry as she tumbled on to the carpet in complete surprise.

Brendan leapt on to her and pinned her to the floor, crushing the remaining air out of her already winded form.

With the noise of the door being forced wide open, Michael, who until this moment had been dozing beneath the duvet with Maggie, come back to his senses and with Maggie's cry, he flew out of the bed and stood there unable to fathom what was happening as he tried to make sense of what he was seeing before him.

He then moved quickly towards Brendan but was stopped in his tracks by the sounds of a recognisable 'click'. He looked towards where the sound had come from and saw Kathleen and a pistol pointed straight at him.

"Get back in the bed Michael," instructed Kathleen calmly.

Michael was not calm, the surprise of the scene unfolding in front of him and the shock of facing a loaded gun caused his breathing to stop and he stood there gawping, his mouth trying to form intelligible sounds through its parched dryness.

"Make a move and I will shoot you," Kathleen stated.

The colour drained out of Michael's face but he managed to shout out, "Brendan?" in an impassioned plea.

His brother's face flickered but he did not turn to meet his brother's request as he replied, "Do what the fuck she tells you to do Michael," and he kept his head down, intent on securing Maggie's silence with the heavy palm of his free hand.

"What the HELL?" Michael shouted but was again cut short by Kathleen's insistent tone and reply of, "Say another word and I will fucking shoot. Get back on that bed!"

Michael did as he was told, unsure whether to fly at his brother or Kathleen and sat there on top of the duvet, his head clamped between his two palms in despair. He sat upright, his legs stretched out in front of him, biding his time, waiting for his brain to unfreeze and to tell him what to do.

Kathleen looked down at Brendan and instructed, "Uncover her mouth Brendan." He did as he was asked.

Maggie took in a deep gasp of air, her eyes wide as she tried to fill her lungs.

"Crazy bitch!" Maggie shouted but due to her reduced lung capacity it came out as a barely audible croak.

"Take some pressure off Brendan," Kathleen instructed again, "let her speak."

This time Maggie didn't curse, grateful for the sense of relief flooding her body as additional air inflated her lungs and reduced the redness in her face.

Kathleen asked, "Maggie, I just want the rest of the papers, I want to finish this and to get some bloody normality back in my life – so come on – tell me where they are, I know that you have them."

No reply was forthcoming, Maggie merely lay there with a strange grin on her face and a glassy look to her eyes.

Kathleen's face grew visibly annoyed, her teeth began to grind together with frustration before she continued, "Just tell me where the papers are Maggie and no one will get hurt – I know that you and Declan had the set from Terry Flanagan and I want to have it, I deserve to have it after all this time and all the work that I did, all the pain I've been through!"

Maggie let a small laugh escape from her mouth before stating, "Why on earth should I help you Kathleen, what have you ever done for me? Hey? You've assaulted me, Michael, who next? You've truly lost it this time."

Maggie was still pinned to the floor but had not tried to extricate herself from Brendan's grip despite the growing numbness in her hands and legs.

Brendan forced his weight down on Maggie again and caused her to cough out a pained cry.

"I know you know where those papers are Maggie and you ARE going to tell me!" screamed Kathleen, waving the gun in the air above her head.

Brendan eased off the pressure again when he noticed that Maggie wanted to reply.

"C'mon Kath, what do you want to know?" What do you think that I know that's going to help you?" she asked quietly.

"Where's Terry Flanagan's safe? Where are his papers? That's what I want to know and I know that Declan and you know!"

"Terry's safe? Have you thought of asking your boyfriend here where his father's safe is? Has the thought occurred to you?"

"Well I wouldn't be asking you if he had a clue now would I Maggie, just answer me please. Where is the safe, did Declan find it? Did Declan get in to it?"

Maggie shook her head. "Declan knew where the safe was but he didn't have the right key for it, it had been hidden in another location . . ."

"I know that Maggie, the key was hidden at Mount Stewart so I've got that now. Brendan did some sterling work on getting that. The thing I don't know is where the safe that goes with it is or even what's in the damned thing!"

"Oh, that's an easy one Kathleen, Kenny Slater opened it for me already, he wasn't going to wait for a ruddy key," replied Maggie sarcastically, "but there was nothing in it that would be of any interest to you!"

"Opened it? I just don't believe you!"

"He got a friend to help get into it Kath, oh God I pity the way that your mind works, waiting to find the key to fit the safe – hah!"

Brendan had been keeping an eye on Kathleen's body language and had seen the mounting anger there and struck Maggie hard with the hand he'd taken away from her mouth. A red wheal formed instantly on Maggie's emotionless face, a little saliva dripped out of her soundless mouth, her demeanor hardened by years of cowardly beatings at Declan's hands.

"WHAT was in the safe?" screamed Kathleen, I nearly know all that I need to know Maggie and you'll get a nice going away gift out of it for you and your sorry excuse of a boyfriend over there if you just tell me what I need to know."

Michael, who had been silent for the last few minutes had started to twitch and rock slightly on the bed, particularly after witnessing his brother strike Maggie. His pent up frustration began to overcome the self-conscious shame he felt at his inability to control the situation and to help Maggie.

"Alright, you can know, I'll tell you exactly what was in there but it won't do you any good!"

"Just TELL me!" Kathleen screamed again, waving the pistol between Maggie and Michael, a motion that had also begun to unnerve Brendan who kept on being put in and out of the line of fire.

"A catalogue," said Maggie, "a page from a bloody auction catalogue. It was of a painting that was for sale. That's it, nothing else, zero. That was the lot."

Kathleen had started to tremble, years of pent up frustration beginning to break down her self-control.

"I don't believe you," she stammered, "if there's a painting . . ." she said, as her mind struggled to put two and two together, "then Terry's had the proceeds and he bought a ruddy PAINTING?"

"Terry?" cried Maggie, "Terry Flanagan is DEAD Kathleen, Declan finished him off. What was he going to do with a painting?" with this she started to laugh, her restricted voice crackling out phlegmy utterances.

Kathleen's rage boiled over and her hand closed on the gun's trigger. Brendan's face darkened to a deep red as he realised he now had the long feared confirmation that his father wasn't coming back and with it, an abject disgust for the form on the floor beneath him and for the situation that Kathleen had caused around him.

Michael's mind exploded with the realisation that his father was not only gone for good, but that he had been killed by his own lover's boyfriend, that his own lover had kept the knowledge of all of this from him over their last weeks of shared passion and that Kathleen had woven this web that surrounded them all.

He sprung up from the bed and rushed towards Kathleen who quickly depressed the gun's trigger. A shot rang out, a woman screamed. The smell of cordite filled the air and blood spilled out into the scene, pumping out and pooling onto the thirsty carpet beneath.

Chapter Thirty Six

A cold, damp November morning some years before. Low cloud enveloped the city in its clammy embrace. The weather seemed to deaden sound, no birds sang, no trees stirred, cars and buses glided through the gloom in subdued solemnity.

Tommy looked down at his watch anxious for the time to move on but cognisant that once it did, he would be enveloped in a battle, one that he was determined to win but still fearful of defeat.

He'd pieced together the fragments of clues, which hid the stolen horse proceeds from the copies of the lists he'd surreptitiously kept. He'd called in favours, deceived, inveigled and obfuscated to gather the information that he'd required.

He now had a substantial amount of cash. Not his cash of course but he saw the opportunity to benefit from the case, to cleanse the dirty money paid out to the masterminds of the theft of 'Who Dares Wins'. The money had been split apart many times, spread around the coded bank account locations. He worked on the discovery through a number of years of calculation and deception.

The money was cleaner now than it had been, laundered by this master of mathematics and visionary of the meanings in seemingly obscure patterns.

The clean money was burning a hole in his pocket.

Tommy had toed the line, been the willing arranger of deceptions and deceit for years and all he had to show for years of working for others was a decrepit flat with tired furnishings and delinquent drains.

His mind thrived on discovery – the more challenging the puzzle, the better. Once he was aware of a separation between Terry Flanagan and Kathleen, he made his move.

Fortune smiled upon him and took Terry Flanagan out of the equation at Declan's hands, taking out the one who could query Tommy's use of the information.

Terry had gradually liquidated the accounts after a sensible time had past and he'd simply stored it in his safe, which had always been the intention of the group, the safe being retained in a secret location.

The code lists not only concealed the details and locations of the original accounts but also the location of the safe itself, the location woven letter by letter into number form with these numbers themselves hidden within the other streams of numbers in the lists.

The key had likewise been hidden in another location, again its own location woven into number form in the coded lists.

Terry had ensured that subtle differences existed in the copies of the codes that had circulated. That way, he was ensuring that only he could decide when they would access the money and who would access the money.

Tommy solved the puzzle though, no ordinary mind deciding that the undoable was, in fact, doable.

Tommy worked out the location of the key and of the safe and he took out all of the cash, replacing it with a page from an auction catalogue. He closed the door of the safe and returned the key to where he had discovered it.

Tommy paced up and down the street outside the auction rooms, waiting for the door to open, waiting for access to the sale.

He peered through the glass of the windows, attempting to see inside and peered again at his wristwatch to make sure that he'd got the correct time.

He was wearing his best suit, albeit an old suit. This one had been in fashion a number of decades before but was of reasonable quality.

He shoes too were antique and the leather on the soles had begun to crack apart creating noticeable fissures as he walked. The wounds in his soles though were largely untroubling given the damp but not wet day underfoot.

The doors were soon opened by a man in a waistcoat who had just turned on the main lights of the auction rooms.

Tommy dashed in, confirmed his registration and collected his paddle before choosing a prime location in the hall, sat well within easy range of the auctioneer.

The room soon filled around him and the noise levels built in eager anticipation of the sale.

After a number of (to Tommy) uninteresting lots, the next one up was the one he had come for.

'Arisphones and Thalia' was an old master by a well-known Dutch artist. He'd first seen the painting on the walls of a local stately home, itself later razed to the ground by dynamite in order to eliminate the running costs.

He'd seen the painting at the top of its main staircase location and was physically arrested by it on first sight, particularly by a figure in the painting itself.

The poor nobleman who had demolished the hall was steadily selling off the family heirlooms to pay death duties.

The canvas, the most valuable of the possessions, had to go and off it went to auction – to this auction that Tommy now sat patiently through waiting for his opportunity to bid.

When the lot came up, Tommy was once again transfixed by the scene – Arisphones himself depicted directing Thalia in a scene from an old comedy, perhaps 'Lysistrata'.

As depicted, Thalia was the spitting image of Tommy's beloved mother, the woman who had faded away out of his life as she had been unable to take enough breath into her diseased lungs to sustain her weakened existence.

Tommy bid on the lot, a fervent determination to possess a piece of his past and preserve it in his own sight.

After collecting the painting and much to the surprise of the auction house, due to its value, he had the canvas and frame wrapped in brown paper and proceeded to carry it in to a waiting taxi, where it only just fit through the doors.

Tommy did not consider his acquisition of the illicit funds, 'theft'. After all, the funds had been obtained illegally and he'd received scant reward for his part in the process.

His conversion of the money into a piece of purchased art satisfied him and ensured that he could gaze upon the artist's seemingly accurate portrayal of his own mother every day.

On his eventual return to the squalid flat, he carefully hung the painting on the wall opposite to his bed so that he could wake up in the morning and sit up in bed with a cup of strong tea that he used to take back to bed with him and gaze upon it as long as he chose, his mouth formed into its characteristic 'o' of concentration, his mind taken back fifty years, his heart at peace.

An ambulance sat silently outside Tommy's flat, accompanied by two police officers and a lot of crime scene tape.

The boys were at the station with their troubled parents and in the flat, Tommy was zipped into a thick black body bag, no longer a man, more a pile of bones held together by decaying skin.

He'd starred in his own detailed forensic examination of the scene and accompanying photo shoot whose other principal players were garbed in white disposable boiler suits and matching white elasticated over shoes.

As the trolley supporting his body was wheeled through the flat, it paused to allow negotiation around the open doorway leading into the bedroom, long enough for his 'mother' to peer down from her elevated position on the wall and on to the remains of her youngest son.

Thalia transformed from the being muse of comedy by The Algea into empty grief and sorrow.

Michael fled the scene, fled the horror of seeing his brother's life ebbing away into the bedroom carpet.

He raced through the downstairs of the house, desperately trying to find a telephone, to help his ailing brother.

On reaching the corridor and the room where Sophie and Kelly were retained, he found it locked and bolted but could plainly hear from inside, cries of, "What's going on? What the hell was that noise, was it a shot?"

Michael rattled and wrenched at the door and finally unlocked it, pushing open the door and letting some welcome light into the room.

Sophie and Kelly's eyes blinked to try and accustom themselves to the light and were startled to see Michael's form hurtle into the room.

"Your 'phone, I need your 'phone!" he shouted, his arms raised in despair to his head.

"What, you want a 'phone?" asked Kelly, fumbling frantically into his pocket for his.

"Oh God, he's been shot!" cried Michael in despair, "Does anyone know first aid – can you help him please?" his body trembling and his face, quite white.

Sophie grabbed Kelly's arm.

"C'mon, we need to go and get help."

Kelly hurriedly switched his 'phone back on.

"There's been no signal at all, hang on there's more of a one down here," he said, moving down the hall and followed by Michael and Sophie.

They all followed the sounds of chaos emanating from the floor above whilst Kelly punched 999 into the mobile and gave the details of their location when his call was answered.

The three of them then raced up to the bedroom and they found the scene much as Michael had left it, Maggie had rolled sideways slightly but was still screaming and was pinned to the floor by Brendan's unconscious body, her own being spattered by his warm blood.

Kathleen was standing upright, her hand still closed around the pistol but she was visibly shaking and kept repeating, "Oh God, Oh God."

The entrance of Sophie and Kelly broke the atmosphere in the room and Kathleen swung around violently, nearly making contact with Sophie.

"The gun!" cried Kelly and Sophie reached down decisively and grasped it from her Aunt's hands.

"Oh God, get him off me, get him off me!" shouted Maggie and Kelly moved across to help her bloodied frame carefully out from under Brendan's.

Kathleen stopped shaking now on seeing Brendan's body slumped on the floor. Her brow creased and her eyes blinked back tears before she raised her head and stated, "I'll err, I'll err, get something to stop the bleeding."

Sophie fixed her with her gaze and said, "We've 'phoned for an ambulance, stay where you are, we'll see what we can do with Brendan, the ambulance service are still on the telephone."

Kathleen shook her head, her mouth unable to form properly to reply before she managed to say, "No, NO, I have to go now, but everything is going to be alright," and she moved steadily towards the door.

Sophie grabbed at her aunt's arm and gripped it hard to get her attention. "No, you need to stay here Kath, you need to help Brendan."

Kathleen tried to shake her off, saying, "NO, I don't, I'm going now Sophie, I can't help him now."

Sophie gripped her even harder whilst Kelly tried to help Brendan.

Kathleen screamed out as Sophie's nails dug into her arm in her attempt to bring her aunt to her senses and she tried to thrash out at her niece.

Sophie fought back though, pulling Kathleen into the middle of the room, saying, "NO, you need to help him, you're not going to run away from this one. There's no way you're going to get away with this!"

'Get OFF me!" shouted Kathleen in frustration, the shock now producing tears that streamed down her face in rivulets of sorrow and despair.

"No Kath, you don't do this again, not after all the years of leaving me and my mother to pick up the pieces. If my mother could see you now . . ."

Kathleen stopped struggling and pushed her face close into Sophie's. "Your mother? Your mother? Ha ha, I AM your mother!" shrieked Kathleen in impassioned rage.

Everything went silent, everyone was frozen.

Sophie dropped her mother's arm as if it were the most poisonous object imaginable.

"No, no, you cannot be serious. This is just one of your games," she said quietly, hopefully.

"Not what you wanted to hear then?" spat out Kathleen, "Poor Sophie, poor innocent Sophie, well welcome to the real world child!"

Sophie was still shaking her head in disbelief and then she reached over and said, "Oh Kelly!"

"Kelly! Oh yes, Kelly will help you for sure Sophie, after all he should want to, he is your half brother!"

Kelly dropped the 'phone, which was picked up by Michael and his mind was stunned and started to race, to put two and two together.

"WHAT? What . . .?" Kelly shouted, 'You mean that you, you and my father?"

Kathleen laughed, "Say hello to your little sister Kelly. I do hope that the two of you haven't been getting TOO close recently!"

Sophie had fallen to the floor, struggling to take in the enormity of the last few moments.

"My father, where is my father?" asked Kelly, pacing towards the demon taunting him, her eyes wide in hysterical ecstasy.

"Oh he's dead," she said, enjoying the blow as it landed on Kelly. "Dead and buried out the back here a long time ago you poor sods. Easier that way though, no questions, no answers."

With that she hurtled out of the room and down the stairs. She grabbed for the keys to Brendan's Audi, to the car that had followed Kelly all along the coast road and she hurriedly started the car, accelerating off down the drive with far too many revs for first gear, the engine screaming in protest and pleading for another gear.

Upstairs, Kelly reached down to embrace his sister. Maggie sat up, her makeup smeared sideways to match her hair and she looked at the pair of them and smiled.

Chapter Thirty Seven

Michael had been drinking heavily and he crashed into the bar of his favourite local, scattering glasses and bottles as he did so, sending them and their residual contents smashing and spilling on to the floor at Elaine the barmaid's side of the bar.

"Hey, hey, watch yourself Michael or I'll have to ask you to leave," she said firmly but tempering her anger as much as she could.

She was aware that Brendan was fighting for his life in hospital and that Michael was severely affected by all of the recent events.

"C'mon now, let's get you sat down," she said, moving out from behind the bar and trying to steady the unstable man in front of her.

"I want another . . . give me another drink," he slurred.

"Now c'mon," she replied, "that's no way to carry on, I'll get you a nice cup of coffee my darlin', that's what you need."

"I WANT another!" he stated but stopped as he saw another woman coming into view.

"Michael, time for home, let's go," said Maggie in soft, reassuring tones.

Maggie was visibly changed, gone the bleached colour of her hair and the hairpiece, gone the thick makeup, replaced by a freshness borne out of a sense of closure and renewal.

Elaine let Maggie take control of her man, "All yours then Maggie," she said with a smile.

"Yes, thanks Elaine, I can take it from here," she replied and started to lead the broken man out from the bar.

She had made this journey of collection nearly every day for the last fortnight, satisfied that Michael needed to forget, satisfied that she knew enough about him to know that he would come out of this phase, that they could start again, free of the poison that had run through their veins before, their blood tainted by others who were determined to control and own their every thought and action.

After the shooting, Maggie had gone to Eamon Gibson and the Police willingly, resolved to put an end to the last years of torment she had suffered at Declan's hands, the years of battling to re-gain her youthful happiness before her father's death at the hands of the thieves of 'Who Dares Wins'.

Maggie had to expunge the evil that was Kathleen, the cause of so much misery and suffering. With Michael's help, she was able to tell the Police where to find Kathleen before she could escape properly and start again.

Kathleen was guilty of the shooting of Brendan but Maggie knew that she would try and deny it and would have been careful to destroy any physical evidence of the event, so she told the Police about Tommy and linked Kathleen with his death.

She told them how Kathleen had gone to see the old man to gain answers and also that Kathleen had confessed to killing him by accident when he wouldn't give her what she needed.

She was happy now in the thought that Declan was dead, finished off by the sea at Carrick-a-Rede, but she felt she owed him some crumb of loyalty for the few good years that she had had with him and much like the victims of kidnap who end up marrying their oppressor, her heart still held something for her one time soul-mate.

So Declan's name would not be linked with Tommy's death, she could give him that at least.

Instead, Maggie was able to describe exactly what had happened at the flat from Kathleen's subsequent visit and she could recount the experience in the bedroom of the flat where

Kathleen had vomited on the bedclothes following the appalling sight of Tommy's body.

This would link her to the scene and at the very least, provide the CPS with more to go on than just Maggie's tale.

Maggie hoped that this would keep Kathleen off the streets for some time, letting others have their chance at a normal life. Letting Michael and her have that chance for themselves.

The pair crossed the pub threshold and stumbled onto the pavement. Above them, a gull soared through the brightening sky and let out a cry as it wheeled through the air.

Maggie looked skyward and for the first time in decades she felt that she could look forward instead of back.

She pulled Michael closer to her and swayed back and forth along the pavement with him, enjoying the beginnings of their dance.

More gulls circled overhead in the azure blue sky at Larne harbour.

Their cries lifted and dropped on the warm wind gusting seaward from the Antrim glens.

Here, the land flattened near the sea, green tracts of land seeped into the sea fringed by blackened rocks and topped by the ubiquitous bright yellow gorse.

Island Magee, or Oilean Mhic Aodha – 'Mac Aodha's island", sheltered the lough from the sea and Olderfleet castle once protected the interests of incomers with designs on conquering this land.

Kelly and Sophie stood waiting for a train to take them east.

They gazed across the North Channel towards Islay and Paps of Jura and were enjoying the sun warming them as they looked towards their future.

The spell was broken by the sound of the train arriving at the harbour railway station.

The Translink service spilled out its passengers on to the platform and Kelly and Sophie headed back from their vantage point to the passenger terminal.

When they arrived, they paused for a moment and let a passenger through the door before them.

An old woman, all coat and arthritis, turned to look at Kelly, her watery eyes blinking at him, her brow knitted together as she stared intently at him.

Kelly realised that it was the old woman from Great Victoria St Station again, the one who had been struggling with her time-table, trying to get to Larne on the fateful day that he travelled to Marino. This was the day that had started with him pausing to peer in at the windows of a shop in the mall there at someone else's memories captured in sentimental sepia. Moments forever frozen in a photographic parody of reality.

The woman's face grew less puzzled as she recognised Kelly and her features brightened.

"Be happy," she said with a broad smile and moved on.

Further along the platform, a figure, bent over in pain, was watching the scene.

Declan Doyle spotted Kelly and Sophie and boarded the same train by the same carriage as them.

All comes full circle, strong links *never* break.

END